It was a time in our ___ ___ ___ ne tenements of teeming ___ ___ d-justing to disillusionm___ ___ ___ en were often as corrupt ___ ___ y. And when a new era of industry and technology was about to dawn, bringing with it unprecedented riches—and un-speakable exploitation . . .

Now, this stunning new mystery featuring Milo Kachigan, a detective who conceals his Armenian background to move up the ranks in the Irish police force, and Helen Sorby, a vibrant young political leader and social worker to the city's poor, continues the powerful historical series by Karen Rose Cercone . . .

BLOOD
TRACKS

MORE MYSTERIES FROM THE
BERKLEY PUBLISHING GROUP . . .

SISTER FREVISSE MYSTERIES: Medieval mystery in the tradition of
Ellis Peters . . .

by Margaret Frazer

THE NOVICE'S TALE	THE SERVANT'S TALE	THE BOY'S TALE
THE OUTLAW'S TALE	THE BISHOP'S TALE	THE MURDERER'S TALE
THE PRIORESS' TALE		

PENNYFOOT HOTEL MYSTERIES: In Edwardian England, death takes
a seaside holiday . . .

by Kate Kingsbury

ROOM WITH A CLUE	DO NOT DISTURB	PAY THE PIPER
SERVICE FOR TWO	EAT, DRINK, AND BE BURIED	CHIVALRY IS DEAD
CHECK-OUT TIME	GROUNDS FOR MURDER	RING FOR TOMB SERVICE
DEATH WITH RESERVATIONS		

GLYNIS TRYON MYSTERIES: The highly acclaimed series set in the
early days of the women's rights movement . . . "Historically accurate and
telling."—Sara Paretsky

by Miriam Grace Monfredo

SENECA FALLS INHERITANCE	NORTH STAR CONSPIRACY	THE STALKING HORSE
BLACKWATER SPIRITS	THROUGH A GOLD EAGLE	*(new to hardcover from*
		BERKLEY PRIME CRIME)

MARK TWAIN MYSTERIES: "Adventurous . . . Replete with genuine
tall tales from the great man himself."—*Mostly Murder*

by Peter J. Heck

DEATH ON THE MISSISSIPPI
A CONNECTICUT YANKEE IN CRIMINAL COURT
THE PRINCE AND THE PROSECUTOR

KAREN ROSE CERCONE: A stunning new historical mystery featuring
Detective Milo Kachigan and social worker Helen Sorby . . .

STEEL ASHES	BLOOD TRACKS

BLOOD TRACKS

KAREN ROSE
CERCONE

BERKLEY PRIME CRIME, NEW YORK

BLOOD TRACKS

A Berkley Prime Crime Book / published by arrangement with
the author

PRINTING HISTORY
Berkley Prime Crime edition / March 1998

The Penguin Putnam Inc. World Wide Web site address is
http://www.penguinputnam.com

ISBN: 0-425-16241-9

Berkley Prime Crime Books are published
by The Berkley Publishing Group,
a member of Penguin Putnam Inc.,
200 Madison Avenue, New York, NY 10016.
The name BERKLEY PRIME CRIME and the BERKLEY PRIME CRIME
design are trademarks belonging to Berkley Publishing Corporation.

PRINTED IN THE UNITED STATES OF AMERICA

10 9 8 7 6 5 4 3 2 1

*For Mom and Dad, Aunt Honey & Uncle Bill,
and everyone else whose memories and memorabilia
of the East Pittsburgh Valley made this book possible.*

BLOOD
TRACKS

1

THE EXPLOSION IN THE BACKYARD WAS ABSO-
lutely the last straw.

The flat crack shattered the midday quiet so vi-
olently that Helen Sorby yelped and dropped the
telephone receiver she'd been half listening to. It
was the same batch of concerned questions she'd gotten from
her Aunt Pittypat every day since arriving in East Pittsburgh.
Wasn't she was still a little *young* to be a settlement-house
director, dearest? Should she really be living in such a dangerous place with her brother only there at night to protect
her? And for heaven's sake, couldn't she at least ring up that
Armenian police officer she'd been seeing and have him check
for criminal records among her tenants? After all, he was still
on the county detectives bureau even if he *had* been arrested
for taking bribes—

With the after-echoes of the explosion still ringing in her
ears, Helen scooped up the fallen telephone bell just in time
to hear her aunt shriek her name. "I'm all right, Aunt Pat.
Something blew up outside the house."

"Blew up?"

"I wonder if it was the Westinghouse plant." Helen leaned
out of the telephone alcove, trying to get a glimpse through
the dirt-streaked settlement-house windows. She could see the
high-rise factories of the Westinghouse Electric Manufacturing
Company half a block away, but no fire whistles were hooting

and the only visible smoke was the normal smudge from its coal-fired power generators. Whatever had exploded, she decided, it wasn't the electric plant. Then she noticed the torn-up clods of dirt scattered across the sidewalk in front of the settlement house, and heard the rattle of rocks and soil rolling down the tar-paper roof overhead.

"*Affangole!*" It was the strongest Italian swear word Helen knew, but it didn't begin to do justice to her feelings. "Aunt Pat, I've got to go. Someone in the house just blew up the backyard."

She slammed the receiving bell back down on the handset, cutting off her aunt's incredulous squeak, then grabbed up her navy wool skirt in determined hands and strode toward the back of the boardinghouse. Unlike most settlement houses, which merely taught classes and handed out charity goods to local immigrants, Essene House actually had low-rent lodging rooms available on its second and third floors. The stairs from those rooms emptied into the back parlor, now thronged with a crowd of gaping tenants. Helen scowled at their static backs, then took a deep breath and shouted, "Move!"

Heads whipped around and bodies hopped nimbly aside to clear her a path. After her first nerve-racking day at Essene House, Helen had made it a law that tenants had to obey her first and complain about it later. The few who weren't intimidated by her scowl and ringing voice had found themselves booted out by her unsympathetic twin brother, leaving a motley but obedient lot behind. Helen went through them like a battleship slicing through an aimless splash of waves. A flock of questions followed in her wake.

"Do you think he's killed himself this time, ma'am?"

"Hey, Miss Sorby, can you see his body?"

"Did he blow the kitchen up? He tried that once before."

All Helen could see in the frost-pinched backyard was a haze of smoke rising beyond the detached kitchen shed. It didn't look as if the wood-framed building had been damaged, although one of the spindly pine trees behind it was leaning at a new angle. She turned to face the last questioner, a carrot-haired girl with bright eyes in a face scarred by childhood pox.

"*Who* blew up the kitchen?"

Molly Slade grinned. Although she was the settlement house's youngest tenant—and formerly one of its resident prostitutes—she had proven to be a surprisingly insightful source of information about Helen's new domain. The distinctly pregnant bulge under her pretty lace shirtwaist showed why she had decided to stay when the other girls, less cooperative about changing their profession, had moved out. "It's old Abraham Maccoun, ma'am. You know, the drunk from the second floor who don't talk to nobody save to spit at them. He's an Antichrist."

"A *what*?"

"An Antichrist. You know, those ones that go around throwing bombs and shooting guns at Henry Clay Frick."

"Oh, an *anarchist*." The world resumed normal functioning, after a moment when Helen suspected she'd been sucked from East Pittsburgh to Oz without the benefit of a tornado. She peered out through the gray December afternoon, seeing no sign of her oldest and most irascible tenant. "But anarchists usually go after rich men or big companies. Why on earth is Maccoun bombing a settlement house?"

Molly shrugged. "Practicing, he says. I think he's just too lazy to go any farther than the outhouse before he throws those flaming bottles of his."

"No doubt." Helen glanced around the ring of expectant, dirty faces surrounding her, sighed, and then grabbed her worn russet coat off of its peg by the back door. "I suppose I'd better go see if he's dead."

She wasn't particularly worried, since even a week's scant acquaintance made her certain Abraham Maccoun hadn't done anything as convenient as die in his own explosion. More likely, he was out there cursing and spitting at his various detached limbs. "Molly, you answer the telephone. If anyone rings up to ask about the explosion, tell them we think it was the gas line. And don't let anyone in unless it's Thomas."

"Yes, ma'am." Face aglow with the honor of minor responsibility, the ex-prostitute swept aside one of the not-so-bright Buchak brothers and scurried toward the front hall. Satisfied that she had done the best she could to hold the fort,

Helen flung her worn wool coat over her shoulders and headed out into the bitter cold.

The kitchen shed was dark and quiet, with Thomas still out surveying for his new fire-insurance map of the East Pittsburgh Valley and no one else trusted to go inside. A well-trodden path led around to the tar-papered outhouse that still saw use when the two indoor bathrooms were inhabited. Helen followed the ribbon of bare dirt to the back end of their lot, where the shadow of the high Pittsburgh, Bessemer, and Lake Erie Railroad trestle loomed over a weed-choked hill slope. She blinked, more in surprise than dismay, when she saw the impressive dirt crater that had been torn out at the base of one spindly pine. A drift of smoke still rose from its edges and a scrawny figure in a much-too-large overcoat stood smack in the middle of it, regarding his achievement with hands soberly clasped behind his back. It was probably the only sober thing about him.

"Mr. Maccoun." Helen strode across the backyard toward him, feeling a frown begin to indent itself into her forehead. "Just what do you think you're doing?"

The old man turned to squint at her, ragged white whiskers jerking and shaking as he chewed his tobacco wad. "Weren't nothing here in the yard but dirt, before," he said defensively.

"That doesn't mean you're allowed to blow it up!" Scowl deepening, Helen skirted a second rag-corked bottle lying in the flattened weeds and went to meet him. His pale gaze seemed unusually alert, despite the smell of cheap whiskey that drifted out from him. "You might have hurt yourself, or someone else."

This time, his answer was a gravelly hawk and spit. Helen's gaze involuntarily followed the stream of brown tobacco juice, and she yelped again. On the far side of the cratered ground, a severed but unmistakably human leg lay beneath the leaning pine.

"Guess I did," Abraham Maccoun said glumly.

Helen's promotion to settlement-house director on December 16, 1905, had been neither planned nor particularly welcome. She'd intended to spend her holiday cocooned in her own drawing room, writing an article on job opportunities for women in the electric industries. This unusual desire for solitude hadn't been caused by the stress of helping immigrant families impoverished by winter layoffs in the steel industry—that had been heart-wrenching but expected. What she hadn't been prepared for was the shock of reading about Milo Kachigan's arrest on bribery charges in the newspapers a few weeks before. His unexplained absence from Sarah Street ever since had turned Helen's initial bewildered sympathy into simmering indignation, whose only acceptable outlet was a feminist editorial tirade. Her long-suffering brother had already warned her that if she snapped at him one more time for no reason, he was going to move in with Aunt Pittypat.

So it had been with a reluctant step that Helen had gone through the open office door of her settlement-house director. In the past two years Julia Regitz Brown had turned Martha Carey House into such a model of social improvement and community service that other settlement-house boards were constantly seeking the benefit of her advice. Helen was vaguely aware that the well-dressed men and women who'd been closeted with Miss Brown since luncheon represented one such board, but she'd been so busy handing out blankets and Christmas hams to unemployed steelworkers that she'd paid little attention to them. Now she paused on the threshold of the office, startled to find herself the object of intense scrutiny from everyone inside.

"Miss Helen Sorby." As usual, Julia Regitz Brown added nothing beyond that terse introduction. The wealthy settlement-house director lavished both her time and her money on her beloved work, but she was a complete miser when it came to talking about it. Helen wasn't sure that she'd ever heard Miss Brown say an unnecessary word on any subject, and certainly not on the subject of settlement houses. "I believe she can do the job."

Silence fell over the office again while the assortment of clergymen in plain day collars and matrons in sober dark dresses scrutinized Helen a little more. She lifted an inquiring eyebrow at her employer, but Julia Regitz Brown evidently felt no further explanation was needed or wanted. It was left to the eldest of the clergy to clear his throat and enlighten her.

"Permit me to introduce myself, Miss Sorby," he said, in a scratchy light tenor. "I am the Reverend Elmore Wheeler, from the Church of the United Brethren in Christ in Trafford City. I have the honor to be president of the East Pittsburgh Valley Christian Benevolent Association. Perhaps you have heard of us?"

"Sorry, no." That sounded too much like one of Miss Brown's curt replies, and Helen searched for something else to say. "I'm afraid I've never visited the East Pittsburgh Valley."

"You haven't missed much, my dear." That deep voice came, surprisingly, from the smallest of the three society matrons in the room. Helen glanced over to see an unexpected twinkle in her eyes. "I believe a *New York Times* travel writer once summarized the main line along the Turtle Creek as the 'ugliest twenty miles of travel in the world.' " Helen's lips quivered in responsive amusement, but seeing the elderly clergyman's frown, she knew better than to laugh out loud. "And he didn't even stop to tour the slums of East Pittsburgh."

"Miss Jarena Lee exaggerates, Miss Sorby," Wheeler assured her. "There are certainly some impoverished and unsightly neighborhoods along the Turtle Creek, as you would expect in a region of such heavy industrialization. But the East Pittsburgh Valley is much cleaner than Pittsburgh and far more conducive to the raising of children. With the aid of the several immigration houses we have established over the past ten years, the influx of settlers from the Old World to the new has been both peaceful and prosperous."

He paused, clearly waiting for approbation from his audience. "That's wonderful," Helen said obediently. "But what has this got to do with me, Reverend?"

Wheeler cleared his throat again, more awkwardly. "We have recently experienced some—er—turmoil at one of our settlement houses in East Pittsburgh." Something less than a murmur and more than a sigh rippled through the other board members. "The problems at Essene House culminated in the sudden resignation of the settlement-house director just two days ago. Without notice," he added glumly. "As you may know, Miss Sorby, the holiday season is the worst possible time to leave a settlement house without leadership.''

"And you want me to take the job?"

The clergyman glanced back at his board and got another ripple of reaction, this time composed all of nods. "On the strength of Miss Brown's recommendation, Miss Sorby, I think we could find no finer replacement. Will you consider an offer of employment from us?"

"I don't know." Helen chewed her lower lip, her rush of pleasure at such a flattering rise in status warring with her mindless desire to spend the holidays curled up in her writing chair in front of a roaring fire. When she added her overdue article to the scales, it tipped in favor of staying home. "Miss Brown might not have told you, Reverend Wheeler, that I also write for the serious press. And I have a manuscript sitting on my desk right now which ought to have been sent to *McClure's Magazine* a week ago. I'm afraid I can't—"

Julia Regitz Brown stirred in her chair, ever so slightly. "Essene House sits directly adjacent to the Westinghouse Electric Manufacturing Company, Miss Sorby. I believe they now employ more women than men in the turbine-building plant there."

That enigmatic comment received a baffled look from Wheeler, but the scrawny Miss Lee clapped her kid-gloved hands in instant comprehension. "My dear Miss Sorby, don't tell me you're contributing to that wonderful series of articles on women's employment in the trades? Wasn't the report by Miss Annie Gibbs on the linen factories in Massachusetts superb?"

"Quite effective," Julia Regitz Brown agreed. "Especially the data she gathered by playing the part of an actual factory girl for several days. 'Going under cover,' I believe it's called."

So many words, coming from the usually taciturn director of Carey House, made Helen turn and stare at her. Her employer met her gaze serenely enough, but her eyes crinkled with secret amusement. "Well, Miss Sorby? What do you think?"

"About what?" the Reverend Wheeler asked, still looking

lost. "The Essene Settlement House job, or the *McClure's Magazine* series?"

Helen ignored him. "Do you really think I could get a job at Westinghouse Electric at this time of year?" she asked Miss Brown in turn. "Everyone else is laying off."

"Not George Westinghouse," said Jarena Lee unexpectedly. "He never lays his men off in the winter if he can help it." Her head tipped with bird-quick enthusiasm. "Of course, I don't know if he applies that same rule to his female employees. It would be interesting to find out, wouldn't it?"

Helen contemplated that and found herself smiling. It *would* be interesting: challenging if she actually got a job at the technology-rich Westinghouse plant and enlightening even if she didn't. It would change her planned article from a tired recital of printed facts to a lively description of true places, real people, actual events. And it would take her miles away from Milo Kachigan. Or from his continued absence, which might be even better.

"I'll do it," she said.

Of course, Thomas had refused to let her go alone. He was a fairly tolerant brother, much too easygoing to worry about Helen's various fits and starts, but he still had a remarkable amount of common sense. No matter how loud she could yell, he'd told her, there were going to be some situations at a rundown settlement house that required a strong arm and a steel-toed boot to resolve. After two grueling days of evicting prostitutes and pimps, sorting out truly hard-up immigrants from malingers and confidence men, and establishing decorum and order in a lodging that had degenerated into near anarchy, Helen had been forced to admit he was right.

She also had to admit that if it hadn't been for Thomas's love of cooking, the entire household would have starved. After one glimpse of the kitchen shed, she'd flatly refused to let the slovenly Buchak brothers resume their former jobs as cooks, even though she herself hadn't the least idea how to prepare meals for fifteen people. Her natural inclination was to hire a cook from the neighborhood, but that was before she'd found out that the previous director of Essene House had absconded with the grocery money and her tenants' monthly rent, not to mention the prettiest of the resident prostitutes. Helen remembered thinking at the time that finding an empty pantry and a bankrupt treasury a week before Christmas would go down in history as the most depressing situation a brand-new settlement-house director had ever faced.

However, that was before she'd seen the results of Abraham Maccoun's explosion in the backyard.

"Who is it?" she demanded, standing on tiptoe to look for the rest of the corpse while she frantically tried to remember whose faces she'd seen in the back parlor. The weeds seemed crushed and darkened in one area, but the leaning pine tree concealed what lay there. "One of the Buchak boys?"

Maccoun chewed meditatively, then spat again. "Don't think it's any of ours," he said at length. "Too expensive."

"Too *expensive*?"

"The shoe."

Helen forced herself to look again at the horridly severed leg across the crater. The old man was right. Beneath the blood-soaked and tattered trouser she could see the anomalous gleam of a polished leather spat. Even if they'd been given a pair of shoes that expensive, none of the lodgers at Essene House would have kept it any longer than it took to pawn for drinking money.

"It must be one of the neighbors," Helen said grimly. This affair was getting worse by the minute. She took a deep breath, tainted by the lingering smell of alcohol smoke, and wished she could make herself move. "We'd better go find the rest of him," she said, more to her wavering self than to her companion. "Just to make sure—"

Maccoun jerked his ragged whiskers into a lopsided grimace. "Don't you think he'd be screaming his head off if he was still alive, Miz Sorby?"

That stilled the tremor of dread that had been clawing through Helen and unlocked her rigid muscles. "True," she admitted. "Which means the police will probably want to arrest someone for killing him." She reached out to grab a handful of the old man's overcoat, preventing him from sliding away. "Don't panic. First of all, let's go see if we know who he is."

Bony shoulders squirmed against her grip, in vain. "I don't know any of the friggin' neighbors," Maccoun grumbled. "If you really want to know who he is, go get our Molly. She probably slept with 'im."

"Yes, but she's not the one who killed him." Helen steered the old anarchist across the crater with some difficulty. Now that the first shock of discovery was over, the alcohol in Maccoun's blood seemed to be reasserting itself, giving him back his usual wavering walk. The only time Helen didn't correct his course was when he made a drunk's exaggerated circuit around the severed leg.

Beyond the crooked pine tree, the patch of crushed weeds was much clearer, and Helen could see an outstretched arm protruding from it. It looked as if it lacked a hand. She took another deep breath, then pushed Maccoun over toward the mutilated body with a little more force than necessary. That way, she had to follow him to make sure he stayed upright.

The corpse lay facedown in the frost-bleached weeds, one handless arm outstretched and the other twisted oddly under its chest. Both legs were cut off abruptly, almost neatly, at the knee. Judging from his broadcloth winter coat and the clean brilliantined shine of his dark hair, the dead man was no laborer or factory hand. And given the impoverished block of East Pittsburgh they inhabited, that also meant he was no neighbor.

"Some rich gent," said Maccoun, echoing her thoughts. He hawked and spat again. "What in hell was he doing sleeping in our backyard?"

Helen frowned, stepping sideways to try to see a little of the unknown man's face where it pressed into the grass. Something about this scene was distinctly odd, but she couldn't put her finger on what it was. "Are you sure he was sleeping?"

The anarchist snorted. "Miz Sorby, I was out here a half hour filling my bottles and tearing up them rags, and I never heard a peep out of this gent. He musta been sleeping."

"In someone else's backyard, in the middle of winter?" She shook her head, her thoughtful gaze sliding back down to the cleanly severed legs. "I don't think so, Mr. Maccoun."

Her companion grunted. "Passed out, then, from drinking."

"Maybe." Finally realizing what was bothering her about this scene, Helen bent to tug at the deceased man's outflung wrist. As she'd expected from the total lack of smell about the corpse, it was ice-cold and completely stiff. "Or already dead. He's frozen solid, Mr. Maccoun. You didn't kill him."

"I didn't?" For a moment the old man's wavering stopped as he regarded her with bloodshot blue eyes. Somewhere behind the drunken haze, Helen caught a glimpse of the intelligent engineering professor Maccoun was reputed to have once been. "You think the cops here will believe that?"

She tilted her head, hearing the approaching sound of police whistles. Someone must have heard the explosion and reported it. "Probably not," she agreed. After the last few days she had very little faith in the untrammeled integrity of the East Pittsburgh police. As far as she could tell, they had been the settlement-house prostitutes' best customers.

"Then don't you think I oughta leg it down to the tracks and hop a westbound train?"

"No." Helen swung the old man around by his overcoat and pushed him back toward the main house. "All that would do is get the rest of us in trouble."

Maccoun's reply to that was a sideways spit that just missed the hem of her skirts. Helen didn't take it personally, knowing he was too drunk to aim that well. "And if I let the cops arrest me to save you all that trouble, what then?" he asked bitterly. "How'm I going to get let out of jail?"

"Let me worry about that." An impulsive idea had come to her, glimmering with both risk and potential. If it worked, Helen would have gained an ally to help her sort out this mess. If it didn't, Thomas would probably kill her. "For now, let's just go and try to explain what happened to the police. If we're lucky, all they'll arrest you for is disturbing the peace."

"And if we're skunked?"

"Then I know a county detective who can investigate and get you free again."

"You do?" Halfway up the back-porch stairs, the old man turned to squint at her in disbelief. "And just how are you gonna bribe him to do that, Miz Sorby? Essene House don't got enough money to buy its own milk, and those county boys cost a mint.''

''I'm not going to bribe him.'' She pushed Abraham Maccoun across the porch toward the sea of expectant faces in the back parlor. From the front of the house, she could hear the authoritative thud of a police fist against the door and Molly's answering squeal of alarm. ''I'm going to blackmail him.''

Maccoun scowled. ''How?''

''By getting myself arrested with you,'' said Helen, and went to meet the police.

2

THERE WAS ALWAYS MILK IN THE ICEBOX NOW. As far as Milo Kachigan could tell, that was the only benefit he'd derived from his recent promotion to the Allegheny County Detectives Bureau.

Bleary-eyed from another late night spent in smoky brothels and gaming rooms, he squinted past the chilly fog descending from the tin-sheathed ice compartment into the food compartment below. Somewhere in that mist, he knew, were two quart jugs full of fresh milk. They came delivered by a horse-drawn wagon every morning, now that he made enough money to pay for that luxury. Even if Kachigan was seldom awake before noon these days, his father always brought them in as soon as they arrived.

But today, amid the bowls of *ghanoush* and jars of grape leaves and rounds of salted cheese, there was no milk. Kachigan sighed and squatted in front of the ice chest, reaching down through the mist to the frigid bottom shelf. No matter how many times he told the old man not to worry if the milk spoiled, Istvan couldn't break himself of the habit of keeping it as cold as possible. The habits of half a lifetime's poverty were hard to break.

Kachigan's fingers hit a familiar shape of frosted glass at last, shoved all the way to the dim back of the shelf. He leaned in to lift it over the paper-wrapped bundles of parsnips and carrots that surrounded it, wincing at the kiss of cold air against his face. Cold always drew a stab of pain from the metal shard buried in his cheekbone, but in the wintertime that was a pain he was used to. He pulled the milk jug out and flipped its foil cap off with a thumb while he rubbed at his cheek to warm it.

"Milosh, where are you?" The thump of walking sticks echoed down their narrow hall, then bumped against the swinging kitchen door and pushed it open. Istvan Kachigan's balding head appeared, eyes narrowed in a scowl made of equal parts irritation and concern. It was an expression Kachigan had seen often enough as a teenager, when he'd run with a gang of wild Slovak and Italian boys his father hadn't trusted. He hadn't seen it again for years after that, not until these last few weeks.

"I'm right here, Pap." Since he knew he was already in the doghouse for something, Kachigan lifted the jug and drank straight from the neck, letting the ice-cold milk wash away the stale taste of last night's cigar smoke and unwanted beer. "What's the matter?"

Istvan growled and swung all the way into the kitchen, still spry despite his arthritis-stiffened knees. He poked one walking stick at Kachigan, hard enough to make him grunt and lower the bottle. "Did I raise my children in a shanty?" the old man demanded. "You drink that from a glass!"

"Yes, sir." Now that the bitter taste in his mouth was gone, Kachigan set the half-empty jug down and went across the kitchen to fetch a glass from their dish drainer. He poured the remaining milk into it, then drank in a more civilized manner. "All right, now can you tell me what you want?"

Istvan grunted disapprovingly. "All you have for breakfast anymore is just milk to drink. All that cream sloshing around your intestines can't be good for you, Milosh. You should be eating some of that new digestive cereal I bought."

Milo made a face. "I refuse to eat anything called 'Grape-Nuts.' And anyway this isn't breakfast, Pap, it's lunch. Are you going to tell me what you called me for, or do I have to play twenty questions with you?"

His father sighed, and jerked his chin back toward the front foyer. "The fat man you go to whorehouses with, he wants you."

"Taggart?" Kachigan paused in the act of reaching into the icebox for the second quart of milk. "He's never awake this early in the afternoon. Did he say why he was ringing up?"

Istvan made an impatient noise. "Did I say he was on the telephone? I said he wants you. He's standing outside our front door, right this minute."

"What?" Letting the icebox door close with a thud, Kachigan circled his father and headed at a brisk trot toward the front door. If there was one thing he'd learned about Art Taggart in the three weeks they'd been working together as detective partners, it was that the big man never stirred himself unless he had to. He wasn't particularly corrupt, at least not compared with the rest of the bureau, and he was far from stupid. But Taggart's primary mission in life was to do as little work as possible. If he had bestirred himself at noon—for him, the crack of dawn—and then come all the way from his East Pittsburgh flat to the South Side, a major crisis must be in progress.

Kachigan wasn't fooled in the slightest by the sleepy look he got when he swung the door open. He'd seen Taggart look exactly that sleepy in the middle of a brothel knife fight. "What's up?" he demanded.

"Call from headquarters." If the big man had taken offense at being left out on the stoop in mid-December, he didn't show it. Of course, taking offense meant expending energy. In some ways, Taggart's indolence made him the easiest of partners. "McGara wants to see us, right away. You ready to go?"

"Of course not. I wasn't expecting to be on duty until suppertime." Kachigan stepped back, this time leaving the door open for Taggart to follow. With him in it, the front hall suddenly seemed much smaller. Despite Istvan's scornful dismissal, the Irish detective wasn't fat so much as he was massive. His oxlike shoulders and back made his barrel chest and beer gut seem correctly proportioned, with only his legs looking mismatched, too stumpy and thin for that heavy torso. Considering how little exercise Taggart got and how much

Chinese food he consumed, it was a wonder he didn't weigh twice as much.

"Why does Big Roge want us in headquarters today?" Kachigan grabbed yesterday's stained collar off the coatrack and slid it under the neckline of his shirt. After a trip through the smoky streets of Pittsburgh, no one would notice it wasn't a fresh one. "Does the mayor need another special favor?"

"Not so far as I know." A quiet ripple of amusement lit Taggart's slitted eyes, hard to see unless you knew what to look for. "Maybe old Judge Detwiler decided to haul us up on those bribery charges after all."

Kachigan snorted and buttoned his collar. "And mess up McGara's leverage on me? I don't think so. The captain knows the first thing I'd do is run to the newspapers with a list of every bribe he's ever taken."

"You couldn't *run* with a stack of paper that big," Taggart pointed out. "You'd have to load it on a dolly and push it."

"True." Kachigan shrugged on his suit coat and grabbed up his overcoat. "Hey, Pap! I'm going down to headquarters now."

Another thud, and the kitchen door swung open from the other side. "You gonna be home for supper?" Istvan asked. "Or you gonna eat some fried meat out at a bar?"

His son gave him a glance of affectionate exasperation. "Actually I thought I'd just drink milk for the rest of the day. What do you care what I eat?"

"Too much meat and not enough vegetables ruins your intestines," the elder Kachigan informed him sharply. "When was the last time you ate a vegetable, eh? Thanksgiving dinner?"

Kachigan winced, reminded not of the sweet-potato soufflé or the endive salad, but the laughing banter between his father and Thomas Sorby as they cooked supper in the kitchen at Sarah Street while he and Helen set the table and argued over voting rights for women. Two days later he'd been arrested by the Allegheny City police for collecting one of Roger McGara's bribes, with the story splashed over the front pages of every paper in town, thanks to his corrupt captain. The friendly dinners at Sarah Street had been put out of reach forever.

"We had beef pies at Max's Tavern last night," Taggart volunteered, when Kachigan stayed silent. His lazy gaze met Istvan's scowl with only the slightest of twinkles. "I think there were a couple of peas and carrot slices in it. Weren't there, Milo?"

"I wouldn't know." Kachigan belted his overcoat and shook soot from his once-gray bowler. "I had the pork and sauerkraut."

There was a flash of teeth beneath his partner's sandy mustache, his lazy version of a smile. "Well, isn't sauerkraut a vegetable? It's made of cabbage."

"Rotten cabbage," Istvan retorted. "I don't call that a vegetable!"

"Anyone who calls Grape-Nuts a cereal should call boiled cardboard a vegetable," said his disrespectful son. He opened the door for Taggart. "Fix yourself dinner tonight, Pap. I promise to steal some oats and carrots from the police stables for mine."

"Better not," Taggart said. "Big Roge would have you on the front pages for embezzling before you even had time to eat them."

The detectives bureau was housed in the Allegheny County Courthouse, a beautiful gray-walled Gothic block with a clock tower that had dominated Grant Street until Andrew Carnegie and Henry Clay Frick put their dueling skyscrapers next to it. Filled with slanting sunshine from its huge leaded windows and the distant muttering echoes from the courtrooms on the second floor, the building always reminded Kachigan of a cathedral. In the winter of 1905, however, this was not the temple of justice its carved inscription proclaimed it to be. With Roger McGara in charge of the detectives bureau, Jacob Detwiler heading the courts, and the mayor's other cronies ensconced in the three county commissioner's seats, Kachigan suspected that the only honest business done inside these walls was the registering of babies and the licensing of dogs. And he wasn't even too sure about the dogs.

"Why can't we ever take the damn elevators?" As usual, Taggart had paused on the second stone landing to let his huffing subside before they climbed the final flight to McGara's office. Kachigan leaned over one rail to admire the play of light through the stone arches and banisters below while his partner caught his breath. "I think you're trying to kill me."

"No, I'm just trying to avoid the traffic jams." The brass elevator doors on the second-story hall were surrounded with well-dressed spectators as well as court stenographers and lawyers. The notorious Stengler kidnapping trial must have adjourned for the day. "You don't fit in the elevators anyway, Art. Not if anyone else tries to get in with you."

"True." Taggart's thin slice of smile showed again. "Maybe I should just do what Big Roge does."

"What's that?"

"Don't wash except on payday, and wear the same clothes for a month. That would keep those East End swells out of my elevator, huh?"

"And make your landlord throw you out." Kachigan gave the big man a push up the last flight of stairs. "You think a Chinese laundry wants their building to smell like Big Roge?"

"Might kill the mice."

Kachigan snorted, and turned the corner into the narrower halls and more closely spaced doors of the administrative third floor. Rumor had it that some of these offices had secret stairs leading down to the courtyard below. Although Kachigan suspected that those had initially been designed to allow county officials to escape angry mobs of citizens, these days they primarily funneled the county's wealthier inhabitants into the courthouse, to grease the wheels of government with the universal lubricant of money. If the stairs really existed, then Roger McGara's office undoubtedly had one, although the entrance was so well designed Kachigan had still not been able to spot it. Of course, most of the time when he was closeted with the detective captain, he needed all his concentration just to keep from murdering him.

In the outer office, McGara's decorative female stenographer glanced up at them over her typing machine, fluttering her gold eyelashes adorably at Taggart while somehow man-

aging not to see Kachigan. She knew who the black sheep of
the department was.

"Detective Taggart." Lucy's voice was a little too high-
pitched to be seductive, and ended up sounding consumptively
breathless instead. "I'm afraid Captain McGara's on the telephone with the mayor right now. Can you wait?"

"No problem. We're getting paid no matter where we sit."
Taggart made a pine chair creak with his bulk. "You just go
right ahead with your work, Miss Jackson."

"Um—I suppose. I mean, of course." She discreetly slid
her makeup mirror off the keys and began to pound them one
by one, with long studious pauses in between to find the right
letters. After a moment she broke a nail on one metal tab and
hissed a curse, then excused herself hastily for the ladies'
room. Kachigan held the door for her and gave his partner a
reproving glance when he sat back down.

"You shouldn't tease poor Lucy like that. I think she likes
you."

Taggart grunted. "No, what she likes is thinking she's making you jealous by flirting with me."

"*Jealous?*" Kachigan said incredulously. "What the hell
have I got to be jealous about?"

"You're the only one in the bureau she hasn't slept with."
Taggart raised an eyebrow at Kachigan's startled look.
"Christ, Milo, she can barely answer the telephone, much less
take dictation and type. What do you think she's here for?"

"To sleep with McGara," he said frankly. "And I'm in
enough trouble with him already, thank you."

His partner snorted. "Big Roge has a wife and two mis-
tresses, not to mention the run of every brothel in the county.
He hired Lucy to keep the troops happy."

"Well, I'm not one of his troops. And it's going to take a
lot more than Lucy to make me happy."

"Sorry to hear that, Kash," said a harsh voice from behind.
"The half-assed way you shake down brothels, Lucy's all
you're ever going to get."

Kachigan cursed, under his breath and in Armenian, but by
sheer force of will managed to keep himself from jerking
around in his chair. Instead, he contented himself with glaring

across the office at his irritatingly lazy companion. Roger McGara's closed door might have muffled the sound of his approaching footsteps, but from where Taggart sat the captain's shadow should have been visible against the frosted glass. Assuming, of course, that his partner had bothered to keep his eyes open.

"Afternoon, Cap." If Taggart was dismayed by being caught discussing his superior officer's sexual activities, it didn't show in either his voice or bland face. "You ready for us?"

McGara grunted, crashing open his office door wide with such force that Kachigan was surprised the glass didn't shatter. "I've been ready for ten minutes. What were you waiting for, an engraved invitation? Get in here."

Kachigan rose but stayed stubbornly silent, leaving Taggart to sigh and explain. "Lucy said you were on the horn with the mayor. She told us we had to wait."

"That's because Lucy couldn't figure out her switchboard unless a bonbon fell out of it every time she pressed the right button." And because McGara liked overhearing what his subordinates talked about when they thought he was otherwise engaged, Kachigan suspected. He took a deep breath, knowing it would be his last pleasant one for a while, and followed his partner into the captain's inner office.

Roger McGara, known to friends and foes alike as Big Roge, had a former boxer's abused face: close-cropped bullet head, gnarled cauliflower ears, bent and flattened nose. His hazel eyes were set just a little too close together in the broad span of his cheeks, giving him a look of constant suspicion. The detective captain always looked clean enough from a distance, but for some reason his stocky body emitted a rank and pungent odor that no amount of imported cologne or expensive pipe smoke seemed able to drive away. Kachigan wasn't sure why McGara never opened the south-facing windows that heated his office to a greenhouse swelter. Taggart facetiously claimed it was because he didn't like killing pigeons.

"You've been making the rounds, you two, but you haven't been reporting in." McGara sank into his richly burnished leather rocker and deliberately turned it so they had to sit on the plain pine stools along the wall rather than the plump up-holstered chairs in front of his desk. "The receipts are looking good, so I know you aren't skimming any off the top. Any problems you're not telling me about, Kash? City police getting in your way? Internal Revenue boys poking around?"

Kachigan shrugged. After the way McGara had "dirtied him up" by deliberately sending him into a staked-out gambling den, he wouldn't have passed such a warning along even if he had one. In fact, the only reason he had continued "making the rounds" was in the hopes of collecting enough blackmail material to force his captain to put him on a real criminal investigation. "Business is down a little with the winter lay-offs," he said neutrally.

McGara scratched a match across his mahogany desktop and held it to his burled pipe. "And I bet the gambling joints want to make a lower payment?"

"Yeah." Taggart cleared his throat. "But we told them police protection is like life insurance. You got to pay the same amount every month, no matter how sick you get."

"Good." Smoke puffed out from the pipe, adding an anomalous cherry flavor to the pervasive stink. "Any new whore-houses show up in Allegheny City?"

Kachigan let out a snort of honest amusement. "Where the hell would there be room for them? There are already girls in almost every house along East Ohio Street."

"Still, it never hurts to check." McGara pointed the pipe stem at him. "You gotta get your priorities straight here, Kash."

"My priorities," Kachigan said between his teeth, "are to solve crimes and help people." He ignored the warning look his partner gave him. "What are yours?"

For once, Big Roge's legendary temper failed to ignite. "To keep people happy by giving them what they want. Sometimes that's whores and sometimes it's cheap liquor and sometimes it's just a simple game of craps." He grinned around his pipe stem. "For you, it's a real criminal case to investigate, huh?"

"Yes," said Kachigan. "It is."

"Well, then, I guess I'll give you one."

Tense silence filled the room after that remark, profound

enough that Kachigan could hear the pigeons squabbling on the ledge outside. He gave Taggart a baffled look and got back an unhelpful shrug. "What kind of case?"

"A murder case." McGara's grin widened at Kachigan's incautious intake of breath. "You've heard about those anarchist bombings they've been having the past couple weeks out in the East Pittsburgh Valley?"

"No." Despite the fact that he and Taggart spent most of their time reading the Pittsburgh papers while he waited for madams and gambling chiefs to count out their payoffs, Kachigan couldn't remember any recent reports of bombings. Given the amount of hysteria anything connected with anarchists usually stirred up in this conservative city, he'd have expected front-page headlines. "Have you, Art?"

His partner grunted. "There's been a few stories about it in the *Westinghouse Valley News*. The bombs have all hit railroad property. As far as I know, nobody's gotten hurt."

"Until this morning." McGara puffed out a thoughtful blue cloud. "When a couple of the anarchists blew some railroad hobo to bits in East Pittsburgh. Evidently they were out testing alcohol bombs in their backyard."

"That was stupid," said Taggart. "Did they catch the anarchists who did it?"

"Hell, yeah. The East Pittsburgh police hustled them right to the local lockup."

"But they're not sure they have all of them," Kachigan guessed. "That's why they asked us to investigate?"

"Good boy." McGara leaned forward to tap his pipe on the huge brass tray spilling over with ashes. The sour smell of stale tobacco fought with his own, and lost. "I can tell you're raring to go, Kash. Don't you worry about collecting receipts tonight. You and Taggart get right on this investigation."

Kachigan hadn't known how frustrated he'd become with his restrictive rounds of whorehouses until he felt freedom pour through him like a cool, sweet waterfall. After the initial relief, however, caution reared its head. This was, after all, the very same captain who'd sent him mercilessly into the arms of the Allegheny City police.

"Why?" he asked bluntly.

McGara didn't pretend to misunderstand. "Why am I giving you boys this case? Well, for one thing, it's right in Fat Art's backyard—you still live in East Pittsburgh, don't you, Taggart? And for a second thing, I know you can't mess it up because they already got the killers." He tamped his thumb into a new load of pipe tobacco and drew through it, releasing another slow cloud of smoke. For some reason, he seemed to be enjoying this. "And for a third thing, Kash, they specifically asked for you."

"The East Pittsburgh police?"

"No." Big Roge grinned again. "The anarchists."

Kachigan didn't know why the Pennsylvania Railroad claimed its main-line service was the fastest to the East Coast. At the lackadaisical rate this eastbound train was making its way through the suburbs of Shadyside, East Liberty, and Swissvale, he estimated it would arrive in New York City sometime in 1906.

"Stop fidgeting." Taggart glanced over the top of his newspaper, half-irritated and half-amused. "You're making me tired. Here, you can have the sports section."

"I don't want the sports section." Kachigan stopped drumming his fingers on the empty seat in front of him and concentrated on the more productive task of brushing soot from his bowler hat. The rush-hour train had been full of city smoke as well as businessmen and office clerks when they left Penn Station. Most of the professionals had gotten off long before they reached the industrial towns of Homestead and Braddock, however, leaving him and Taggart alone in the dusty car. "Is East Pittsburgh the next stop on the line?"

"Unless they've built a new station since I came home yesterday, it is." Taggart turned to the theater page and scanned the vaudeville and nickelodeon listings. Kachigan wasn't sure why, since he never went to any shows. "Did you know Evelyn Nesbit plans to tour next spring in *Gold-digger's Daughter*?"

"No, and I don't care either." Kachigan watched the gray December landscape slide by as they gathered speed. After leaving the Monongahela River behind at Braddock, the main line had curved east into a flat-bottomed valley whose slopes were stripped of timber and blackened by railroad smoke. A small stream meandered along the tracks for a while, then was pushed aside by an astonishing swath of brand-new buildings, including a ten-story tower rich with gleaming windows. It seemed like an odd place to put a skyscraper.

"Taggart, what's that building?"

"Westinghouse Electric Manufacturing," his partner said without looking up. He began to fold his paper as the train braked with a whistle of compressed air. "Everything up the valley from here is Westinghouse plants, except for the big Pennsylvania Railroad yard at Pitcairn."

Kachigan whistled, impressed. Compared with the sprawling steel mills he'd grown up with in Monessen and the dirty glass plants that hulked over the South Side, this factory's narrow loft and elegantly arched windows seemed ridiculously futuristic, like something from a world's fair postcard. "Is this where they make the air brakes for the railroad?" he asked, following Taggart off the train and through the small crowd of workers gathered to board it.

"No, that's further up at Wilmerding, where the local Westinghouse headquarters is. They make electric motors and windings down here." He led Kachigan away from the drab industrial railroad depot and over a sturdy iron trestle bridge that led directly into the towering factory complex. At four-thirty in the afternoon, a last trickle of men and women were emptying from the factories into the central road, some heading back toward the railroad station and others hurrying to catch the streetcar that waited down at the intersection. A cold wind whistled between the tall brick buildings, carrying the roar of powerful generators and the hum of turning belts with it.

"None of the Westinghouse properties were bombed by our anarchist ring?" Kachigan asked, shouting to be heard over the din. "Only the railroad installations in the valley?"

"According to the local paper, yeah. But you never know." Taggart dodged the sparking streetcar, hopping nimbly enough over the tracks for all his bulk. "Maybe old George Westinghouse paid their reporters some hush money, the same way the railroad did with the city papers.''

"Maybe.'' On the far side of the street, a second railroad line loomed high over East Pittsburgh, its solid steel trestle casting oddly lacy shadows against the lower stories of the Westinghouse factory. Arched openings allowed three streets to pass beneath it, as well as a spur of the streetcar line. Another cold blast of wind fought them all the way through the underpass, but by now Kachigan was used to it.

They emerged into a ragtag scatter of confectioneries, dry-goods stores, and tobacconists, wedged in between dozens of hotels and bars. Electric signs glittered in the winter twilight, each trying to outflash the others in an attempt to attract George Westinghouse's departing workers. Despite that superficial glamour, East Pittsburgh's downtown looked tired and grubby, as if it had been built cheap and used hard ever since.

"The town hall's up a block, on Linden Avenue,'' Taggart offered. "That's where their lockup is.''

"How do you know?''

His partner grunted. "Used to work on the police force here, a while back. It wasn't such a bad beat during the week, but there was just too damn much work to do on weekends.'' They turned down another hotel-jammed street. "When the bars and bowling alleys stay open all night long, you're up till dawn stopping fights and kicking drunks out of people's backyards.''

Kachigan snorted. "Is that any worse than staying up till dawn collecting payoffs for Big Roge?''

"Sure is.'' Taggart ducked around the town hall's main door and headed for a smaller, cellar entrance marked POLICE in fading paint. "Big Roge's clients never throw up on my shoes. Hey, Danny, how's it going?''

The burly older cop at the front desk looked up, his beard splitting with a delighted smile. "Art Taggart, you son of a gun! They send you in to investigate our bombing case?''

"Not me, buddy.'' Taggart helped himself to a piece of apple strudel that sat on an adjacent counter. "The man you want is my new partner here. Milo Kachigan, this is the East Pittsburgh chief of police, Dan Turchan.''

"Detective Kachigan!" Turchan leaned forward and shook his hand with surprising warmth. "Glad you boys could come so quick. You want a piece of strudel before I take you to meet the anarchists? The wife made it just this morning."

Kachigan shook his head at the dripping slice Taggart offered him. "How many suspects did you arrest, Chief?"

"Just the two." Turchan rattled his keys out of his pocket, then led them down a dimly lit basement corridor that smelled of urine and old vomit. Kachigan grimaced, remembering Taggart's comment. "One of them's a stranger. The other's a bad-tempered old drunk I've seen around town for years. I'm having a little trouble believing he could have pulled off all those railroad bombings, to tell you the truth."

"So the first man's your prime suspect?"

"Seems like." Turchan fitted the key into a solid oak door. "The problem is, it's not a man."

"Not—" Kachigan fell silent, scowling at the horrible premonition that had just washed over him. *No,* he told his clamoring instincts while the door swung open to reveal two barred cells. Common sense ruled that there was no way Helen Sorby could be inside this stinking lockup, miles from her comfortable South Side home.

But the sober face and dark eyes that gazed back at him through the trellis of ironwork were all too familiar. "About time you got here, Milo Kachigan," Helen said. "I was starting to think I'd have to call Aunt Pittypat to bail me out."

So much for common sense.

3

HELEN'S TEMPER ONLY LET HER GET AS FAR AS the front step of East Pittsburgh's town hall before it exploded. After two weeks of simmering over Milo Kachigan's unexplained absence, she hadn't realized what a powerful mixture of relief and irritation would blast through her when she finally saw him. She'd done her best to keep a lid tamped on her roiling emotions, but one simple, overheard statement had lit the fuse on them.

"Did you *bribe* that man to let me out?"

"No." In the gathering twilight, it was hard to see the detective's expression, but she thought it looked more exasperated than guilty. "What makes you think that?"

"You said you'd make sure he wasn't sorry he released me." Helen scowled up at him, heedless of the laughing conversation back in the lockup, where the other county detective was still talking to the police chief. "What did that mean?"

Kachigan snorted. "It meant I'd do my best to stop you from publishing that list of 'humanitarian abuses' you insisted on reciting while I was trying to get you released."

"But, Milo, you could see it was all true! Those cells *were* airless and lightless, and the sanitary facilities—"

"Wouldn't be used by Saturday-night drunks, even if they existed," he said shortly. "Any more than your anarchist friend back there would use a spittoon."

Helen grimaced, unable to argue with that. She'd forgotten how annoyingly observant Kachigan could be. Her only defense was to round stubbornly back to her original accusation.

"If you didn't bribe that police chief to release me, then why is Mr. Maccoun still in jail? He's no more guilty of murder than I am!"

Kachigan's gaze never wavered from hers, but she knew him well enough to recognize the slight stiffening of his face as embarrassment. "I'm not disagreeing with you," he said. "But you told us yourself that Maccoun set off an explosion in a residential neighborhood—"

"Which would have only gotten him a fine and a lecture from the local magistrate, if it hadn't excavated a body!"

Kachigan raised his voice to be heard over the roar of a train on the high trestle that shadowed all of East Pittsburgh's downtown. "We're not talking about some railroad laborer using a stick of dynamite to blow up a stump! Practicing with bombs implies use of bombs in later criminal activity."

Helen raised her own voice to match his. "So just because Mr. Maccoun's political views are unpopular, he automatically becomes a criminal? Then why didn't you leave me in jail, too?"

"Because Chief Turchan would have started crying if I did," Kachigan shot back. "The question you should be asking, Miss Sorby, isn't whether I offered him a bribe to let you out, but if I took one from him to get rid of you."

For some reason, it was the formal "Miss Sorby" rather than the insult buried in his words that infuriated Helen most. "Well?" she demanded, before her better judgment could intervene. "Did you?"

The dirty glow of gaslights along Linden Avenue wasn't bright enough to show her the color of Kachigan's face, but it threw the quick clench of muscles along his jaw into sharp relief. Knowing what he was capable of on the rare occasions when he lost his own deep-seated Armenian temper, Helen braced herself for a furious reply. To her surprise, what she got back was a bitter bark of laughter.

"No," said Kachigan. "But only because I wasn't in the mood for apple strudel." He glanced back at the door to the police station. "Art's probably taking a slice for the road, though. Maybe you could still write us up as an example of police corruption."

The cold slam of a wind gust caught Helen's retort and shoved it back into her throat before she could make matters even worse. She turned her back to the wind and let it whip at her worn wool coat, noticing as she did so that Kachigan was rubbing irritably at his scarred cheek. By the time the wind died and the rumble of the passing train had faded into silence, she'd forgotten what she was going to say. The pause stretched into a grinding silence, broken at last by the heavy smack of footsteps behind them.

"You guys just made Danny Turchan the happiest man in East Pittsburgh." As predicted, Kachigan's partner was indeed wolfing down a slice of sweet-smelling brown pastry. Helen glared up at him, and got back a look that was equally amused and sleepy. "He was starting to think he might have to bring the wife down for the night to be Miss Sorby's chaperon. That wouldn't have gone over real big."

"I should imagine not, given the stench and squalor of that place!" Helen snapped.

"No, he was just worried about ruining her bingo night." The sandy-haired detective wiped his hand on his coat flap, then held it out to Helen. She took it reluctantly and was surprised by the equable firmness of his grip. Most big men shook hands squeamishly with women, as if they were afraid to crush them. "I'm Art Taggart, by the way, since Milo didn't see fit to introduce us back there. And you're Helen Sorby, his anarchist social worker from the South Side."

"She's not an anarchist, she's a socialist," Kachigan said, between his teeth. "And she's not mine."

Helen lifted her head, as defiantly as she could with the wind yanking her hair across her face. "I'm not a social worker either, Mr. Taggart. I'm the new director of Essene Settlement House." She deepened her voice, trying for Julia Regitz Brown's tone of magisterial authority. "In that capacity, as an official representative of the East Pittsburgh Valley Christian Benevolent Association, I demand that your bureau fully investigate the death of the man in my backyard.''

"Don't worry,'' Kachigan said. "We intend to.''

The body had apparently been left where Abraham Maccoun's
blast had scattered it, although the path back to it was now
guarded by a tall young patrolman. He kept the curious settlement-house residents at bay on the back porch with an occasional twirl of his stick, meanwhile trading banter with Molly
Slade over the rail. Beyond him, a warm glow of gaslight lit
the kitchen shed and scattered shafts of golden light across the
side and back yards. Thomas must have opened all the shutters.

"County detectives bureau.'' Kachigan reached into his
pocket and showed the young man a new brass badge. The
patrolman straightened abruptly. "No one's disturbed the body
since you arrested the suspects this afternoon?''

"No, sir. I only let one guy back there, to turn the gaslights
on in the shed.'' The patrolman's respectful tone startled Helen. She wondered if it reflected the power of the Allegheny
County Detectives Bureau or Milo Kachigan's brusque voice.
"I figured you could use the light to see by.''

"Good.'' Kachigan turned back to Helen, his thin face expressionless. By dint of great self-control on her part, the three-
block walk from the lockup to Essene House had been
accomplished in polite silence, but it didn't seem to have soft-
ened the detective's mood. "I'd like you to stay here while
we examine the body, Miss Sorby. I don't want the grass
around it to get any more trampled than it already is.''

"Can I at least go back to the kitchen and let my brother
know I'm out of jail, Mr. Kachigan? Or do I have to shout
the news at him from here?''

"You already *are* shouting,'' he informed her. "I doubt Mr.
Sorby needs any more reassurance than that.''

Helen clamped down on a strong desire to hit him. "Then
I suppose I'll just have to go inside and start ringing up the
Pittsburgh papers to see who's interested in an article about
humanitarian abuses in the East Pittsburgh lockup.''

Kachigan gave her a frowning look, but it was Taggart who
responded to the unsubtle threat. "I really think you should

go back and talk to your brother, Miss Sorby,'' he said. ''I'm sure he's very worried about you.''

Kachigan didn't look as if he shared that conviction, but he gave the patrolman a reluctant nod. Helen gathered up her skirts and scurried past him before he could change his mind.

The steamy warmth of the kitchen, sweet with the smell of frying onions and baking peaches, greeted her like a hug after the cold night air outside. She pulled the kitchen door shut and headed straight for the back windows, squeezing her way between stacked burlap potato sacks so she could watch what Kachigan and Taggart were doing.

''There you are, Helen.'' Her twin stopped slicing onions into an enormous black skillet just long enough to glance up at her. He didn't sound surprised or relieved, just mildly curious. ''How many more will there be for dinner tonight? Just the patrolman, or will Milo be staying, too?''

After twenty-six years, Helen had thought she was wise to every trick a twin brother could pull, but this nonchalant question made her turn and stare at him. In fact, she even went so far as to demand, ''How on earth did you—'' before her wits woke up and rapped at her brain for admittance. ''No, don't tell me. You heard his voice outside?''

''No.''

''You heard me yelling at him?''

''No.''

She paused, considering what she would have done in Thomas's place. ''You called the detectives bureau when you found out I was arrested and asked Kachigan to investigate?''

''Actually, I rang up Aunt Pat.'' Thomas took a last swallow of beer from the open bottle in his hand and splashed the rest of it over his skillet full of veal and onions. Helen didn't bother to give him the usual scold for that. After seeing what the Buchak brothers had considered clean enough to go into a skillet, half-drunk beer seemed like the ultimate in hygienic food. ''After she finished having hysterics, I told her to call her godson in the county commissioner's office and get Kachigan put on the case. I figured that would be a lot cheaper than bailing you out of jail.''

''Hmmph.'' Helen turned back to the window, rubbing off

steam so she could peer through at the beams of refracted light
that lit the backyard. She couldn't see much, but it looked as
if Kachigan had climbed far up the steep, weedy hillside below
the railroad trestle while Taggart loitered to examine the bare
dirt of Maccoun's crater below. "It might have been cheaper,
but it wasn't any quicker."

"Yeah, I know. But I figured it was worth the wait to get
Kachigan back so you could yell at him instead of me for a
change—Helen, don't throw that potato at me! Molly said you
wanted your detective friend to investigate this case."

She glared at him, fingers clenched around the sprouting
missile she'd grabbed up. "He's *not* my friend. And what I
wanted him to do was get Abraham Maccoun out of jail, which
he hasn't yet made the slightest move to accomplish!"

"Well, what's your hurry?" Thomas threw a generous
handful of black pepper and parsley into his sizzling pan. "Let
Maccoun spit at the East Pittsburgh police instead of us for a
while. At least he can't blow up any more of our backyard
while he's in there."

Helen's sigh put more mist on the cracked kitchen window.
Thomas Sorby might be an uncommonly supportive brother,
but no one had ever accused him of having a social conscience.

"Maccoun is in jail for a crime he didn't commit," she
reminded her twin. "That's unfair. And you know the police
just want to find someone to blame. If they can't find the real
killers, Abraham Maccoun would be the perfect person to
frame. No one would miss him, and no one would lift a finger
to defend him."

"Except you," Thomas said. "So why aren't you out there
helping Kachigan investigate?"

"Because he doesn't want or need my help, that's why!"

Her twin threw her an amused glance. "I don't recall that
stopping you the last time you worked with him." He uncov-
ered a giant tub of boiling water, releasing still more steam
into the kitchen shed. "Now, how many more people are we
having for dinner? I need to know before I start the noodles."

"Three." Outside, Helen saw Taggart look around as if
summoned, then reluctantly plod up the hill in the direction
Kachigan had gone. She took a deep breath and rebuttoned

her winter coat. "Assuming I don't manage to make Milo so mad at me that he leaves before you're done cooking."

She left her brother pouring a small avalanche of egg noodles into his tub and stepped down into the unlit back pantry. The mossy stone floor was covered with an unexpected sheen of water, cold enough to make her yelp when she stepped into it. Helen stopped and let her eyes adjust to the dark so she could survey the extent of the flooding. This, too, was damage caused by Maccoun's bomb blast, she realized—none of the settlement-house tenants had been allowed back to empty the meltwater tray under their ancient icebox since noon. Not that they would have anyway, without her here to nag them about their assigned chores. Helen sighed and picked her way across the puddled stone floor, adding "mop pantry" to her list of things to do tomorrow.

A narrow back door let her slide behind a scraggly, brown-leaved forsythia hedge and cross into the backyard undetected. The light spilling through the unshuttered kitchen windows was surprisingly bright, she discovered, once she was actually out in the darkness it illuminated. She could see the severed leg beside Maccoun's crater, now discreetly draped with an old linen towel. A ragged blanket had been used to cover the rest of the corpse, but even as she watched, it was lifted by a wiry shadow she recognized as Milo Kachigan. Taggart's larger silhouette loomed behind him, itself dwarfed by the overhanging shadow of the railroad trestle. Helen lifted her skirts past her ankles and hiked up to join them.

The crunch of her footsteps across frost-stiff weeds brought both their heads jerking around to stare at her. Kachigan scowled as he recognized her. "Helen, I thought I told you—"

"Not to come back here. I know." His words might have been sliced off abruptly, but Helen found the familiar flare of exasperation in his voice reassuring. Anything was better than the cold silence she'd endured on the way over from the lockup. She climbed the rest of the way up to join him. "I'm not going to interfere. I just came out to make sure you're investigating this case."

His frown deepened. "As opposed to what?"

"As opposed to looking for evidence to frame the suspect

you've already arrested.'' She threw him a challenging look across the facedown corpse. ''If you kick me out of here now, that's what I'll have to conclude you're doing. I was careful to follow where Mr. Taggart walked. The grass couldn't get much more trampled there—''

''If an elephant had walked on it,'' the big detective finished politely. Helen threw him a wary glance, but saw only amusement on his broad face. ''She's got you there, Milo.''

Kachigan didn't bother to reply, instead going down on one knee beside the body. Taking that as tacit acceptance of her presence, Helen tucked in her skirts and hunkered down across from him, taking a long, somber look at the dead man's fatal wounds. Now that the first shock of discovery was six hours behind her, she could think more intelligently about what might have caused his savage mutilation. The approaching rumble of a Pittsburgh, Bessemer, and Lake Erie engine on the trestle overhead supplied an answer so obvious she wondered why it hadn't occurred to her before.

''He was run over by a train, wasn't he?''

Art Taggart snorted. ''See there, Milo? I told you there was no need to go climbing all over that damned hillside to figure that out.''

Kachigan grunted, brushing several mud smears off the dead man's expensive wool suit and onto his palm to eye them more closely. ''I wanted to know exactly where on the tracks he was hit.''

''Well?'' Helen demanded, lifting her voice to be heard over the clatter of the passing train. ''Where was it?''

The detective didn't answer her, leaving his partner to reply. ''From the bloodstains on the rails and the weeds he crushed when he rolled down the hill, it looks like he was up on the trestle, almost a third of the way across.''

''Hmm.'' Helen bent over to sniff at the slice of the dead man's face that wasn't pressed down into the dirt. There was a thin hint of cologne water and the faint sickly tang of frozen blood, but no trace of whiskey, gin, or rum. She straightened to find Kachigan and Taggart both staring at her in surprise.

''I wanted to see if he was drunk,'' she said defensively. On the track overhead, the locomotive's chuffing faded into silence. "But he's not. So, why on earth was he up on that high rail?"

"Probably because someone left him there." Kachigan felt around the back of the dead man's head, first probing at the brilliantined dark hair, then sliding his fingers beneath the edge of the rumpled collar. With a grunt of satisfaction, he tugged the collar free to show Helen and Taggart the crushed and fiercely purpled bruise beneath it. "From the size and color of that contusion, I'd say he was knocked unconscious several hours before he died."

"Was he robbed?" Helen demanded.

Kachigan gave her an irritated look. "That's what I'm trying to find out. Quit distracting me."

She bit her lip and sat back on her heels, forcing herself to pay strict attention to what the detective was doing. She had to admit that if he was planning to frame Abraham Maccoun, his investigation showed no hint of it. Kachigan ran careful fingers around the bloodstained edges of trousers and shirtsleeve where the missing legs and hand had been, then lifted the remaining cold-stiffened limbs up to inspect the crushed and darkened weeds beneath. After each observation, he jotted down another line in his evidence book, writing with his usual meticulous slowness. Finally, just when Helen was about to explode with impatience, he slid his fingers into the dead man's trouser and coat pockets. He pulled a torn-across train ticket out of one and a few paper-wrapped cough drops out of another, but nothing more.

"He *was* robbed," she said in satisfaction.

"Maybe." Kachigan rose and nodded at Taggart to help him lift the corpse and place it faceup several feet away. "Don't step on the place he was laying," he said over his shoulder to Helen.

"I won't." It wasn't hard to avoid, outlined as it was in scattered smears of blood. She made a wide circuit around it, ending up beside Kachigan when she joined them this time. He glanced down at her cautiously, but didn't try to prevent her from seeing the man who'd died in her backyard.

The dead man had a blunt face, high-browed and accented with a long handlebar mustache. Although death had pressed his nose and cheeks lopsided against the grass where he'd been flung, Helen suspected that in life they'd been regular, perhaps even handsome. He looked to be in early middle age, his body thick through the waist but still broad-shouldered and athletic. The hand that had survived his accident was well manicured and wore a heavy silver signet ring. Helen frowned and pointed to it.

"Maybe he wasn't robbed after all. Wouldn't thieves take that?"

"If they could get it off." Kachigan squatted to tug at the ring. It resisted his pull, but the movement dislodged the dead man's coat far enough to see that he still wore a thick gold watch chain dangling from the pocket of his vest. Taggart whistled softly.

"Definitely not robbed. There'd be no problem getting *that* off, and it's the first thing thieves take after the wallet."

"I know." Kachigan made a careful note in his book, then slid his fingers into the dead man's watch pocket. The watch he came out with was as gold as the chain it was attached to, with an unusual design engraved into its cover. Helen leaned closer, trying to decide if the crossed tools above the oil lamp were compasses or calipers.

"That looks like some kind of scientific symbol."

"Mm-hmm." Kachigan clicked open the case to reveal a plain white face with gold Roman numerals and an inscription on the inside of the lid. He angled it toward the distant gleam of kitchen light. " 'American Association of Mechanical Engineers,' " he read slowly, " '1905 Inventor of the Year.' "

"Sounds like he might have worked for Westinghouse," Helen said. "Is there a name?"

"No." Kachigan snapped the watch shut and turned it over, but the back was annoyingly blank. With a frown, he unclipped it from the dead man's watch chain and slid it into his own vest pocket, tucked into his evidence book. "But whoever he was, this man certainly wasn't stupid."

"And he wasn't drunk," Helen said.

"And he wasn't robbed." Taggart draped the ragged blanket back across the body. "So, why did he get conked and left on the railroad tracks?"

A stymied silence fell between them, broken after a moment by the rusty clang of the old horseshoe Thomas used as a dinner bell. With a growl, Helen's stomach reminded her that she hadn't eaten since breakfast.

"We're having veal and noodles for supper at the settlement house," she said abruptly. "Are you staying?"

Kachigan rose and glanced down at her, his expression turning remote again. "Are you inviting us?"

"She just did," Taggart pointed out. "And I can smell how good it is from here. Come on, Milo."

The detective frowned and shook his head. "No, I don't think so. There's something Miss Sorby has to understand before we go any further. This is now a case of murder."

"I managed to figure that out for myself, Mr. Kachigan. What does that have to do with supper?" Helen tilted her head, remembering the last murder case they'd investigated together. In the course of that week the detective had missed more meals than he'd consumed. "Have you decided that you're not allowed to eat until you've solved the case?"

"I can eat," he said. "But I can't release Abraham Maccoun from jail."

After her initial jerk of surprise, Helen wasn't sure what she felt most—bleak satisfaction that she'd been right about the detective's reluctance to free Maccoun, or even bleaker disappointment. She'd been so sure, a month ago, that Kachigan's unwanted transfer to the corrupt Allegheny County Detectives Bureau couldn't affect his fundamental integrity. Although her faith had been shaken by his arrest and even more so by his subsequent disappearance from her life, she realized that she'd never quite lost that inner core of sureness. Until now.

Her voice, when she found it at last, surprised her by being quiet instead of loud. "You're actually going to charge Maccoun for this murder? Even though you know he had absolutely nothing to do with it?"

"Not charge him, no. Just hold him in jail."

"Why? Because the motto of the county detectives bureau is 'arrest first, investigate later'?"

"No." Kachigan reached out and caught her elbow when she would have swung away. The fierceness of his grip startled

Helen, revealing an anger that his rigid face still hid. "Because if we don't have a suspect in custody, Art and I will get yanked off this case before you're even done with supper."

Helen stared up at him. He held her gaze steadily, the dark blue fire in his eyes burning brighter than usual. "Why?" she demanded. "Doesn't your boss trust you to solve it?"

It looked as if Kachigan's teeth had locked so tight that he couldn't get a word past them. Taggart answered for him. "Miss Sorby, our boss doesn't trust us to collect his payoffs without an arraignment hanging over our heads. He's certainly not going to let us handle a murder case that could make him look bad if we blow it."

"So he's going to throw it to some of his detective cronies. Men he can be sure *will* frame someone for it." Kachigan cleared his throat. "And then any chance of finding the real murderer, and clearing your friend of the crime, will be gone. Trust me, Miss Sorby, the safest place for Abraham Maccoun right now is right where he is."

Helen blew out a frustrated breath. "All right," she said in resignation. "I'll let you keep Mr. Maccoun in jail. I'll even keep my mouth shut about the East Pittsburgh lockup. But there's one condition, Mr. Kachigan."

"I know. You want me to let you help with my investigation so you can write it all up for some New York magazine."

Helen straightened to glare at him. "No," she said, and had the pleasure of seeing his eyes widen in surprise. "I want to run my own investigation, and I don't want you to interfere with it. In return, I promise not to get in your way, or nag you with any questions. Is it a deal?"

Kachigan looked as if he wanted to argue with her, but a quick poke in the ribs from his partner made him grunt. Taggart said, "Sounds like a deal to me, Miss Sorby. Can we go down to supper now?"

She nodded, smiling in satisfaction. "There should be plenty of veal and noodles, Mr. Taggart, but you'd better hurry if you want peach cobbler. The tenants tend to eat their dessert first."

The big man's smile flashed in the darkness. "Yes, but they can't get to it until we give young Otis permission to let them back to the kitchen. I think I'll let you do that, Milo, while I size up the cobbler situation.''

He strode downhill with long strides that belied his usual lazy amble. Helen watched him go with raised eyebrows. "He can move fast enough when food's involved, can't he?'' she commented critically.

"Don't underestimate Taggart,'' Kachigan said. "If he wasn't so lazy, he'd be a damned good policeman. He's twice as smart as he looks, and half as corrupt as any other detective in the bureau.''

Helen bit her lip to keep from asking the obvious question. Instead, she asked, "Are you really going to let me investigate this murder case?''

"Are you really going to stay out of my way?''

"Yes.'' She led the way back toward the main settlement house so Kachigan could give permission for her tenants to get their supper, forcing herself to ignore the empty grinding in her own stomach. No one had ever told her that being a settlement-house director was this hard. "I have a magazine article on women's employment in the electrical trades to finish by Christmas, Mr. Kachigan,'' she said truthfully enough. "Between that and my work here at Essene House, I'm not going to have time to get in your way.''

"No requests to read my police files? No demands to accompany me during questionings?''

"No.''

"Not even any suggestions that we share information while we ride the train back to the South Side?''

She cast him a frowning look. "I don't take the train back to the South Side. You'll be safe enough taking it home.''

"So Thomas not only escorts you out here every day, he hires a cab to do it? It sounds like your promotion to settlement-house director is going to cost him more than your salary brings in.''

This time, Helen slowed to a stop to give him the full benefit of her scowl. "My salary includes free board and lodging, Mr. Kachigan, and it's not costing Thomas a cent! He's just been kind enough to reschedule a mapping project he needed to do for the Sanborn Map Company in the East Pittsburgh valley so he could keep me company while I settled into my employment. By the time he's done, I'll have Essene House in such good order that he can go back to Sarah Street without me.''

Kachigan's eyes narrowed to slits. "You're planning to live by yourself in a church-run tenement? In the middle of the slums of East Pittsburgh?"

The clear ring of condemnation in his voice ignited Helen's temper once again. "Well, at least it's better than spending all my nights in whorehouses and gambling dens!"

This time, the clear light from the unshuttered kitchen windows ruthlessly revealed the dark rush of color in his cheeks. "True," Kachigan said, in a stiff voice. "Excuse me, Miss Sorby, please. I've got to give permission for your tenants to have their supper."

"And then?" she demanded, already knowing what his answer would be.

"And then I'm going to take the train back to the South Side and go home. For once." He tipped his bowler hat to her with infuriating formality. "Good evening."

Helen bit down hard on all the things she wanted to say. Instead, she watched him walk up the path to the back porch of the settlement house, pause briefly by the steps to speak to the young patrolman, and then disappear into the dark alley that separated Essene House from its nearest neighbor. It didn't improve her temper in the slightest to observe that he never once looked back at her. Standing in the darkness, she faced up to the annoying truth that this first meeting after Kachigan's arrest really couldn't have gone much worse.

Her only consolation was knowing that with a murder to solve, the detective would be back.

KACHIGAN HAD ALMOST FORGOTTEN WHAT MORN-
ing looked like.

He paused on the slate sidewalk that bordered
Linden Avenue, content for a moment just to
watch winter sunlight pour through a rift in the
cloudy sky and listen to the soft winter chatter of sparrows
from the eaves of the boardinghouse across the street. A mid-
morning quiet had settled over East Pittsburgh's run-down
business district, hovering between the early rush of Westinghouse workers and the more leisurely excursions of local
housewives. Despite the occasional glitter of sun, the air was
cold and still and smelled of sulfur from the coal smoke cur-
dling above each house chimney. Except for the absence of
ash drifting from steel mills, Kachigan could have been back
in the South Side walking his old morning beat.

But instead of getting up early to direct horse traffic and
help schoolchildren cross busy streets, he'd taken an empty
predawn train out of the city and spent the last few hours
visiting one rank boardinghouse and tavern after another, talking to men who'd just come off third-trick shifts at Westinghouse and Edgar Thompson. Kachigan blew out a long breath,
wishing he could expel a morning's worth of frustration along
with the lingering reek of cigar smoke and stale beer. It was
always hard getting men to talk after ten or twelve hours hard
labor, but when they'd trudged home at dawn to a quitting-

time beer that also served as breakfast, getting anything out of them but yawns or shrugs seemed almost impossible. Until he'd left, of course, when a consistent rumble of laughter usually trailed in his wake. Kachigan wondered if it was the anomaly of a county detective actually doing his job that amused them, or just the folly of expecting them to remember anything that occurred at the end of a late-night shift.

Down where Linden ended against Electric Avenue, a trolley clattered to a stop and discharged a bustle of housewives. Their cheerful Italian and Slavic accents chased away the morning stillness, but it was the excited whoops of their children that made the sparrows across the street burst into a flurry of startled flight. Within minutes, every child had clustered around the window of the nearest bakery shop. A man in a white apron stained from several hours work leaned out the door to banter with them, then elicited more shrieks of delight by tossing them a generous handful of cookies.

It occurred to Kachigan that tired factory men and drunks weren't the only ones awake in the early-morning hours when a corpse was tossed from the high iron railroad trestle into Helen Sorby's backyard. And industrious local merchants might have better memories. He headed down the street, searching in his vest pocket for a dime to buy a bear claw or maple gob. Today was the first time in three weeks that he'd actually left for work before the milkman had arrived, and his stomach was starting to growl at him about it.

Inside, the bakery was summer warm and smelled of yeast and melted butter. There was only a single glass case but it was bursting with sweet rolls and strudels, nut breads and cheese tarts, and loaves in all shapes and sizes. The burly baker stood behind the counter, shoveling an astonishing amount of bread into paper bags. His customer wasn't one of the kerchiefed matrons, however. It was a broad-shouldered young man in a surveyor's vest, whose face lit with a grin when he saw Kachigan.

"Hey, Milo. You missed a good supper last night."

Kachigan winced. He had never been sure, even when he'd been on the best of terms with Helen Sorby, just how seriously to take her twin brother's teasing. "I'm sure Taggart ate enough to make up for my absence," he said, to avoid making excuses he knew he couldn't justify. "I hope he didn't run you out of peach cobbler."

"Actually, he did." Thomas Sorby loaded the bread into the netted market bag he had slung over one shoulder. It already bulged with greens and potatoes from the grocers up the street, and large cuts of meat wrapped in damp butcher paper. "But he made up for it by playing a mean hand of poker after the dishes were done. By the way, didn't you say you would get the milk?"

Kachigan opened his mouth to deny making any such promise, but found that Sorby wasn't looking at him anymore. With a jolt that wasn't quite remorse and wasn't quite irritation, he swung around to see Helen peering at him from the bakery door. The expression on her face was hard to read, since the militant set of her mouth clashed with distinctly cautious dark eyes.

"Miss Sorby." Kachigan took off his hat and stepped back to allow her into the enveloping warmth of the bakery. Just because they weren't cooperating on this case didn't mean he couldn't impress her with his politeness. In fact, it was probably all he had left to impress her with. "Good morning."

"Good morning, Mr. Kachigan." She gave him as much room as she could when she passed him, but he still saw the involuntary wrinkle of her nose that meant she'd smelled the taint of beer and smoke on his clothes. Knowing Helen, he knew what was coming next. "Or should I really be saying good night?"

"Three bear claws," Kachigan told the baker instead of answering her. By the time he'd paid for the glistening golden pastries and handed the extra two to Thomas Sorby, his spurt of temper had faded to resigned disgust. "If you were a really observant reporter, Miss Sorby, you'd have noticed that I have on different clothes than yesterday. That would have told you I hadn't spent the entire night crawling through bars."

"Then why do you smell like one?" she demanded, ignoring the pastry her brother held out to her. "Does the county detectives office serve beer instead of coffee in the morning?"

Kachigan snorted. "No, but only because all the judges in

the courthouse would demand a share of the profits.'' Three dark-haired matrons chattering in what sounded like Greek crowded into the small bakery, pressing up against them with the cheerful disregard of space that most immigrants emerged from steerage with. Thomas stepped back into the baker's storage area, setting his market bag down on a convenient stack of flour bags so he could devour his pastry. ''I've been questioning the local third-trick men about what they might have seen on the railroad trestle the night before last—but since you don't want to cooperate with my murder investigation, Miss Sorby, I don't suppose you're interested in the results.''

That earned him the frown he'd expected, but not the indignant reporter's demands that he'd thought would come with it. ''I don't need you to tell me your results, Mr. Kachigan. I know what they are already. No one saw *anything* up on the Bessemer, Pittsburgh, and Lake Erie tracks, night before last.''

Thomas's disgusted snort blew pastry flakes off his mustache. ''If that was all the information you could get out of the butcher, the greengrocer, and the oysterman, Helen, what's your excuse for forgetting the milk?''

His sister's face reddened slightly. ''The milkman got mad at me for insisting that he must have seen something while he was making his rounds. He wouldn't sell me any.''

For some reason, that confession took the annoying edge off Kachigan's own futile morning rounds. He relaxed enough to take a bite of his bear claw, and was surprised by the unexpected Greek flavors of honey and lemon mixed with the usual sweet walnut filling. He'd noticed before that even the most American of foods, like apple pie or hamburger, tended to mutate in flavor from neighborhood to neighborhood as each of Pittsburgh's diverse immigrant races added the spices and flavorings they liked best.

''I suppose that means I'll have to go get it myself, or there won't be any pudding for dessert tonight.'' Thomas sounded resigned but not particularly upset. Kachigan suspected this wasn't the first time Helen Sorby had alienated some local merchant with her socialist principles and overactive conscience. ''Are you going to take this bear claw, Helen?''

She accepted the pastry and even gave it an absentminded

bite before scowling as if she'd just remembered where it came from. "As long as you're going down the street, Thomas, would you mind stopping at the Chinese laundry and asking them—"

"No," he said bluntly. "My Chinese isn't any better than yours, and I'm already late for work."

"But somebody must have seen *something*—that man didn't get flown up to the trestle by angels of the Lord!" She dropped her half-eaten bear claw on the floor, giving Kachigan a defiant glance as she did. "And all we need is to know the time he was killed to clear Mr. Maccoun of the crime."

Kachigan forced his face to stay expressionless, but he couldn't suppress the involuntary clench of his fist that crumbled the rest of his breakfast into drifting crumbs to join hers. Helen knew that the minute she got her drunken anarchist out of jail, he'd be yanked off this murder investigation. "I realize you'd rather not cooperate with me, Miss Sorby," he said in the coldest voice he could manage. It was effective enough to make Thomas Sorby throw him a startled look, although it didn't seem to make the slightest dent on his sister. "But I wouldn't try to get Maccoun released if I were you."

"Why?" she demanded. "Because you'd rather pretend to investigate this murder than go back to shaking down bars and brothels for Roger McGara?"

"Helen—"

"Because you really don't want to find out just how corrupt the rest of the county detectives bureau is!" Kachigan lifted his voice to override whatever angry comment she was trying to make. "If you eliminate Maccoun as a suspect and get me thrown off this case, all my boss is going to do is find another local anarchist to arrest on no evidence. And then *neither* of us will be able to find out who really killed that man on the railroad tracks!"

Silence crashed across the bakery after that furious exchange, obvious enough for even Helen Sorby to notice. She glanced past Kachigan at their audience of wide-eyed Greek matrons and frowning baker, and the olive tint of her cheeks turned to rose. "I think we'd better leave," she said to her brother in a stifled voice.

"I think so, too." Thomas Sorby hefted his market bag, giving her and Kachigan a jointly exasperated look. "I also think you two ought to reconsider this idea of separate investigations. It's obvious neither of you can think straight on your own."

"Just what do you mean by that?" Helen demanded.

"I mean that you can badger merchants and factory men along this street until you're blue in the face, and you still won't find anyone who saw anything happen up on those tracks. And I know why."

Kachigan added his frowning look to Helen's. "Why?"

"Because it doesn't take angels of the Lord to drop an unconscious man onto a forty-foot-high railroad trestle," Thomas Sorby said impatiently. "All it takes is a railroad car."

"Taggart, I'm an idiot."

"Yeah, I knew that." His partner didn't even glance up from the morning newspaper he was reading. Their trolley lurched and sparked to a stop at a house-dotted hillside, letting out a cluster of shoppers before it resumed its journey up Airbrake Avenue toward Pitcairn and Wilmerding. Another trolley passed them in the opposite direction, and Kachigan had to shield his eyes against the glare as one east-facing window after another caught a mirrored flash of sun and reflected it back at them. "I could have told you myself that the best way to drop a guy onto a trestle was from a train. You should have just slept in and asked me."

And spared himself another incendiary encounter with Helen Sorby, Kachigan thought in resignation. Although he'd never had a very clear idea of how he was going to reintroduce himself into her life once he'd gotten his name and reputation reasonably cleared, he knew that springing her free from jail last night had been the worst possible way to do it. No matter what excuses he had given her, the glaring fact remained that what he had done was neither legal nor aboveboard, any more than a corrupt detective springing his favorite bookie. When you added in his equally unethical decision to keep Abraham Maccoun in jail just so he wouldn't get thrown off the case, you had a recipe for guaranteed disaster. In fact, the longer he thought about it, the more it seemed like a miracle that she hadn't spat in his face this morning and walked out without a word.

Taggart interrupted those gloomy thoughts by smacking him with his folded newspaper. "Are you listening to me?"

"I am now," Kachigan said, and straightened his bowler hat.

His partner grunted. "Then tell me why you think we're actually going to get to talk to George Westinghouse about our dead guy."

"Because of this." Kachigan extracted the dead man's watch from his vest pocket. "Westinghouse is an inventor as well as a factory owner. I'm betting that even if he didn't employ him, he's going to want to know why the '1905 Inventor of the Year' is dead."

"That doesn't mean he's going to want *us* to know." Taggart braced himself on a hanging strap as the Eighty-seven Ardmore streetcar swung right, lurching onto a bridge over the main Pennsylvania Railroad line. Another hillside town climbed the barren valley slopes ahead of them, its houses grading from brick to insul-brick to tar paper as they straggled up to the poorer top streets. The streetcar bridge crossed directly over a complex of long factory buildings, as ultramodern in their graceful fanning shapes as their taller cousins back in East Pittsburgh. "Asking George Westinghouse questions he doesn't want to answer might get us thrown off this case just as fast as letting that old man out of Dan Turchan's jail."

"You think Westinghouse might be involved in the murder?" Kachigan asked in disbelief. Every story he'd ever heard about the electricity magnate emphasized how he stood head and shoulders above the corrupt steel, coal, and rail barons who were his Pittsburgh millionaire peers.

Taggart shrugged. "There's been a lot of stories in the New York papers lately about industrial secrets being stolen in the electric industry. Just the other day, the *New York Herald* had a cartoon of Thomas Edison and George Westinghouse hanging on to live electric wires, one alternating current and one direct. The caption said only one of them would come out alive."

"Just because they can't stand each other's electrical inventions doesn't mean they'd actually kill people over it."

"Doesn't it?" His partner threw him a skeptical glance. "Do you know how much money George Westinghouse made on the Niagara Falls power plant?"

"No, how much?"

The trolley clattered to a stop at its short loop turnaround in Wilmerding before Taggart could reply. "Enough to build that headquarters building," he said, and pointed up the street ahead of them as they got off the car. "Does that answer your question?"

"Mm." Kachigan eyed the gleaming citadel of brick turrets and spires that towered over the homes and shops of Wilmerding, and steeled himself for his first encounter with a millionaire. "Let's go see if he'll still talk to the county detectives bureau."

He led the way up Station Street to Commerce Avenue, then caught sight of the time on the Westinghouse headquarters tall clock tower and took the stairs to the main entrance at a pace that made Taggart grumble. The minute hand had slid only a little past eleven by the time they walked through the doors, but the generously freckled young man who came forward to meet them still looked as worried as if they'd been long overdue.

"Detectives Kachigan and Taggart?" He had a self-effacing voice, as genteel and modest as his soft handshake. "I'm John McCaplin, Mr. Westinghouse's private secretary. I'm afraid Mr. Westinghouse has already left for the holidays. The receptionist said she told your secretary that—I don't know why she still made the appointment."

Either because Lucy hadn't heard a word at the other end of the telephone connection, or didn't care if their trip was wasted, Kachigan thought, but he didn't let his anger show. Although McCaplin's tone had been respectful enough, there was a reserved look in his eyes that told Kachigan the reputation of the Allegheny County Detectives Bureau had spread even to this quiet eastern valley. "We're investigating a murder in East Pittsburgh, Mr. McCaplin. If Mr. Westinghouse can't see us, we'd like to talk to someone else who could help us identify the victim. We think he was a company employee.''

That news dug even deeper furrows into the secretary's face. ''Mr. Westinghouse employs upward of a thousand men in the East Pittsburgh Valley, Mr. Kachigan. You'd need to talk to plant foremen from every factory and every shift in order to identify your—er—victim.''

''We have reason to believe that the dead man may have worked right here in Westinghouse's office. In fact, you yourself might have known him. Here.'' Kachigan pulled the gold watch from his pocket and dropped it into McCaplin's well-manicured hand, clicking the case open as he did to show the inscription inside the lid. ''Does that look familiar?''

McCaplin's breath hissed between his teeth. ''I think you'd better come up into the engineering offices, Mr. Kachigan,'' was his answer. ''Right away.''

He turned on his heel and strode down the hallway without even giving them a chance to reply. Taggart whistled and lifted an eyebrow at Kachigan as they followed. ''That hit a nerve. I wonder why.''

''Maybe they're worried about their missing engineer. He's been dead since yesterday night, remember.'' Kachigan pursued the secretary's neatly trousered legs up the iron-railed staircase at the end of the hall, outdistancing Taggart in half a flight. He caught up to the younger man at the top landing, tugging at his sleeve to stop him. ''If you could wait for my partner?''

McCaplin threw a remorseful look down over the railing, where Taggart's huffing slowly preceded him up the steps. ''Sorry about that. It's just that—'' He broke off, glancing down a hall lined with open office doors. Kachigan could hear the high-pitched whir of motors and the whine of a metal saw, overlain with a rumble of arguing voices. ''This news won't be easy for them. Everyone's been very concerned.''

''I'm sure.'' Kachigan extracted his notebook from his coat pocket. ''While we're waiting do you think you could tell me the name of the man who owned that watch you're holding?''

The secretary glanced down in surprise at the watch he still clutched in his hand, then thrust it back toward Kachigan. ''Sorry—I didn't mean to keep it. You did say this was a murder case, didn't you? I suppose it must be evidence.''

"Yes.'' Kachigan tucked the gold watch back into his pocket. "Can you tell me whose it was?''

"Osborne's.'' McCaplin took a deep calming breath. "Mr. Lyell Osborne, I mean. He is—he was—one of the senior engineers here.''

"I see.'' Kachigan wrote the information down, slowly enough that Taggart had joined them and caught his breath before he was done. McCaplin promptly swung around and started down the hall. He paused at the first office door they passed but did not enter, instead bracing his hands on both sides of the doorway as if to keep himself from falling in. Seeing the astonishing clutter of jumbled books, rolled blueprints, and haphazardly stacked machinery that obscured the view within, Kachigan could see why he did it. "Leo, there's a policeman out here who needs to see you.''

"Policeman?'' The muffled voice was mildly accented, but what really surprised Kachigan was the fact that it belonged to a woman rather than a man. "Have the dogs gone over the fence again? I wish I could convince the neighbors that they'd rather play with their children than eat them.''

"Not the Adderly police, ma'am. The Allegheny County Detectives Bureau.'' McCaplin cleared his throat. "It's about Mr. Osborne.''

Something sizzled abruptly behind the walls of clutter, followed by a flood of passionate Italian curses. "*Maron, maron, maron* . . . Giovanni, why must you say such things while I'm connecting circuits?''

"Sorry, ma'am.'' McCaplin stepped back, his mouth twitching a little at the corner. "We'll meet you in Mr. Sparenberg's office in a few minutes, all right? It's very important.''

"*Si, si* . . .''

The secretary led them past a large multiple office, where three young men in rolled-up shirtsleeves were arguing over a circuit drawing pinned to a steeply pitched drafting table, then past a room full of lathes and vises, where a senior machinist with greasy hands was nodding intently at the instructions he was getting from another dark-haired woman engineer. Taggart whistled softly when he saw her, and got a fierce glare in reply.

"Are these *all* company engineers, Mr. McCaplin?" Kachigan inquired, after they'd passed the machine shop.

"Except for the odd machinist and draftsman, yes. And there's another whole bunch of them in the main headquarters building downtown." McCaplin led them past a second shared office, then paused before the last doorway along the hall. Unlike all the others, the heavy oak door to this one was closed. The secretary tapped on it politely, then swung it open just far enough to peek around the edge. "Mr. Sparenberg, if you're not busy—"

A gravel-deep snort rolled through the slivered opening. "At the rate things are going, John, I'm going to be busy until 1908. What's the problem now?"

"The Allegheny County police are here to see you. It seems they've found Mr. Osborne, murdered."

"What?" The roar thundered out into the hall, loud enough to silence the multiple conversations behind them. "Well, don't stand there like a bump on a log, send them in! And go get Leo!"

"She's already coming." Like any good secretary, Kachigan noted, McCaplin had the uncanny ability to guess what the boss was going to want and arrange for it in advance. The young man swung the door wide, ushering them into the plain plastered office on the other side. Like the others along this hall, it was centered around a large drafting table and edged with groaning bookshelves full of technical manuals. "Should I telegraph the old man, sir?"

"No." The portly engineer swung around on his high drafting stool, running a hand across a mostly bald pate and leaving streaks of india ink behind. "I'll do that myself, as soon as I know what's what. My name's Sparenberg, gentlemen, Oliver Sparenberg."

"Milo Kachigan." He shook the engineer's ink-stained hand, impressed by the lack of condescension with which it had been thrust out to him. "This is my partner, Art Taggart."

Sparenberg swung around and pumped hands with the big man, too. "You say Lyell Osborne's been murdered? How?"

"Indirectly," Kachigan said. "The immediate cause of death was being run over by a train on the Pittsburgh, Bessemer, and Lake Erie trestle in East Pittsburgh. But he had been knocked unconscious beforehand and deliberately left there, probably dropped from a train car."

"From a train car?" Sparenberg frowned. "Was he set upon and robbed by hobos?"

"Only of his identification." Kachigan pulled out the gold watch and showed him the engraved cover. "The killers left this behind. Do you recognize it, sir?"

"I should." Sparenberg lifted his own plain steel watch chain to show them an identical timepiece. "It's an AAME award watch. I got mine in 1887. Does that one say '1905'?"

"Yes. Would that make it Lyell Osborne's?"

"It would." The engineer's dark eyes glinted shrewdly through his thick spectacle lenses. "Of course, it might have already been stolen from Osborne. Can you describe the man you found it on?"

Kachigan flipped a page in his notebook. "Five-nine, about one hundred and eighty pounds, mid-thirties. Dark-skinned, dark eyes, dark hair worn short and oiled. Hand-tailored gray wool suit worn with a silk brocade vest and linen collar, opal cuff links, and black calfskin spats."

Sparenberg heaved a deep, resigned sigh. "That's Lyell, all right. Damn."

Kachigan lifted an eyebrow at Taggart, who'd gone to lean his bulk against one of the bookshelves. Although there had been a wealth of regret and frustration in Sparenberg's gravelly voice, he hadn't heard much in the way of sorrow. "If I may ask, sir, were you on close terms with the dead man?"

An inelegant snort from the doorway answered him before Sparenberg could. "No one was on close terms with Lullio. And I think that was just the way he liked it."

They all turned to face the diminutive silver-haired woman who had just entered the office. The seeming clash of her pale skin and alpine-blue eyes with an Italian accent and a generously curved nose led Kachigan, wise in the many strands of ethnic diversity that ran through Pittsburgh, to conclude that she was most likely Swiss. Her serge skirt and masculine

jacket were as dark and plain as her younger coworker's had
been. The only clashing note was the bright red-and-yellow
silk scarf that she'd wound like an ascot around her neck.

"This is Frau Doctor Leonora Grissaldi," Sparenberg said,
his voice softening with what might have been either amusement or gentle affection. "She shared an office with Lyell."

"For my sins." Grissaldi shook hands with both of them,
as strongly and simply as a man would. Her hands were del-
icately boned but reddened and callused from long years of
manual work. "Lullio was not an easy man to get along with."

Kachigan wrote that in his notebook, too. "Do either of you
know when Mr. Osborne was last seen alive?"

"Wednesday," said Sparenberg promptly. "He left at five
o'clock, just as he always did. We expected him back at seven
the next morning, but got no word of him after that."

"I saw him at the trolley stop on Station Street, quarter past
five on Wednesday," added Grissaldi. "I'm afraid I didn't see
which line he took."

Kachigan wrote that down, too. "Does he have a wife or
family? Next of kin who'll need to be notified about his
death?"

"No wife," Sparenberg said. The two engineers exchanged
thoughtful looks. "How about his parents, Leo?"

She shook her head. "No, I don't think so. I remember
when his mother died in 1902, he said his father was already
dead. Perhaps there was a brother or sister, but Lullio never
said much."

"About his family?"

"About anything!" Grissaldi declared. "From morning to
night you were lucky to get ten words out of him. 'Hello,'
'good-bye,' 'hand me the ruler,' and 'please shut up.' "

"Leo's exaggerating," Sparenberg said, but the smile that
tugged at his mouth told Kachigan it wasn't by much. "It's
true, though, that Lyell kept mostly to himself."

"Do you know where Mr. Osborne lived?"

"Pitcairn," Grissaldi said at once.

Oliver Sparenberg frowned. "No, Leo, not Pitcairn. Wall."

"Wall?" The little Swiss engineer looked dubious. "But
I'm sure I saw him take the Eighty-seven Ardmore to Pitcairn,

several times this month. I live myself in Adderly, on that same trolley line," she added, glancing at Kachigan. "That's why I noticed."

Sparenberg grunted. "The front office should know his address, and maybe even who his next of kin are. They've started keeping these things called personnel files." He sent a sardonic look at McCaplin, who'd effaced himself remarkably well into a corner. "Gives them an excuse to hire more secretaries."

The younger man didn't look particularly intimidated by that remark. "Would you like me to check on Mr. Osborne's file for you, sir?"

Kachigan cleared his throat. "I'd prefer to do that myself, on my way out. With your permission, of course."

Sparenberg grunted. "As long as you don't take anything out of it. You can leave directions for picking up the body, too. I'm sure Mr. Westinghouse will want to pay for the funeral." A distant whistle blew in the valley, and he glanced at his gold award watch. "I've got to meet some plant foreman for lunch today. Did you have any other questions for me?"

"Just one, and it's for all of you." Kachigan flipped back a page in his evidence book, to the one word he had circled and underlined on the previous night. "As you may or may not know, the most important thing in a case of murder is the killer's motive. Who would have wanted to kill Mr. Osborne?"

There was a long and not-quite-blank silence after that question. Kachigan kept his gaze focused on Oliver Sparenberg, knowing that from his vantage point, Taggart could see both McCaplin and Grissaldi. There wasn't much to be read in the chief engineer's blunt face, however, aside from a wince of slight discomfort. And that could have been just the distaste of a cultured gentleman confronting the harsh realities of crime.

Leonora Grissaldi answered first, with an unexpected snort of laughter. "Around here, Mr. Kachigan, I don't think anyone found Lullio more annoying than I did. But I give you my word, I didn't murder him. It made him more silent, not less, eh?"

"I don't know that he had any—er—personal enemies,"

Sparenberg added. "Of course, I don't know that he had any personal friends either. He wasn't a social man."

McCaplin shrugged. "I didn't know Mr. Osborne at all well, myself. All I can tell you is that Mr. Westinghouse trusted him implicitly, and said that he had quite a future as an inventor."

Taggart spoke up for the first time, lazily. "Could he have been murdered for some invention he was working on? Something worth a lot of money if it fell into someone else's hands?"

The not-quite-blankness of the silence deepened abruptly. Kachigan let it stretch, lifting an eyebrow at Oliver Sparenberg. The engineer cleared his throat, shifting on his drafting stool.

"That's—well, that's a little hard to say. Lyell never talked much about his work, either. All I'm sure of is that he was in charge of our South American hydroelectricity projects." Sparenberg consulted his watch again, a little more desperately this time. "I'm afraid I really must be going—perhaps you gentlemen can come back after the holidays if there are other questions you need to ask."

Kachigan folded his evidence book closed, shooting Taggart a quick glance to be sure he got the hint. "We appreciate your assistance, sir. If one of you could authorize our looking at Mr. Osborne's personnel file—"

"Yes, of course. John, if you would—"

"Of course, sir." The secretary led them out of the office and through a nearby steel door, then down a different staircase than the one they'd ascended. Kachigan followed him down, emerging into such a clattering bustle that he could barely hear McCaplin calling for the office manager. Rows of young women and young men with gartered sleeves glanced up from their adding and typing machines without a pause in their flying fingers.

"We don't both need to read Osborne's file," Taggart said, beneath the din. "Why don't I get us something to eat while you finish up here? By the time you're done writing down everything you want to have in your notebook, it'll be past one o'clock."

Kachigan opened his mouth to deny that, but his stomach

concurred with a growl. "All right. Fresh milk for me, if you can find it—and none of your smelly Chinese food!"

Taggart snorted. "Coward. It doesn't smell any worse than your rotten sauerkraut—and the chop suey even has enough vegetables in it to make your old man happy."

"In that case," Kachigan said, "I definitely don't want it."

To Kachigan's annoyance, he heard the Westinghouse clock strike one just as he emerged from the main office, head aching from the noise and fingers cramped from too much writing. He found Taggart waiting for him in the castle's narrow front lobby, already munching on the roast-beef sandwiches and delicatessen pickles he'd brought for lunch. His partner didn't look a bit annoyed by the delay, either because of his natural indolence or because his bench gave him a close-up view of the stenographers and typists passing by in their tight-laced shirtwaists and bright poplin skirts. At least Taggart wasn't whistling at them.

"Find out anything?" he asked lazily.

"Not much." Kachigan sat down beside him, reaching first for the waxed-paper carton of milk that waited beside his own paper-wrapped sandwich. He drank it down in three long, grateful swallows, then rubbed at the pain its ice-coldness had sent through his damaged cheekbone. "Osborne did live in Wall, not Pitcairn. He graduated from Johns Hopkins University in 1881. Went to work for Westinghouse at Union Switch and Signal that summer and hasn't had a holiday since then. And he definitely deserved that inventor-of-the-year award. The company's patented a couple dozen of his ideas, from switches to turbines to train couplers."

"A real Boy Scout," Taggart agreed. "So why did he end up getting sliced to smithereens on a railroad track?"

"Good question."

"Yeah," said his partner. "But I've got an even better one for you. If your Miss Sorby is getting paid to run that East Pittsburgh settlement house, why would she need to apply for a job here at Westinghouse, too?"

Kachigan paused in mid-bite. "Who says she did?"

"I do," Taggart told him. "Because I just saw her do it."

5

THE WESTINGHOUSE HEADQUARTERS WAS A CAS-
tle.

Not an enormous castle, Helen Sorby thought
critically. More the size of one of Andrew Carnegie's public libraries than his purchased Scottish
fortress. But like any good medieval estate, its elegant turrets
and gabled roofs overlooked the fiefdoms and dominions of
its lord. Immediately at its foot were the long low buildings
of the Westinghouse Airbrake plant, which manufactured the
first of George Westinghouse's many successful inventions.
Farther down the valley in East Pittsburgh and Turtle Creek,
she could see the gleaming windows of Westinghouse Electric
Manufacturing and Westinghouse Machine Company. Farther
up, past the immense sprawl of the railroad yards in Pitcairn,
she knew a dedicated foundry had just been built on the out-
skirts of elite new Trafford City. It was the very model of a
modern electric empire, bustling with wealth, innovation, and
efficiency.

And prejudice.

Helen took a deep breath and climbed the rest of the way
up to the castle entrance, nearly tripping over the disgustingly
frilly skirts of the outfit she'd borrowed from Molly Slade that
morning. The last time she'd applied for a job here, two days
before Abraham Maccoun had blown up the backyard, she'd
been summarily rejected as an electric-factory worker. It

hadn't been the refusal to hire her that had infuriated Helen, though—it had been the reason why. "You're far too well educated to take a factory job, Miss Sorby," the chicken-plump office manager had explained, in an irritatingly solicitous voice. "And much too—um—well-bred, if you know what I mean. Now, can I interest you in a nice stenographer's position?"

"Does a stenographer make as much as a factory-line worker?" Helen had asked, doing her best to keep her seething temper in check.

"Well, er . . . no," the office manager admitted. "The work's not as demanding, you see, and there's just not the same amount of overtime."

She *had* seen, and she'd been more than willing to share her insights with every unenlightened Westinghouse functionary in earshot. Either George Westinghouse had a bad case of misplaced morals, she'd informed the office manager, or he had a well-justified fear of how an educated woman would react to the appalling work conditions in his factories. In either case, it was contemptible to offer a woman a lower-paying job just because she knew how to read and write. Would they have done the same thing if she'd been a man?

The question had never been answered, since she'd slammed out and left the office manager staring after her in stunned silence. It wasn't until she reached the Wilmerding trolley station two blocks away that Helen's reflexive flare of anger had transmuted into pure exhilaration. It wasn't often that she got the chance to throw the sins of capitalism right into the sinners' teeth. She'd decided then and there that undercover reporting was definitely her forte.

Now she was having second thoughts.

"Well, Miss Sorby." The office manager's prim smile made him look even more like a chicken. "I certainly didn't expect to see you back again."

"I'm sure," Helen muttered. Until a man who was probably a Westinghouse employee had ended up dead in her backyard, she hadn't expected to find herself back there again either. Her article on women working in the electrical trades had coalesced nicely around her discovery that no educated females were allowed to take such jobs. All it needed now was a few interviews with actual women electrical workers to be complete.

But that was before Milo Kachigan's insistence on keeping Abraham Maccoun in jail had spurred her into a rash declaration of independence. Once her temper had cooled, it hadn't taken Helen long to realize just how difficult an independent investigation of this murder was going to be. Between the iron-fisted secrecy of the Pennsylvania Railroad and the loyalty that George Westinghouse inspired in his employees, there wasn't much left in the East Pittsburgh Valley for a reporter to uncover. It wasn't until she'd awakened from restless sleep an hour before dawn this morning that it had occurred to her she'd already paved a way to investigate Westinghouse from within.

It took an effort of sheer will, but Helen forced herself to look up at the fowl-faced office manager with what she hoped was a properly mortified expression. "I'm sorry I lost my temper. It's just that I was hoping to get the higher-paying job, Mr. Jenkins. With my parents dead and my brother laid off for the winter . . ."

"I understand." His air of smug solicitousness deepened. "I presume you haven't found any other offers of employment in the meantime?"

Helen heaved a dramatic sigh. "Just for shopgirl positions, and that's only until after the holidays. So if the stenographer position is still open . . ."

"Fortunately for you, Miss Sorby, it is." Jenkins swung around on his tall secretary's stool, searching through the neat stacks of paper on his desk. Behind him, the productive clatter of adding machines and typing machines created a mind-numbing roar. It struck Helen that for all its gentility, the main office of a large company was almost as inhumane an environment as a factory floor. "Your pay will be three dollars a week, and your hours will run from eight A.M. to five P.M. on weekdays and until noon on Saturdays, with one half hour released for lunch. You'll be allowed five days off per year in case of sickness—unpaid, of course—and you'll receive as holidays Christmas, Thanksgiving, and Independence Day. And keep in mind that should you happen to marry during your employment, your job will be terminated at once." He slanted her a speculative glance, as if waiting for another explosion. "Are those terms agreeable?"

"Yes," Helen said between her teeth.

"Good." He unscrewed the cap of his steel fountain pen and tapped it to start the ink flowing. "From the appropriateness of your attire, I presume you can start today?"

"Yes," she said again, but this time it was in quiet satisfaction. Jenkins had just unwittingly confirmed a hypothesis she'd formed two days ago when she'd first visited the Westinghouse front office. As she stood among the sea of female secretaries and office-machine operators—all professional women like herself—it had startled Helen to realize that her plain skirt and severely tailored jacket were the exception rather than the rule. Although she suspected most of her fellow workers considered their elegant ruffles and flounces a privilege that set them off from factory drabs, to Helen they smacked alarmingly of social labels. How seriously could you take a stenographer when her clothes were—in her case, literally—those of an East Pittsburgh prostitute?

Fortunately, her future employer couldn't overhear the radical socialist speculations swirling inside her head. "Good," Jenkins said, and signed his name on a short typewritten form. "All I need is for you to fill this out for your personnel file, and I'll have Miss Walroth show you to your slot." He handed her the form and the pen, then watched critically while she wrote in her name, birth date, East Pittsburgh address, and nearest living relative. "Superb penmanship, Miss Sorby," he commented. "I noticed that the last time you were here. I think you'll make a good addition to our Westinghouse family."

"Thank you," Helen said sweetly. She wondered if the office manager would like her penmanship quite as much if he knew that she had honed it writing manuscripts for the *Progressive Worker's Weekly* and *McClure's Magazine*. "Where do I go now?"

Jenkins stood, wincing a little as he straightened what must have been an aching back, then led her down a noisy aisle of typing machines to the small desk at the far end. Miss Walroth, a slender older women with a serious face, glanced up from an accounting ledger as they approached. She welcomed Helen with a nod and a quick notation in her book, then handed her a stack of what looked like scribbled grocery lists.

"Do you think you can transcribe these supply requests, Miss Sorby?"

Helen glanced at them and frowned. It wasn't the cramped handwriting that troubled her, since her brother's scribbles on the first drafts of his fire-insurance maps were every bit as illegible. But among the jumble of words and abbreviations were many terms she simply didn't know. "I can read them, ma'am, but I'm afraid I may misspell the scientific terms. Is there a dictionary I can look them up in?"

"Oh, good. You're a questioner, not a bluffer." Walroth's smile was a quick flit across her face, but it warmed her eyes with humor. "I'm afraid no dictionary on the planet has all the scientific terms the old man uses. The only thing you can do is ask one of the other girls who's been here a little longer." She handed Helen a sheaf of linen bond and a cheap hard rubber fountain pen, then pointed to one in a long line of stools along the back wall of the room. "Sit there, next to Miss Howards. She can help you, but no extraneous talking, please." The head stenographer dipped a warning look in the direction of their departing boss. "Mr. Jenkins thinks it interferes with our productivity."

"Of course," Helen said, doing her best to sound sincere instead of cynical. She headed for her station and promptly tripped over the wretched flounce at the bottom of her dress. Fortunately, Miss Walroth didn't seem to notice her muffled yelp, but it did catch the attention of the long line of girls perched on the secretarial stools. A barrage of critical gazes swept over Helen, taking in her cheap poplin skirts and over-ruffled shirtwaist with lifted eyebrows. Helen gritted her teeth and kept walking, more angry at the warmth in her own cheeks that meant she was blushing than she was at them. It occurred to her that the dress code she was seeing among the secretaries might not be entirely due to male prejudice.

She slipped onto her empty stool at last with a sigh of relief loud enough to attract the attention of her nearest neighbor. Dark eyes met hers with unexpected sympathy, despite the glorious mop of chestnut curls and elegant aquamarine dress that made this secretary look more like an authentic Gibson Girl than a stenographer.

"You all right?"

"Just embarrassed," Helen admitted, trying hard to keep her own voice down to that same discreet level. "Are you Miss Howards?"

"Guilty as charged. Call me Bonnie." Her pen never paused in its swift travels. "You?"

"Helen Sorby. I'm the new stenographer."

That got her another sparkling look, this one a little more amused. "So I see." She tapped a buffed fingernail on Helen's stack of scribbled lists. "Let me know if you need any help with those. They can be hard to decipher."

"Thanks." Helen spread out her papers and tapped the ink down into her pen nib, frowning as it blurted out an annoying spray of droplets. She already missed her reliable Waterman Ideal with its smooth gold-plated nib. "What's '1sp 5VCu'?"

"One spool of five-volt copper wire."

"Oh." She worked her way down through a list of other wire voltages, her curiosity growing. "Bonnie, who *is* the 'old man'?"

"George, of course. Mr. Westinghouse."

"He does—" Helen felt more than saw the hushing motion that rippled through the rest of the stenographers and lowered her voice. "He does the supply ordering for the whole *company*?"

Bonnie Howards shook her head. "No, just for the little machine shop he uses himself, down inside the Airbrake. He still makes a lot of his own gizmos and gadgets, I guess."

"Oh." Helen copied down three types of switches, then paused to puzzle over another abbreviation. "What about '3dz SB'? Three dozen of what?"

"Shortbread cookies. The old man has a sweet tooth," Bonnie said with a not-so-discreet gurgle of laughter. From across the room, Helen saw Jenkins give them a warning look and another hushing ripple traveled down the secretarial line. "I've never taken notes in a meeting with him that I don't get sent out for coffee cake or chess tarts or divinity." She leaned over, the attractive scent of French violet perfume floating around her like invisible lace. "All those 'Tr's are transformers, by the way."

"Thanks." Helen finished transcribing the first scribbled list, blotted her paper, and set it aside to start a second. "How long have you worked here?"

The other woman gave her another amused glance. "Only since November—that's why Miss Walroth put you next to me. Don't worry, though. You'll get the hang of all these electrical terms in no time."

"Miss Howards." It was amazing, Helen thought, how quickly the office manager's voice had gained the ability to send a guilty start down her spine, just like the nuns at St. Peter's School. She glanced over her shoulder, expecting to be lectured for too much talking, but instead saw Jenkins cupping a telephone bell to his chest and looking worried. "The senior engineers need a steno up on third. *Now*."

"Yes, sir. I'm on my way." Bonnie scrambled up from her seat, capping her fountain pen and scooping up her yellow steno pad and pencils along the way. On her feet, she was a bigger girl than Helen had realized, strong-boned and generously fleshed inside the exaggerated hourglass of her fashionable dress. She gave Helen an unexpected wink before she left. "If you run into too many abbreviations, finish my memo for Mr. Sparenberg," she said in a tiny whisper. "Then we'll both do the old man's shopping lists when I come back."

"Thank you," Helen said politely. It wasn't until half an hour later, though, that she realized how grateful she really was. The last of George Westinghouse's lists was full of arcane symbols that looked more like one of Thomas's old Greek texts than a catalog of electrical parts. She waited until both Jenkins and Walroth were engaged in fixing an adding-machine operator's twisted paper tape, then silently slid Bonnie's stack of memos over to her section of the table. To her relief, she saw that the other woman's shorthand was the standard variety she'd learned at St. Peter's, and that their handwriting was in that same grammar-school style. With only a little modification of her capital letters and slant, no one would ever know they'd switched assignments.

. . . contracts are in hand and we have all the power circuits diagrammed and modeled for resistance. The initial estimate of twelve turbines may need to be revised upward as it does not appear that the amount of flow during dry periods will be sufficient to meet operating standards . . .

At least hydroelectricity was a subject Helen knew a little about, from her research into the coil-winding work that women did in the Westinghouse Electric Manufacturing Plant. She only had to stop and puzzle out a few technical terms as she translated from shorthand to longhand. Mostly the memo seemed to be a collection of assurances, veiled in engineering language, that meant the work was well in hand and nearing completion. With a twinge of pure curiosity, Helen glanced through the previously written-out pages until she found the intended recipient. To her surprise, it was addressed to the Honorable Philander Knox, United States secretary of state. A quick glance past the salutation told Helen why. The hydroelectric system in question was destined for Brazil, one of the fledgling South American democracies President Theodore Roosevelt had pledged to support.

From somewhere near the front of the office, what sounded like a dinner bell rang through the din. Helen glanced up in surprise as all around her, stenographers and machine operators stood, stretching and shaking the circulation back into their fingers before they headed en masse to the water coolers out in the hall. A mid-afternoon break was more progressive work policy than she'd expected from such a large company— and more consideration than she ever gave her own ink-stained fingers. Since she'd barely begun to write, Helen didn't bother to join the exodus. Instead she worked through the blessed silence, making her way down to the end of the Knox memo. There she paused with lifted pen, unsure of the official Westinghouse style for the sign-off.

A telephone shrilled into the silence, making Helen jump and splatter ink all over her just-written page. She cursed beneath her breath at the cheap rubber pen, resolving to smuggle in her own dependable Waterman for the next workday. Before she could even clean her ink-flooded nib, however, the approach of urgent footsteps warned her to drop a sheet of blotting paper across her work. A moment later Jenkins's plump shadow fell into her light.

"We have a problem on the third floor, Miss Sorby. Miss Howards has fallen ill in the middle of an engineers' meeting." He cast an impatient glance out at the mill of workers in the hall. "I'd rather send Miss Bosserman, but it would take me five minutes just to find her. Here."

Helen took the blank yellow sheaf of papers he thrust at her, then caught at his elbow when he turned away. "How do I get to the third floor, Mr. Jenkins?"

He made impatient shooing motions toward a corner of the office. "Just go up those iron stairs, right there. Mr. Sparenberg's office is the one at the end of the hall. And whatever you do, don't take that pen! Engineers *hate* it when you spill ink on their blueprints. Our stenographers all take shorthand in pencil."

"Yes, sir." Helen put the uncapped pen down on her blank pages, knowing it would probably leak a blue puddle onto them while she was gone, then scooped up a stub of pencil from Bonnie's work area and hurried up the stairs. She half expected to meet the other stenographer returning the same way, but there was no sign of her either on the stairs or amid the quieter but equally industrious bustle of the third-floor offices. Puzzled and beginning to be worried, Helen hurried over to the closed oak door at the end of the hall and tapped on it lightly. No answer came. She rapped again, this time using her knuckles on the wood.

"*What?*" The young man who'd swung the door wide to confront her would have been handsome if it hadn't been for the unpleasant scowl that marred his features. He had the pure flaxen hair that most blond children lose when they grow up, gray-green eyes, and the kind of clean-cut face you usually saw only on the models for Arrow collars. His scowl faded when he saw Helen, but it was replaced by what she considered an equally unpleasant speculative look. "Who are *you*?"

"The stenographer you sent for." Helen slid past him, since he didn't seem inclined to step back, smelling the blend of cigar smoke, cologne, and whiskey she always associated with wealthy men. The young man turned to watch her as she passed, his gaze dropping to survey her cheap dress and her figure with startling frankness. "Where should I sit?"

"On my lap would be fine," he said with a smile that she supposed was meant to be charming.

"Alessandro, stop it." It wasn't the Italian accent or the curt dismissal that swung Helen's gaze around in amazement to find the owner of that voice, it was the soprano pitch. A tiny silver-haired matriarch with a powerful jut of Roman nose returned her gaze with an equally dismissive frown. "We don't have time for you to play games with the little office girls. This is a *crisis*."

The young man sighed and backed a step away from Helen. "Leo, has anyone ever told you you're a pickle?"

The burly older engineer sitting at the drafting table cleared his throat and intervened. "Please sit here, Miss—"

"Sorby."

"Miss Sorby." Despite his more polite voice, he obviously didn't feel any need to introduce himself or his coworkers to the brand-new stenographer. Instead, he nodded at the quiet, freckle-faced man beside him, who handed her a half-written leaf of yellow paper. "Now, where did we leave off on that memo?"

Helen took a deep breath, scanning down to the last line of Bonnie's shorthand. " 'Given the encumbrances on the current government of Brazil—' "

"And the extra time we'll need to redesign the entire generating assembly," the silver-haired woman said pointedly.

"Leo, we can't say that!" Mr. Arrow Collar strode across the room to glare down at the older woman. "Can't you get it through your dense engineer's head that the Brazilian government doesn't issue binding contracts like ours does? I'm telling you, if they find out we've lost the plans for the Vale Brissa plant, they're going to jump straight to Consolidated Edison!"

"Why?" she demanded, looking not in the least intimidated by his glare. "It's not as if Edison's engineers wouldn't have to start from scratch just like we will. And we'll still design a better power plant."

"But not by the deadline we agreed to meet. Not by the

deadline they're going to pay us *extra* to meet.'' He leaned over, scowling and poking a finger at her to make his point. "The banks who hold notes on the old man's assets are counting on those Brazilian bonuses to cover the interest, Leo. If they don't get it, all our jobs are going to be foreclosed on.''

"Greer, sit *down*." The senior engineer, who must have been Sparenberg, said it with the kind of irritable emphasis that meant it wasn't the first time the order had been given. "And get it through *your* head, banks or no banks, the damned deadline's going to broken. Whether or not we find Osborne's original plans, the project's not going to stay on track without him.''

The young man flung himself into one of the leather-upholstered side chairs, looking remarkably sulky. "Well, why do the Brazilians have to know that? Can't we just lay low until they pay the first installment and then push the deadline back a few months?''

The quiet young man at the other end of the table cleared his throat to call discreet attention to himself. "I'm afraid we can't, Mr. Greer. The contract you negotiated for us says we owe Brazil a compensation fee if we are late.''

Leo Grissaldi snorted. "Some salesman!''

"Hey, the old man insisted on that!'' Greer said indignantly. "I told him he was going to break his jaw on it but he wouldn't listen to me. Why didn't *you* do something about it, McCaplin, if it was so stinking bad?''

Sparenberg exchanged resigned looks with the freckled man. "Greer, you know John is just the old man's private secretary, not his business adviser. And none of us can change the way Westinghouse likes to do business. What we *can* do is explain to the Brazilians that the engineer who was in charge of designing their power plant has died in a most unfortunate accident, and politely request an extension of their deadline.'' He swiveled back toward Helen. "Now, where were we, Miss—uh—Miss—''

"Sorby," she said again with what she hoped was the same secretarial self-effacement that McCaplin exuded so well. She kept her eyes trained on the shorthand pad to make sure none of her flaring excitement showed. "I believe we were at 'the encumbrances on the current government of Brazil,' sir.''

"Right." He cleared his throat. "Add to that, 'and given the time we'll need to recover from Mr. Osborne's untimely death, we believe it to be in both our interests to delay the completion of the Vale Brissa hydroelectric generating station until at least the fall of 1907.' ''

Helen glanced up from her pad inquiringly. "Their fall or ours, sir?''

Sparenberg gave her a startled glance, as if one of his office chairs had suddenly gotten up and walked itself across the room. Helen bit her lip, seeing that her natural curiosity had betrayed her into unsecretarial behavior. "What do you mean?''

Greer chuckled maliciously. "She means that the seasons in the southern hemisphere are the opposite of ours, Oliver. Are you talking about May of 1907 or November?''

"November," the older female engineer said bluntly. "That's the earliest we could possibly hope to be done.''

"Then we'll make the request for December," Sparenberg decided. "That'll give Greer a little negotiating room when he goes back." Helen noticed that it didn't seem to occur to any of them to thank her for correcting a mistake that might have cost the company millions of dollars. "Finish with the usual polite closing and have the final draft on my desk by five o'clock.''

"Yes, sir." Helen rose to her feet, giving Greer the iciest look she could muster when he jumped up to hold the door for her. The last thing she needed was for some Westinghouse salesman to decide she was fair game just because she took shorthand and wore ruffles. Fortunately, when he showed signs of following her out the door, an irritated female voice snapped, "Alessandro! Come back here. We still haven't settled Lullio's other projects.''

His handsome face twisted into an even more unpleasant grimace. "Coming," he said, and shut the oak door in Helen's face with a lack of consideration that startled her, given his obvious masculine interest. Apparently, even an attractive stenographer didn't rate being treated with politeness.

She'd half expected to find Bonnie Howards back in place

beside her, since the only "illness" that seemed consistent with the other girl's high color and buoyant spirits was an unexpected monthly onset of what her Aunt Pittypat laughingly called "the curse of all womankind." But the other stool remained empty for another long hour. Helen transcribed Sparenberg's most recent memo into her best longhand, checked with Miss Walroth to find out what "the usual polite closings" should be, and then recopied the last page of Bonnie's earlier memo as well. In both cases, the original shorthand notes got folded and slipped into the inner pocket of Molly's skirt. It wasn't until Helen had delivered both finished memos—a good quarter hour before the deadline Sparenberg had set—and was coming back down the iron stairwell a second time that she caught a glimpse of familiar aquamarine through the open steps.

"Bonnie." Helen hurried down the stairs to catch up with other girl, seeing from her pallor that she really had been ill. "Are you all right?"

"I've been better." Bonnie's smile was tight and didn't make much impact on the lines of pain that had furrowed the corners of her eyes. They deepened when she and Helen entered the frenetic clatter of the front office. "It's the migraine. I've been lying down in the ladies' room, hoping the quiet would help, but I think I'd better just go home."

"It's almost quitting time," Helen said in concern. "If you wait a little, I can come with you."

"Thank you," Bonnie said, and winced. "And I don't need to worry about waiting. By the time I finish explaining what happened to Mr. Jenkins and filling out whatever paperwork he gives me, you'll be the one waiting for me."

Her prediction proved accurate. Helen took her time cleaning up her station, checking again with Miss Walroth to see if she should give back the supply lists that had been left undone and even scrubbing off the dried splatters of ink left from her earlier accident. But she was still left loitering out in the building's narrow foyer, watching the last straggle of secretaries, machinists, and engineers depart while Bonnie got what sounded like a severe scolding in the front office. Helen watched them through the semifrosted glass of the door pane, frowning so intently that she never noticed the approaching footsteps until a familiar voice spoke in her ear.

"Waiting for me, Miss Sorby?"

She swung around, disturbed by the transmitted warmth of a male body standing far too close. "No, Mr. Greer. I'm waiting for a friend."

"Well, I'm a friend." It shouldn't have been possible to take such handsome ingredients—straight nose, firm jaw, sensitive poet's mouth—and turn them into a detestable combination, but Greer's utterly self-centered smile managed to do it. "Wouldn't you really rather walk home with me?"

"No," Helen said between her teeth, goaded. "In fact, I'd rather walk to hell."

Instead of alienating the Westinghouse salesman, her fierce response seemed to intrigue him. "We're not quite the usual little stenographer, are we? But you know, it's one thing to correct old Oliver Sparenberg on his antiquated geography and another thing to spite me, Miss Sorby. I have strong connections with this company. *Very* strong."

Helen took a step back from his too-close face, wishing she had an umbrella she could hit him with. "Are you threatening to get me fired?" she demanded.

"Oh, no," said an unexpected female voice behind her. "Alexander Erskine Greer would *never* stoop to that, not with so many other women fainting at his feet. He's just having some fun with you, Helen, that's all."

Greer turned, the flash of dismay on his face quickly fading into another self-infatuated smile. "Bonnie, my love. I thought you were already home, recovering from your headache."

"And so I would be, if the wretched Jenkins-creature hadn't taken a quarter of an hour just to tell me I'd be fired if I got sick one more time." Bonnie's pinched look had faded a little, allowing some of the sparkle to return to her dark eyes. "Of course if that happens, you'll use your *strong* connections to the company to save me, won't you, Alex?"

"Of course!" His boyish voice might have seemed more sincere if his gaze hadn't skated from her upturned face to her Gibson Girl curves with such outright relish. Thus engaged, he completely missed the mocking look Bonnie threw past him at Helen. "I always enjoy helping my *friends*."

"So do I." A little of Bonnie's amusement spilled out into her voice as she slid her arm through Helen's elbow and turned her toward the exit. "And so does Helen, which is why she waited so nicely to see me home tonight. Say good evening to Alex, Helen. He's an important international salesman and I know he has lots of work left to do."

"Good evening," Helen said, trying so hard not to laugh that her voice came out sounding more stifled than anything else. Bonnie swept her through the door before Greer could even open his mouth to reply, and they left him staring after them in vaguely sullen frustration. Halfway down the stairs that led to Commerce Avenue, they exchanged amused looks, then both burst out laughing.

"Dumb as a stump, isn't he?" Bonnie asked at last, still breathless with mirth. Her migraine seemed to have faded as soon as they walked through Westinghouse's revolving doors. "Doesn't it make you wonder how on earth he does his job?"

In the darkening winter haze of twilight, Helen could see the electric lights of the trolley cars glittering like will-o'-the-wisps as they clattered down the bridge and onto the Wilmerding loop. She didn't bother hurrying, since she knew the valley lines ran every few minutes. "Actually, what it makes me wonder is how on earth he *got* his job. He can't have deserved it."

"Oh, he says he's a relative of the old man's wife, back through some Scottish connections." With each step away from the Westinghouse castle, Bonnie's face and voice regained more of its normal vivacity. She shook her head, encouraging her sensuous chestnut curls to unravel a little more in the chilly wind. "Personally, I think the real answer is that he's one of the Johnstown Flood orphans."

"But George Westinghouse wasn't even one of the investors who owned the fishing dam that broke in Johnstown," Helen protested.

"I know. But the old man is a sucker for a sob story." Bonnie squeezed her arm, then released her as they reached the trolley stop. "Tomorrow, see if you can get Miss Walroth to tell you about all the widows he's supported, not to mention the immigrants he's sent back to the old country to take care of supposedly dying mothers. You'll see why the valley loves him and the banks and the railroads hate him.''

Helen's investigative instincts sparked alive. ''The railroads hate him? Why? I thought he made all their air brakes.''

''He also gives the men who make those air brakes retirement pensions,'' said Bonnie Howards, with surprising insight. ''The electric workers don't get them yet, but in another few years everyone in the company will. And when that happens, the workers at the Pennsylvania Railroad are going to explode.''

Helen opened her mouth to ask another question, but the sizzle of an arriving trolley drowned her out. She followed Bonnie toward the boarding door, seeing that it was the eastbound car that went to Trafford City. ''Do you want me to come all the way home with you?'' she asked, when the squeal of brakes had finally faded.

''Oh, no. My headache's gone now.'' Bonnie's smile was almost devilish. ''There's nothing like snubbing an overbearing boss to make a girl feel better. You go on home yourself, Helen Sorby. Tomorrow, if you want to hear more dirt about what goes on at Westinghouse, just come out to luncheon with the rest of us secretaries. We know more about that company than its board of directors.''

''I can see that.'' Helen smiled and stepped back to wait for her own streetcar, now chugging its way slowly across the factory-spanning bridge. ''Thanks, Bonnie. For everything.''

''Anything for a fellow stenographer,'' her coworker said, still sounding amused, then stepped into the press of homeward-bound factory workers and was gone.

6

THERE WAS NO PLACE TO LIVE IN PITTSBURGH that wasn't far from railroad tracks. Kachigan had grown up with trains running just beyond his backyard fence in Monessen, and his house on the South Side lay only a few blocks from a railroad line. But even the poorest of South Side immigrants hadn't built their houses jammed in as dangerously close to the tracks as the row of flats where Lyell Osborne lived. They faced onto an avenue that was really nothing more than the slag-covered shoulder of the railroad bed, with the tracks barely ten feet down from their dirty stoops. Kachigan eyed the fresh black creosote on the nearest ties and decided that the inhabitants of Wall probably hadn't built their houses that close on purpose. The tracks had come to them.

Here where the Turtle Creek's floodplain made a pregnant bulge between the surrounding hills, the artery of shining tracks that was the main line to Philadelphia had branched into a mile-wide carpet of steel rails, punctuated by the busy smoke and echoing clamor of a roundhouse full of riveters. Everything that wasn't railroad had been summarily evicted from the valley floor—trees, hills, ponds, even the streams themselves. Most of the hillside tributaries simply vanished into culverts beneath the tracks; the larger Turtle Creek had been shoved into an arbitrarily straight path and jammed as close to the northern hill slopes as it could go.

The space left for people to live and work in this stretch of the East Pittsburgh Valley looked even more grudgingly given: a narrow roadway perched on either side of the railroad yard to carry foot and trolley traffic while the houses scrambled for footing up the steep hillsides themselves. Across the valley, the town of Pitcairn had managed to nestle itself into another small creek junction with some success, although many of its houses still climbed rank on rank up to the flat, steeple-dotted hill crest. But here on the southern side, nature had provided no such space. Kachigan wasn't sure where Wall Station had first gotten its name, but it certainly suited the little town's long and narrow shape.

A train rumbled down the nearby spur, making the entire set of flats shake in alarming sympathy with the sound. Kachigan watched from the narrow stoop while the locomotive squealed to a halt, then sat rumbling and steaming in the afternoon sunlight, waiting its turn for entry to the roundhouse up the tracks. Between the noise of the constantly passing trains and the sharp percussive hammering of the riveters, Kachigan wondered how Lyell Osborne had ever gotten any sleep.

A pair of women in babushkas and shawls walked down the railroad shoulder, their footsteps lost under the noise from the yard. Kachigan saw how suspiciously they eyed him and turned back toward his partner, whose considerable bulk hid whatever he was doing to Osborne's front door. "Haven't you gotten that lock jimmied yet?" he demanded, not trying to soften his voice. Even from a few yards away, there was no way the neighbors were going to hear him unless he shouted. At least that was one thing the clamor from the train yard was good for.

Taggart grunted. "No. Just like a damned engineer to put a high-class dead bolt on a dump like this. Hang on. . . ."

The sharp crack of breaking glass made Kachigan wince and look around. Fortunately, the neighbor ladies had already vanished into the bar at the end of the street. "Did you have to do that?"

"You're the one who wanted in so bad you couldn't be bothered to find the landlord," his partner retorted, knocking the last few shards of glass out of the door pane with the heel of his hand.

"Yes, but if we had to break a window, wouldn't it have been better to pick one around the back?"

"Hell, no." Taggart wriggled his hand carefully through the gaping pane and groped for the inside latch. "If you're going to break and enter, you should always use the front door. That way, people assume you have the right to do it."

Kachigan gave him a caustic look. "Where did you learn that? From some burglar you arrested?"

"Nope. From Roger McGara." With a creak the door swung open and Taggart stepped back, letting him enter first. Kachigan paused on the dim threshold to scrape a match alight and then turn on the gas in the living-room light fixtures.

The steady, hissing glow of the wall sconces revealed an almost unnatural neatness. Lyell Osborne's living room was bare of draperies, paintings, or anything else that might have added to the inventor's creature comforts. A long table covered with electrical equipment and carefully rolled blueprints took the place of a couch, and the single cracked leather chair had been placed not beside the gas fireplace but conveniently close to a bookcase full of scientific journals and engineering texts. Through a narrow doorway, Kachigan could see the only other downstairs room, a small and equally barren kitchen. A narrow side stair presumably led up to the bath and bedrooms.

"Upstairs or downstairs?" he asked Taggart.

The big man measured the flight of stairs, undoubtedly weighing the effort of climbing against the likelihood of much less work up above. "Upstairs," he decided. "But I get dibs on any beer in the kitchen."

"Help yourself." Kachigan pulled out his evidence book and began examining the engineer's worktable while Taggart took him literally enough to head for the kitchen before the stairs. He came back carrying two bottles and looking disgruntled. "It's Fort Pitt," he said, in answer to Kachigan's inquiring look. "And it's warm. No one's put ice in that chest for days. It's barely damp inside."

"Smell much?"

"Nope. No food in there either."

Kachigan grunted, remembering his own empty-ice-chest days, before his father had moved in and insisted on saving every leftover scrap. "Osborne probably ate at a boarding-house or in the bars, and just came here to work and sleep."

"And drink an occasional beer." Taggart held out a bottle and snorted when Kachigan shook his head at it. "You're not a flat-footed patrolman anymore, Milo. You're allowed."

"Well, I shouldn't be."

His partner sighed, tucking the extra bottle into his coat pocket. "You know, that steel-company police chief who bribed McGara to make you a county detective last month must have been crazy to think you belonged here."

"Bernard K. Flinn?" Kachigan grinned. "No. He was just damned mad at me."

"Figures." Taggart climbed to the second floor, his heavy step creaking across the cheap floorboards. "What are we looking for here?" he asked, his voice carrying downstairs with ease.

"Some clue to where Lyell Osborne spent his last few days." Kachigan trailed a cautious finger across one of the electrical engineer's devices, wondering if the exposed wires and metal plates would spark under his touch. When they didn't, he pressed gently on the central spring and watched a poised metal bar spring up to mate with a pronged connector. It looked like a small model of a railroad decoupler. "Recent store receipts, bankbooks, letters from friends—"

He unrolled a few of the blueprints, scanning them more for names and dates than because he understood what they meant. Most were undated and much-erased drawings of the same kinds of electrical gadgets that sat on the table in front of him. Some of the oldest ones, yellowing with age, were an odd mixture of drafted diagrams and elegant little sketches of buildings and landscapes and people's faces. Kachigan wondered if that meant Osborne had once dabbled in architecture, or in art.

Overhead, he could hear the creak and slam of drawers opening in a dresser, then the soft thud of a mattress sliding from its bed. "Does a pack of nude girls on postcards count?" Taggart asked.

"Only if they wrote him notes on the back." Kachigan moved on to the case full of books and magazines, pulling them out and shaking them for any slipped-in letters or lists. The books were disappointingly blank, but torn paper slips fluttered out of the first magazine like snow. Kachigan scooped them off the leather chair where they had fallen, but they were all blank, meant only to mark some article of interest to the engineer. He began to shake the next one, then paused and sat down with it instead, slowly paging through the electrical journal to see what Osborne had thought important enough to mark.

"You're supposed to be gathering clues, not reading *Collier's*." Taggart came down the stairs with something bright and flimsy thrown across one ox-wide shoulder.

Kachigan gave him a sardonic look. *"The Transactions of the American Society of Electrical Engineers* isn't exactly my idea of light reading."

"Was it Osborne's?"

"Apparently." He held up the page marked by one torn slip of paper. "He seems to have been particularly interested in electrical triggers and switching systems."

"Well, isn't that one of Westinghouse's specialties?"

"Sure, out at Union Switch and Signal where Osborne used to work. But his job now was designing hydroelectric plants for the electric company, like the one at Niagara Falls." Kachigan closed the journal and slid it back into place along the shelf, then went back to frown down at the table full of experimental devices. Having seen similar sketches in the journal articles Osborne had marked, he no longer thought they were scaled-down models. "I wonder if Osborne was selling this work on the side?"

"What did he need extra money for?" Taggart pulled the second bottle of Fort Pitt beer from his pocket and levered the cap off against the fireplace mantel. "He probably didn't pay more than ten dollars a month in rent for this dump. And he bought cheap beer."

"He was wearing expensive clothes and jewelry when he died."

The other detective grunted. "That's true, he did have more

than the usual two good suits a professional man owns, and all his shirts looked hand-tailored. He also had this, but I don't think he wore it.''

Kachigan caught the flimsy length of primrose silk with one hand, wincing as the smooth fabric snagged on his callused skin. He shook it out, expecting to find the square shape of a man's formal stock. Instead, the folds of fine silk fell into the voluptuous and unmistakable lines of a thin-strapped chemise. A drift of sweet scent, half perfume and half woman, floated out from the fabric while it wrapped itself around his hand in a clinging embrace. It was so obviously not an everyday sort of female undergarment that Kachigan felt his face tighten with embarrassment just from holding it. He began to see why it had ridden downstairs on Taggart's shoulder.

''Where'd you find this?'' he asked, carefully folding it back up to cover his uneasiness.

Taggart's grin told him his ploy hadn't succeeded. ''Hanging off the doorknob in the bathroom. I don't think Osborne was using it to study static electricity. Pretty racy little souvenir, huh?''

''Uh-huh.'' Kachigan began to stuff the silk garment into his overcoat pocket, then thought of how far its telltale scent might carry and held it back out to Taggart instead. ''Here, you hang on to it.''

''Afraid your Miss Sorby might get the wrong idea?''

Kachigan didn't bother to answer, since he couldn't think of an excuse that Taggart wouldn't see right through. ''Now we know where Osborne's money went,'' he said instead.

His partner gave the silk chemise a dubious look before tucking it away. ''Not many whores I know who would invest in this kind of quality and then leave it at the customer's house.''

''True.'' Kachigan made a final note in his evidence book, then went to turn off the gas. ''But they might have, if something had happened to interrupt the—er—transaction.''

''Something like Osborne getting conked on the head and hauled away to be murdered?'' For all his physical bulk and laziness, there was nothing sluggish about Taggart's intellect. ''Wouldn't bother a cheap crib hussy, but it might make a two-dollar girl rattled enough to leave a layer of frills behind."

"Then we need to see if there are any two-dollar girls available here in Wall." His partner's snort told Kachigan the answer before they had even closed the door behind them. An early December twilight was falling across the massive Pitcairn railyard, lit here and there by the dim reflected glows of coal fires from steam locomotives. He raised his voice to be heard over the clamor of riveting. "All right, you used to walk a beat in this valley. Where would you go to get a two-dollar girl?"

"Allegheny City." Taggart laughed at Kachigan's irritated look. "Or maybe Pitcairn. Railroad bosses come there from Philadelphia sometimes, to test out new brakes and couplers in the main yard. I hear they have a taste for fancy dishes."

"Then let's go check out the menu." If there was one thing the past few weeks of working for Roger McGara had cured Kachigan of, it was embarrassment about walking into a brothel. "If we're lucky, we might even get to talk to some of the entrées."

To get around the massive railroad yards, they had to take the trolley west to Wilmerding, cross the air-brake plant to the northern side of the valley, then retrace their route back east toward Pitcairn. It was a long, bumpy, and—at this hour—crowded journey. Kachigan began to see why young railroad roustabouts and poor immigrant girls routinely got hospitalized with severed limbs from illegally crossing the tracks. An irate story in last week's *Gazette* had trumpeted that railroad accidents were the leading cause of tragic, preventable death in Pittsburgh. Nice sentiment, Kachigan thought, but until some philanthropist threw enough money at poor railroad communities to erect track-crossing bridges and trolley lines, the toll would undoubtedly continue to mount.

The trolley rolled past a long shale bluff and through the dusty smoke plume of a brick works before it clattered down into Pitcairn. From close up, the railroad town's business district looked even more lopsided than it did at a distance, with all its bustling stores and sidewalk merchants perched on the steep side of its main street and nothing but the straightened

Turtle Creek and railroad on the other. Kachigan glanced out
the trolley window at the enormous roundhouse, more clearly
visible from this side of the valley. It was surrounded by a
scatter of storage buildings and workshops, all of them drowning in a vast sea of railroad cars waiting to be transferred from
one train to another. The small, dark-timbered depot building
that they passed a moment later looked like a tacked-on after-
thought to the industrial yard, its narrow access bridge a reluctant concession to the fact that the human beings who lived
in Pitcairn needed some way to board the train.

The trolley paused for a long time in front of the large hotel
that faced the roundhouse, letting off a crowd of Westinghouse
factory and office workers into a din so ferocious that the roar
of passing railroad engines was actually lost amid the clang
and crash of rivets biting into steel. Judging from the com-
muters' unworried expressions, Kachigan realized that this appalling level of noise must be normal for Pitcairn. The clamor
was as startling to him as Pittsburgh's choking smoke was to
out-of-town visitors, and it was probably just as unnoticeable
to its acclimated inhabitants. He watched some scatter into the
restaurants and stores that lined the main street while others
began the climb to hillside homes, all without so much as a
glance at the roundhouse that was emitting all the noise.

"We don't get off here?" Kachigan shouted at his partner
as the trolley remained motionless.

"Nope."

With a jerk, the nearly empty car resumed its journey. Two
blocks later sparks flew as it swerved from one set of tracks
to another, and the conductor called out, "Last Pitcairn stop,"
in a bored voice. Kachigan followed Taggart out the door,
seeing that they'd ended up at the steep end of town where
each row of the houses towered above the next. He eyed the
astonishing slant of one brick-paved street and wondered if
even a brothel could induce anyone to climb such a slope.

"Not that way," Taggart shouted over the noise, and led
him past the last street to an ungraded hillside road. It bordered
a creek whose ravine had apparently ended the sprawl of Pitcairn's business district. A last few careless houses had been
shoved into the mouth of the creek, actually built across it on

wooden beams and concrete-block pillars. Despite their sloppy design and cheap insul-brick siding, the wood trim was freshly painted and fine lace curtains gleamed behind cheap window glass.

"The brothel district," Taggart said succinctly. "Also the illegal-beverage district. The railroad makes sure that the rest of Pitcairn stays dry."

"That must keep business here booming." Kachigan took a deep breath as he walked toward the door of the first building, then wished he hadn't. The smell of sewage hung in the still evening air, where shallowly dug outhouses had leaked into the stream below. "Allegheny County Detectives Bureau," he said to the Negro who opened the door to him. "Is the lady of the house in?"

"Yes, sir." A desultory tinkle of piano music and the clink of glasses being washed and dried at the bar confirmed that this wasn't a busy time. No girls were even present in the outer room, although Kachigan could see a ripple of satin and pale flesh pass beyond the curtain of hanging jet beads that veiled the inner room. "I'll fetch her for you—but may I say what this visit's about?"

The doorman's wary look made Kachigan wonder if this far-flung brothel had ever been visited before by any of his rapacious coworkers. They were close to the edge of Roger McGara's kingdom here, barely a mile from the county line. "I'm looking into a murder that occurred in East Pittsburgh. There are a few questions I'd like to ask."

"Ah." The doorman's dark face betrayed no trace of surprise. "Will you sit at the bar while I'm gone, sirs?"

"Yes," said Taggart, before Kachigan could reply. He opened his mouth to argue, then realized it was pointless since there was nowhere else to sit except the curtained inner room. He followed Taggart to the bar with a sigh while the doorman vanished into a back office.

"Drinks on the house, sir?" asked the lighter-skinned Negro behind the bar.

Taggart grunted. "Beer for me and a ginger ale for my detective partner. He's taken the pledge."

He deliberately said it loud enough to stir the handful of

men at the bar into putting down their unfinished drinks and leaving. If Kachigan hadn't spent so many years patrolling the seedier streets of the South Side, he might have attributed that abrupt departure to hostility toward his badge. As it was, he recognized it as the simple caution of men who'd probably only stopped for a beer and a look at the half-dressed girls before they headed home to wives and children. The last thing they needed was to be arrested by a county detective.

The Negro barman pulled an amber glass from his illegal tap and set a dusty brown bottle of ginger ale beside it. Taggart dove into the cold beer and emerged with foam on his mustache and a contented sigh. "You want to ask the madam about Lyell Osborne, too, or just get her permission to talk to the girls?"

"Both." Kachigan sipped at his ginger ale with distaste, wishing it were milk. "Is this the only place in Pitcairn Osborne's girl is likely to have worked?"

"Yep. The other cribs in town would have rolled Osborne rather than served him." Taggart looked over Kachigan's shoulder with amusement. "But you'd never do that, would you, Sally Lowry?"

"Not unless he was a county detective," came the sharp reply. Kachigan swung around to see a massively heavy woman with faded blue eyes perch herself onto the stool next to him. "I've told you before, Art Taggart, if you try to make me pay off that stinking boss of yours, I'll just move across the county line. Trafford City's getting big enough to need some girls."

"We're not here to collect, ma'am," Kachigan said, his respect for her reluctantly kindled by the scorn in her voice when she'd spoken of Roger McGara. "We're investigating the murder of a Westinghouse engineer down in East Pittsburgh the night before last."

"I heard about it." Lowry scooped up a handful of peanuts with fingernails so long and smoothly buffed that they didn't seem to belong to her plump, age-spotted hands. "And what I heard is that he got blown up by a drunken old anarchist. Shouldn't you be checking out socialist clubs instead of cribs?"

Kachigan sorted through the facts of the case for the ones he was willing to release for public consumption. "Osborne got conked and rolled before he got blown up," he said at last. "And it looks like he might have had a fancy girl with him the night it happened."

The madam gave him a snapping glance. "You think we rolled him here and shipped him rail freight down to East Pittsburgh? Where he just kind of coincidentally fell into someone's backyard and got blown up?"

"No, but I think one of your girls might know what actually happened. Which of them was at Osborne's house in Wall the night he died?"

Lowry shook with breathless, consumptive laughter. "None of them, honey. How the hell would they even get there? Take the trolley down to Wilmerding in their nighties? Or skip across all the tracks in the buff?"

"Sal, your girls have street clothes," Taggart chided. "And that would have been a slow night. You sure Osborne didn't stop by and take someone home with him?"

"Positive." She poked a sharp nail at Kachigan's chest, hard enough that he could feel the pinch through his vest. "I don't want you waking up all my girls to ask them about this, so I'm going to tell you everything I know about Lyell Osborne. And then you're going to take yourself right out my door. You hear?"

He met her gaze for a moment, seeing what he thought was a gleam of sincerity beneath the faded patina of greed and self-interest. "All right, I hear you."

"Well, then." Sally Lowry sat back, clasping her hands across her massive chest to keep her balance. "It's true Lyell Osborne was a customer of mine. Came here for years, once a week, usually on a slow night. No special girls, no special requests, and he never made a lick of trouble."

"Did he drink much?" Taggart asked.

Lowry bounced a peanut at him. "Stop jumping ahead, I'm getting to that part. Osborne liked an Iron City with his girl, like most of the boys around here do, but he never did much other drinking that I knew of. Until about six weeks ago." She glanced across at her quiet black barman. "There was a couple of weeks there where we couldn't pour the whiskey fast enough for him, could we, Robbie?"

"No, ma'am."

"And then what happened?" Kachigan asked.

Sally Lowry's satin-draped shoulders raised and lowered in a massive shrug. "About a month ago the boy just stopped coming in. Not for drinks, not for girls, not for anything. Took the pledge, I figured. Either that or he found some cheaper dive to get drunk in."

Kachigan took another sip of bitter ginger ale and considered the possibilities. "I don't think the girl he had before he died came from anyplace cheap." He nodded at Taggart, who pulled out the scrap of perfumed silk they'd brought with them. "Do you recognize that?"

Lowry shook out the chemise and snorted. "Honey, this didn't come from *any* of the crib girls in the East Pittsburgh Valley. That's real silk and French perfume, not some department-store imitation." Her eyes narrowed, bringing the shrewdness of her face into sharper focus. "You sure Osborne hadn't gone and got himself a girlfriend?"

This time it was Taggart's turn to snort. "Right now we're not sure of anything. Except that whoever killed Lyell Osborne, it wasn't that drunken old anarchist in East Pittsburgh."

Kachigan scowled at his too-informative partner. Fortunately, the slam of the brothel's front door and a cold blast of winter wind and railroad noise interrupted before Taggart could spill any more specific details. Sally Lowry glanced over her shoulder at the newcomer, and her face grew shuttered and still.

"Good evening, Mr. Dettis," she said, wrapping her sharp voice in surprisingly cotton-soft deference. It gave Kachigan an unexpected glimpse of what she must have been like in her commercial prime. "What can we do for you, sir?"

"Leave."

Kachigan swung around on his stool, not sure whether that rasping command had been intended for Sally Lowry or for him and Taggart. The man staring at them from the open doorway seemed oblivious to the night wind blowing past him, although he wore only an old-fashioned frock coat and stovepipe hat. At first glance, he looked like nothing more than a local businessman, but the trio of husky men in railroad-police uniforms who pushed past him to secure the room made the madam's behavior understandable. The Pennsylvania Railroad ruled the communities around its main yards as powerfully as any coal mine or steel mill ruled its company towns.

With an irritated sigh, so soft only Kachigan could hear it, Sally Lowry pushed herself off her stool. "Is the next room far enough away, or should I go upstairs?"

"Upstairs, and take your whores and black boys with you. I don't want anyone spying on me." The railroad boss didn't come into the room until all the staff had been gathered and herded up the steps. By then, most of the room's heat had drifted out into the night, leaving the brothel cold enough to make the shard of metal in Kachigan's cheek ache. Dettis scowled over his shoulder when the last of his men would have closed the door behind him. "Leave it," he growled. "I don't want to stink like a whore when I leave here."

"But the girls—" The police guard glanced up the stairs, where the half-dressed stock-in-trade had disappeared.

"They'll be hot enough when they get to hell." It wasn't the callousness or contempt in Dettis's voice that startled Kachigan. It was the pure, hardheaded conviction.

"Railroad-police chief?" he asked Taggart, deliberately turning his back on the approaching man.

His partner's narrow grin flashed out in appreciation of that tactic. "No, the superintendent of the Pitcairn yard. O. X. Dettis, better known—"

A hand dropped on Kachigan's shoulder and yanked him rudely around again. He met the glare of bloodshot eyes without faltering, although the flare of anger he saw in them startled him. Dettis was a small, powerful bull of a man, not as broad-shouldered as Taggart or as tall as Kachigan. His fleshy face had the constant high red color of someone with a heart condition, and the sparse stubble of hair below his hat's brim was iron gray. Despite all of that, however, the shake he gave Kachigan was both brutal and fearless.

"Don't turn your back on me, county boy. I came here to talk to you."

"Really?" Kachigan knew he should watch his tongue around a railroad autocrat, even one as local as this, but something about Dettis's arrogance made it impossible. "And here I thought you just stopped by for a two-bit whore."

That got him another shake, this one almost strong enough to dislodge him from his bar stool. "Careful," Dettis said between gritted teeth. "Your boss McGara owes me more favors than he owes the mayor. Too much lip out of you and I can have your job."

And welcome to it, Kachigan wanted to snarl back, but the image of Helen Sorby trying to solve this murder on her own stuffed the words back into his throat.

"Sorry, Ox," Taggart said placidly. "Kachigan's new and don't know all the ropes yet. And he's had a long day."

The railroad-police chief's color deepened, but he didn't snap at Taggart for using his nickname. "So what's stopping you from going home? It's past five by my watch."

"I still have work to do." Kachigan watched one of the railroad policemen circle the cheap pine counter to watch them from the other side. His face looked familiar, but it wasn't until the gaslight silhouetted his dark Italian face that Kachigan recognized him as one of the men who'd been drinking here when he and Taggart first came in. That let him guess what Dettis might have gotten exercised enough about to come running coatless from the yard. "Don't worry, I'm not here to collect payoffs from the brothels in Pitcairn. If McGara says this is your turf, that's good enough for me."

Dettis scowled but didn't deny it. "So why are you here?"

"Just trying to close out a murder down in East Pittsburgh."

"Oh, the Westinghouse engineer." The railroad boss's tone was a little too casual to be real. "Don't you have a guy in jail for that already?"

Taggart answered while Kachigan was still searching for a good excuse. "McGara wants us to make sure we collar the whole anarchist ring. You know how nervous he gets when people start running around throwing bombs at millionaires."

Surprisingly, that brought a wave of deeper and more angry red washing up Dettis's fleshy face. "You can tell McGara that no one's throwing any more bombs around this valley. You got that straight, Fat Art?''

"Why makes you so sure?" Kachigan asked, before he could stop himself. "Just because we caught that one old guy down in East Pittsburgh—''

"You caught more than one anarchist in East Pittsburgh!"

For one chilling moment Kachigan thought that angry shout referred to Helen Sorby. He opened his mouth to ask Dettis how he knew, but the police chief's explosion didn't stop there. With a violent crack of palm against glass, he sent Kachigan's half-empty bottle of ginger ale flying off the bar to splash against the brothel's far wall.

"Goddamned anarchists, thinking they've got the right to destroy what honest men worked like dogs to create! And for what? They never even tell you what the hell they want. Serves them right to get blown up with their own damn bombs!"

"With their own . . .'' Kachigan's voice trailed off as he realized what had sparked this ranting fury. He glanced over at Art Taggart and saw his partner looking as incredulous as he felt.

"Ox, are you saying that Lyell Osborne was an *anarchist*?" Taggart demanded.

"Hell, yes!" The superintendent's snarl sounded resentful enough to be genuine. "That damned George Westinghouse has an entire nest of anarchists working down in his electric factory. Hiring all those foreigners and college-educated women like he does—most of them are bound to be socialists and radicals!"

Kachigan frowned. "Do you actually have any proof that Osborne was one of them?''

"Maybe." This time, the infuriated smack of Dettis's hand was against his shoulder, hard enough to knock him back against the bar. "But the railroad didn't hire me to do your job for you, county boy. They hired me to keep their property and their workers safe, and that's exactly what I do.''

Kachigan rubbed at his aching shoulder. He was getting a little tired of Ox Dettis and his volcanic temper. "By getting rid of troublemakers like Lyell Osborne?" he asked recklessly.

"No, by getting rid of troublemakers like you.'' Dettis gathered his waiting railroad policemen with a jerk of his chin. "You've got five minutes to make the trolley back to Pittsburgh, boys. Take any longer than that, and you're going rail freight to the end of the line."

7

SATURDAY DAWNED COLD AND CLOUDY, WITH A wet feel to the air that warned of sleet or snow. Helen listened to the wind bang at the shutters and rattle the loose slate tiles of Essene House, and tried not to think of how cold she was going to be in Molly's second-best dress, a gauzy confection of nauseating strawberry-pink tulle and white satin ribbons more appropriate to July than December. Instead, she concentrated on scowling at her twin brother across the long dining-room table. Even though it was nearly seven, they were the only ones sitting there—an unusual enough occurrence in this hungry household that Helen had quizzed her brother on what he'd done last night while she'd been trapped on the telephone with Aunt Pittypat. The answer hadn't gratified her.

"You gave them *how* much?"

"Two bits each. Not enough to get drunk on, just enough for trolley fare." Thomas avoided her gaze, but she couldn't be sure if it was out of guilt or because he was trying not to burst into laughter. "Helen, be realistic. You can't just hand the tenants a sketch and tell them to make the rounds of all the local bars with it. You have to give them an incentive."

Her exasperated sigh blew steam off the lumpy oatmeal that was all she'd managed to make for breakfast, in between trying to fasten all the tiny hooks and pins of Molly's dress. "I *did* give them an incentive! I told them that if they found someone who'd seen Lyell Osborne on the night he died, I'd give them a free month's rent.''

''Which would have sent them all out to the nearest bars on Linden Street, and nowhere else,'' her brother retorted. ''And what good would that have done? If Osborne had been drinking down here the night he died, don't you think Kachigan would have already found out about it?''

Helen's scowl deepened. ''He didn't have a sketch of Osborne to take with him when he visited all those bars.''

''And whose fault was that?'' Thomas sounded more exasperated than he usually could be bothered to get over his sister's fits and starts. ''You might have suggested it to him that first night he came here, but you decided to fight with him instead.'' He gave her a surprisingly serious look. ''Helen, you know those bribes Kachigan got caught with weren't meant for him. Why are you being such a puritan about it?''

Stung, she opened her mouth to inform her oblivious brother that it was Kachigan's reprehensible behavior, not his trumped-up indictment, that infuriated her. Unfortunately, the slam of the front door opening interrupted her diatribe before she could even launch into it.

''Miss, miss, are you still here?'' Molly came darting into the dining room, surprisingly light on her feet despite her rounded stomach. She smelled of beer and cigar smoke from a night spent in the bars, but excitement lit her face to a bright-eyed glow. She waved a bedraggled, half-torn copy of one of the sketches Helen had spent the previous night reconstructing from memory. ''I found out all about that dead guy for you, truly I did! Do I get the steak-and-ice-cream supper tonight?''

Helen frowned at her brother. ''More incentive?''

''You wanted the information as soon as possible, didn't you?'' Thomas scraped the last of his oatmeal out of his bowl, then clattered his spoon down into it. ''And the Linden Hotel is having a one-dollar steak special tonight. I thought we could let the Buchaks cook dinner for once and go out on the town.''

''You didn't happen to mention that to Kachigan's partner when you were playing poker with him the other night, did you?'' she asked suspiciously.

''No.'' Her twin shrugged into his surveyor's vest, tapping

all the pockets to make sure his tapes and rulers and pencils were in place. "He mentioned it to me."

"Thomas—"

"Molly and I are going whether you come or not," he informed her curtly, giving the ex-prostitute a pat on the head as he went past her. She giggled in delight. "And it would be a shame if you didn't join us, when you're already so nicely dressed—"

Helen threw her spoon at him, cursing in Italian, but Thomas knew her too well. He'd already ducked out into the main hall, the explosive sound of pent-in laughter drifting behind him. Helen saw the bewildered look that Molly gave her and sighed in defeat. How could she explain to the owner of this coquettish outfit that it would take a team of cart horses to drag her into any place where Milo Kachigan might see her in it?

"What *did* you find out about the dead man, Molly?" she asked instead.

"Lots." The ex-prostitute finished ladling oatmeal into her bowl, then added a liberal handful of the coarse brown sugar that was all they could afford. She came to plump herself down next to Helen companionably. "I took the streetcar up all the way to Pitcairn, since the Buchaks said they was going to Wilmerding and I saw Lester and old Jess get off at Adderly. I still know a lot of the working girls up there, especially the ones from Missus Lowry's place. I just had to wait until they got off at four and could come out for a drink."

Helen blinked, impressed by the girl's dedication although somewhat taken aback by her sources. "What did the girls tell you? Did Mr. Osborne have—um—I—mean, did he—"

"Use any of them the night he died?" Molly finished matter-of-factly while Helen searched for less embarrassing words. "No, and that's the funny thing. He'd been to Missus's Lowry's a slew of times before, Lil and Nan told me, but when they saw him at the Gold Eagle Bar that night, he acted like he didn't even know who they were."

It didn't take the intellect of an electrical engineer to figure out what that meant. "Who was he with?"

Molly grinned, exposing the crooked tooth that made her look even younger than she was. "You're smart, Miss Sorby.

He had a lady with him at the bar, all dressed up in fancy satin and lace. Lily figured her for his sister, 'cause they looked a lot alike, she said. But Nan said she was thought it was just another working girl, one of the high-class, uppity ones from Allegheny City.''

Helen chewed on her lip, thinking about that. "Did your friends see Osborne meet anyone else besides this lady?"

"No, but Nan saw where they went when they left that night." Molly looked up from her oatmeal, her eyes intent. "You've got to promise me something before I'll tell you, though."

Helen restrained the urge to strangle her brightest and most annoying charge. "You can have as much dessert as you want, for the rest of the week," she promised recklessly. "And free rent for *two* months."

Molly shook her head. "All I want is for you to come to supper with us tonight, ma'am."

"No."

The younger woman's smile faded, and her face grew troubled. "I know you're mad at that county detective for not letting Abraham Maccoun out of jail, but I thought—well, he might not even be there. And if you came along, then it wouldn't be all just men."

That wistful observation made Helen blink again, this time in surprise. "Molly, are you *afraid* to be alone with Thomas and Art Taggart?"

The ex-prostitute's earthy Irish snort answered that better than any words could have. "Miss, I played poker with the both of them until past midnight the other night—and cleaned their pockets of all but the lint, too. No, it's just that I've never been in a fancy hotel restaurant that the waiters didn't pinch me or whistle at me. I thought if I went with a real lady, it would be—I don't know. Nicer."

Helen sighed again, unable to resist that plea. The fact that Molly Slade had turned to selling herself so young was the inevitable consequence of a system that made no provision for orphans of poor immigrants. But the fact that she had never known the respect that middle-class girls like Helen took for granted was a crime. "All right, I'll come. But only if I get home early enough." To change into my plainest shirtwaist, she added with mental resolution.

Molly clapped her hands in delight, like the sixteen-year-old she really was. "It'll be good fun, Miss Sorby, you'll see. And I promise to eat polite."

"You can shovel in ice cream with both hands, so long as you finish telling me what you managed to find out from your friends in Pitcairn," Helen retorted. "Where did Osborne and his lady friend go after they left the bar?"

"To the railroad station," Molly answered. "Nan saw them there while she was out—um—taking the air for a while. She said it was strange how they waited, since it was way too late for any of the passenger trains to be running. But what really knocked her on her—well, what surprised her was that a train came and got them anyway."

"A train stopped just for them? Did they both get on it?"

Molly shook her head. "Just the Westinghouse guy, not the fancy lady. She left then, but Nan didn't see if she got on the trolley or went into another bar." She tipped her head, regarding Helen with shrewd eyes. "That's not the strangest part, though. You know what is?"

"What?"

"The railroad car that picked your dead guy up—Nan said it was one of those real fancy private ones that only the millionaires ride in. And the sign on the back of it was a big letter 'W' in a circle. You know what that stands for?"

"Yes." Helen took a deep breath. "Westinghouse."

Helen hadn't realized, from her initial day of work, just how annoying her new secretarial position really was. It wasn't until she found herself in the thick of the morning crowd milling through the front doors of the Westinghouse castle, with a steady stream of young engineers and draftsmen bumping into her and then charmingly begging pardon, that her real powerlessness sank in. Most of the other young stenographers looked flushed and happy with this flurry of masculine attention, but it made Helen have to clench her teeth to keep acid comments from boiling out. It wasn't the politeness of the men's voices or their easy smiles that disturbed her. It was the underlying sense that she was not really a person but a thing, an office accessory to be paid attention to or ignored with as much concern for her feelings as she might give her fountain pen.

That message got hammered home again a short while later, and it wasn't because she'd gotten a barrage of even more dubious looks from her fellow stenographers when she'd shed her coat to reveal Molly's second-best dress. That feminine disapproval at least assumed she was a person, even if she had no taste and less virtue. It wasn't until she'd settled herself at the desk she'd been assigned the day before and started translating another of George Westinghouse's illegible supply lists that the trouble started.

"Miss Sorby," Jenkins said from behind, his voice so cold and unexpected that she jumped. To one side, she saw Bonnie Howards grimace down at the bookkeeping ledger she'd been assigned to copy. Somehow, Helen didn't think it was the rows of numbers that had inspired that sour expression. "May I ask where you got that fountain pen?"

Helen glanced down at the brushed steel Waterman in her hand. "It's mine," she said in surprise. "I brought it in from home this morning so I wouldn't spill so much ink on my work."

Jenkins made an odd little noise, halfway between a cluck of disbelief and a snort of derision. "You just happened to have a ten-dollar fountain pen at home?" He reached out and snagged it from her hand. "I don't think so, young lady."

"Hey!" Helen made a grab after the pen, but he'd already slid it into a vest pocket. "You can't take that! It's mine."

The office manager gave her a dismissive look. "Of course it's not. You told me yourself yesterday that your brother was laid off and you had no other sources of income." He swept another glance down her bright pink dress and his nostrils pinched in distaste. "Or perhaps no other sources that you cared to put on your application. So where did you take it from, Miss Sorby? Mr. Sparenberg's office?"

Helen felt her face burn with mortification. "I was given that pen by my Aunt Pat for Christmas," she said between her teeth. "And you have no proof that it's not mine."

"I don't need proof." Jenkins glanced down at the work she'd done and his mouth tightened to match his unhappy nostrils. "Make sure you keep up that superb handwriting, Miss Sorby. Right now it's all that's keeping you employed."

His prissy footsteps clicked down the silenced row of secretaries and machine operators. Helen gritted her teeth on the Italian curse she wanted to fling after him and instead swung back to her work to avoid the sidelong glances she was getting. For a long time, though, the odd Greek symbols Westinghouse used just danced and slipped through the rows, refusing to stay in focus.

"Hey." A hand crept across the counter to give hers a comforting squeeze. "Don't worry, Helen. I know where that old fart keeps all the stuff he confiscates from us. He's got my perfume atomizer in there, too—we'll make a raid after he leaves today."

Helen took a deep breath and found her voice, although she couldn't yet manage a smile. "Thanks, Bonnie."

"No problem." The other stenographer's magnificent curls danced with the defiant toss of her head. "I'm starting to think this job's not worth the snootiness we have to put up with, even if it does pay fifty cents a day."

"It's not snootiness." Helen fell silent, slowly rolling the ugly Westinghouse-issue pen back and forth in her fingers. "To Jenkins and those engineers upstairs, we're not even *people*. We're just things to use, like the typing and adding machines."

"You've noticed." The dry note in Bonnie's voice didn't escape Helen. She glanced up at the other new stenographer and saw how crooked her smile had become. "Welcome to the world of the twentieth-century office, Miss Sorby. Where your boss will dictate the most amazing things to you because he assumes you won't remember any of them five seconds later."

Helen chewed on her lip for a moment, then threw caution to the wind. "Bonnie, that meeting we took notes on yesterday—"

"Hush!" That was Miss Walroth's steely voice, echoing up the line of scratching pens. "No extraneous talking, girls, you know that. Miss Sorby, if you have a question on those lists you're transcribing, bring them here to me.''

With another grimace, Bonnie went back to her work. Helen reluctantly rose and passed through the hostile gauntlet of female scrutiny to reach her frowning supervisor. She brought the list of Greek symbols with her. ''I'm sorry, ma'am,'' she lied, glancing down at the list in what she hoped looked like a distraught fashion. ''But this last list has been so hard to copy. . . .''

Walroth glanced at it and her frown melted into a startled look. ''Good heavens, no wonder! That's not a supply sheet, Miss Sorby. That's one of the old man's worksheets of equations for some new invention.''

''Oh.'' Helen held the page out in genuine relief, but instead of taking it from her, Walroth paused. ''Why don't you just take that upstairs to Dr. Grissaldi, yourself?'' she suggested after a judicious moment. ''She'll know where it should be filed, I'm sure. And perhaps she can—er—shed some light for Mr. Jenkins on the origin of your fountain pen, if you happen to mention it to her.''

The sympathy in her voice was unmistakable, and melted the cold knot that seemed to have lodged itself somewhere in Helen's windpipe. This time, a smile was easier to find. ''Yes, ma'am. I'll take it up to her right away.''

She threaded her way through the noisy clatter of the office, better able now to ignore the speculative looks she got. The iron stairs that led up to the engineer's office were cold and drafty enough to make her hurry up them. Through the slitted windows that pierced each landing, Helen could see a whirl of snow flurries spangling the sky outside. She paused beside the last one long enough to stand on tiptoe and check to see if the snow was laying. A moment later a hand fell on her shoulder from behind and swung her around to meet a familiar handsome face.

''Mr. Greer.'' Helen tried to step away from him and felt the steel-railed wall hit her back. She froze her voice to its iciest pitch. ''Let me go, please.''

The young man's smile was insufferable. ''Are you really

asking me that, or just putting on a pretty female show of modesty?''

She scowled up at him, heedless for once of her meek secretarial cover. ''I'm not *asking* you anything! I'm warning you that if you don't release me, I'll scream loud enough to bring every engineer down from the third floor.''

''And then you'll lose your job.'' His sweetly beguiling voice belied the ugly words. ''Mr. Westinghouse doesn't like secretaries who are loose.''

''How does he feel about salesmen who are castrated?'' Helen deliberately let her voice rise to the fierce, ringing shout it became whenever she was truly infuriated. ''By the half-Italian brothers of women who didn't really want to be raped in a stairwell?''

Greer was wincing by the time she finished, although she didn't know if it was from her blunt words or the harsh echoes her voice had bounced off the metal stairs. ''All right, take it easy,'' he said, letting her go. His voice had turned cautious and calming, as if she was suffering from nothing more than an inexplicable attack of hysterics. Helen knew from experience that this was the way men usually reacted to women who intimidated them, but that didn't make it any less maddening. ''I was just kidding around.''

For once, Helen didn't allow her temper to draw her into an argument. Instead, she gathered her tulle skirts in her hands and pushed past Greer, running up the rest of the stairs to the third floor. She didn't care if it looked like retreat. Right now physical exertion was the only thing that could burn off her seething, impotent rage.

She burst out from the stairwell into a cluster of men gathered around a water cooler, barely managing to skid to a stop before she slammed into them. Several pairs of eyes turned to survey her with curiosity and concern. ''Sorry,'' Helen said breathlessly. ''Which is Dr. Grissaldi's office, please?''

''That one, Miss Sorby.'' A freckled young man pointed at a doorway almost blocked by a stack of copper electrical coils, then gave her a discreet smile that actually acknowledged she was a fellow human being. It wasn't until then that Helen remembered why he knew her—this was the self-effacing private secretary from the engineer's meeting yesterday. "Be careful when you go in, though. Leo's got live wires running everywhere."

Helen nodded at him gratefully, then hurried down the hall before Greer could emerge behind her. If he had any sense, the salesman would go downstairs instead of up to avoid gossip, but she had very little evidence that sense was numbered among any of the virtues Alexander Erskine Greer presumably had.

Her tentative rap on the door frame of the cluttered office got her only a grunt of reply. Helen waited, then pushed the door wider open and took an even more tentative step inside, looking for wires. Her path was blocked almost immediately by a bookshelf full of leather-bound volumes with titles in German and Italian as well as English. Behind it, a sizzle and snap were followed by a familiar Italian curse.

"Dr. Grissaldi?"

"Si, si . . . avanti!"

Helen took a deep breath and rounded the bookshelf into chaos. A scatter of equipment, drawings, and open textbooks drowned the long worktable, and rolled blueprints crowded every nook and cranny around it, spilling down under the table in a messy pile. One of the two desks inside was stacked with memos, notebooks, and stained teacups. The other was surprisingly bare of clutter, like an island of sanity amid a creative maelstrom. Draped lengths of wires connected from an overhead electric fixture to some of the equipment, sparking an occasional whir or clatter when the miniature turbines were started by the elderly genie in their midst. Leonora Grissaldi's hair was as ruffled as a busy housewife's and her fingers as ink-stained as a journalist's, but the look of intense concentration in her blue eyes could only have belonged to a scientist or engineer.

"If you don't mind, I have a paper of Mr. Westinghouse's that you need to look at. . . ."

Helen's voice trailed off at the astounded look she got from the female engineer. It wasn't until the older woman cleared her throat and asked in fluent Italian, "And what paper would that be?'' that Helen realized she had instinctively used the same language when she spoke.

Since it was too late to deny her heritage, Helen continued to speak the language her mother had taught her. ''A page of experimental notes, we think, that got mixed in with his supply lists.'' She stepped forward, carefully ducking beneath a hanging copper wire, and handed the paper to Grissaldi. The female engineer scanned it, grunted, and tossed it over to join the piled-up layers of similar papers on her desk.

''Old notes, from the Brazilian project,'' she informed Helen, in English this time, then tipped her head to regard her with interested eyes. ''You are the new secretary from yesterday's meeting, eh? I don't remember that your name was Italian.''

''I'm only half, on my mother's side. My father was Irish.''

''*Mezzo-mezzo,* just like me,'' the older woman said, with a surprisingly cordial smile. ''Except my mother was Swiss, and my father Italian from Lake Como.'' Another shower of sparks, blue and gold and fire white, burst out from one of the coiled copper cylinders on the table, seemingly at random. For a few minutes the office smelled of sharp, burned air, like the aftermath of a thunderstorm. Grissaldi ignored it. ''You read and write Italian as well as speak it?''

Helen took a deep breath, then nodded. She knew she was admitting to more knowledge than a grammar-school girl should have, but there was a serious note in Grissaldi's voice that had caught her journalist's instincts. The female engineer grunted again, turning to scrabble something out from the closest pile of memos on her desk. When she turned back, she was holding a different piece of paper out to Helen.

''Write this letter out in English for Olivio, eh? He needs to see it today, but I have to have these condensers finished for the test circuit we're making up tomorrow.''

Helen glanced down, seeing the frilly slant of European handwriting that covered both sides of the sheet. ''When do you need it done, ma'am?''

''Right now, here. That way, if there are any technical words you don't know, you can ask me about them.'' Grissaldi kicked out the chair from the neat desk that stood beside hers.

"Don't worry," she said, when Helen hesitated. "Lullio isn't alive anymore to yell at me about using his desk. You have a pen?"

"No, ma'am." Helen cleared her throat, but before she could launch into the story of her purloined Waterman Ideal, Grissaldi startled her by tossing her the pen in her own hand. Helen caught it with a wince, expecting a shower of spilled ink, but its gleaming nib never spilled a drop. She turned the polished silver barrel in her fingers and caught her breath as she saw the elegant Mont Blanc insignia. She was being entrusted with an even finer pen than the one she had lost.

"Use mine," Grissaldi said unnecessarily. "And Lullio should have some writing paper in that top drawer—go ahead and take a sheet."

Helen pulled the drawer open, almost nervously. This chance to look into the work space of the man whose murdered body she had found had come so unexpectedly and under such odd circumstances that she had to remind herself to take her time pulling out a sheet of paper so she could see what else was in the desk drawer. Unfortunately, it wasn't much. Lyell Osborne's spartan neatness had extended from the surface of the desk into its deepest crannies. Besides the stack of thick linen bond, only a neatly tied bundle of drafting pens and pencils, a gleaming steel ruler, and a scatter of tacks resided in the drawer. She closed it with a faint tinge of disappointment and bent to her task of translation.

The letter was dated *diciassette novembre,* or November 17, 1905. *Gentile Signor Professore Osborne,* ran the usual effusive Italian salutation. *Io scrivo in grave afflizione informare....*

After three minutes Helen turned to stare at Leonora Grissaldi. "Signora, have you *read* this letter?"

"Mmm." The engineer didn't look away from the coil she was winding additional copper wire onto. "What word don't you know?"

Helen took a deep and steadying breath, looking back over the letter she'd just read. There were two words she hadn't recognized. *"Molla."*

"Spring. The mechanical kind, not the season."

"And *scatto*?"

"Trip switch. Or trigger."

Unable to stand it anymore, Helen threw the expensive Mont Blanc down on her blank page and went to stand beside Grissaldi. She waited in tense silence until the older woman looked up from her electrical device.

"What's the matter?"

"Signora, that letter is a confidential message to Lyell Osborne!" Helen said in vehement Italian. "Warning him that someone has stolen his—his spring-trigger invention or whatever it is, and is filing patents on it all across Europe. And if Professor Ferraris is right, the person who stole it was someone who works for this company!"

Grissaldi gave her a steely look. "Well? Don't you think Mr. Sparenberg should know about that?"

"I don't think *I* should know about it!" Helen's exasperation heated her voice almost to a shout. "Signora, I've only worked here for one day!"

"Precisely."

Helen took another deep breath, staring down at the female engineer. "You asked me to read it on purpose, to see if I was the spy? But this trigger device must have been stolen months ago! I wasn't here then."

"No, but some other flighty young stenographer surely was." Grissaldi tapped a live wire to her copper coil and showered both of them with a spray of brilliant, biting sparks. Helen had to sink her teeth deep into her lower lip to keep from jumping away. "Although I don't remember meeting one quite as smart—or quite as careless—as you, Signorina Sorby." The older woman's voice had turned fierce and sharp as the crack of a whip. "Who hired you to work here and steal Westinghouse secrets?"

Helen stared at her for a silent moment, seeing no space for mercy or doubt to bloom in those glacial blue eyes. And Milo Kachigan kept telling her she was a terrible liar, anyway.

"*McClure's Magazine* hired me, signora," she said flatly, her gaze never wavering from her accuser. "But the only secret I was supposed to steal from your company was how badly its women workers were treated. You can telegraph the editor yourself if you want to confirm it.''

Whatever Leonora Grissaldi had expected her to say, that wasn't it. Her silver eyebrows arched up across her forehead in a look so astounded that it was almost comical. *''McClure's Magazine?''* she demanded. ''For their investigative series on women in the trades?''

''Precisely,'' Helen said, deliberately echoing Grissaldi's own words.

The engineer frowned for a moment. ''Then what are you doing here in the main office?''

''Finding out how badly the stenographers are treated, too!'' Helen retorted. ''And trying to discover why Lyell Osborne got killed and thrown into the backyard of my lodgings in East Pittsburgh a few nights ago. I don't know whether you're aware of it, signora, but a local settlement-house resident was arrested for your coworker's murder. I think he's innocent.''

Grissaldi's frowning gaze shifted to the bare desk beside her own. ''You're investigating the office to see who might have wanted to murder Lullio? So you can write a newspaper article about it?''

''Yes.''

''Maron.''

There was a long silence after that heartfelt comment, during which one of the whirring coils on the table cracked and then whispered to a stop. After a while Grissaldi put down her live wire and reached out to touch the malfunctioning equipment.

''Lullio would have known how to fix this just by looking at it,'' she said, sighing. ''It's going to take me days to figure it out, and more days after that to fix it. He may have had no humor and no personal life, but he was beyond doubt a genius.'' She looked back up at Helen, her eyes darkened with worry and fear. ''I'm afraid the old man's electric company is going to bleed to death without him.''

Helen frowned and crouched beside her so their gazes were on a level. ''Could that be why Osborne was killed? To sabotage the company?''

''I don't know. I hadn't thought—but then that letter came in the mail for him yesterday.'' Grissaldi threw up her hands in a fatalistic gesture that reminded Helen strongly of her mother. "If the old man's enemies hate him badly enough to murder us for it, then only God can help us now."

"God or the freedom of the press." Helen caught Grissaldi's callused, bony fingers in her own. "If we can find out who did it and expose them, we can swing the tide of public opinion so strongly in Westinghouse's favor that no bank would dare foreclose on him!"

"Maybe," Grissaldi said doubtfully. "But Signorina Sorby—ah, I can't keep calling you that English name while we're talking Italian! What is your first name?"

"Helen."

"Helena," she said, nodding. "And you call me Leo, eh? How are we supposed to find out who killed Lullio? We aren't the police, to ask questions up and down the whole valley."

Helen gave her hands a reassuring squeeze. "Don't worry, I have that part covered. What you need to help me do is figure out which of George Westinghouse's employees might be sabotaging him."

"But that's the problem!" the older woman protested. "No one who works for the old man for more than a week could *possibly* want to hurt him."

"No one at all?" It was Helen's turn to be doubtful. "Not even someone like Alexander Erskine Greer?"

"A conceited boy and not too bright," Grissaldi agreed. "But he knows what side of his bread has jam on it. No other company would hire him at half the salary the old man pays him. So why would he cut his own throat?" She shook her head, hair flying like silver gossamer. "It has to be someone who doesn't know him, someone new like you."

"Then who else has been hired recently? Have you checked the office staff?"

The older woman gave her an indignant look. "Of course I've checked. Our only new engineer has been down in Brazil since September, clearing the site for the Vale Brissa plant. All the draftsmen and mechanics have been here for years and wouldn't lose their new pensions for anything. And the only new stenographers besides you all left between October and

November. It might have been them, but how can we find them to check?''

Helen frowned. ''There's one other new stenographer,'' she said reluctantly. ''The girl that was taking notes on your meeting before me, Bonnie Howards.''

''Yes, yes.'' Leonora Grissaldi ducked her chin in an impatient Italian gesture. ''But if there is anyone here who wouldn't have wanted Lullio dead, Helena, it was that poor girl. He got her the job because she was some sort of second cousin of his. . . . I could have hit Olivio for forgetting that yesterday! What a *capo tosta*!''

. . . He had a lady with him at the bar, all dressed up in fancy satin and lace. Lily figured her for his sister. . . .

This time, it was Grissaldi who turned her fingers inside Helen's grip to give her a little shake. ''Helena, what is it? You look like a goose just walked across your grave.''

Helen released her and scrambled to her feet, checking the time on the engineer's wall clock. Half past ten, just about time for the morning break. ''Leo, do you really need that letter translated for Mr. Sparenberg?''

''No, I already told him about it—why, where are you going?''

''Back to the main office,'' Helen said. ''To have a talk with Bonnie Howards.''

8

THE CALL CAME EARLIER THAN KACHIGAN HAD expected Saturday morning, while he was still in the bathroom dipping his toothbrush into tooth-scrubbing powder. After the seventh ring, he knew who it had to be—no local operator would have kept trying the connection at this hour for a purely social call. It wasn't until he heard the scrape and thunk of his father's walking sticks from next door, however, that he even bothered to push the bathroom door open.

"Don't get up, Pap. I'm going to get it."

"Huh." From the edge of his rumpled bed, Istvan frowned across the hall at his son. Downstairs, the telephone shrilled through another series of rings. "What are you waiting for?"

"I know who it is." Kachigan spat, rinsed his mouth, then spat again. "And I know he won't hang up."

"Well, answer anyway, before the neighbors come banging on the doors," his father growled. "That damned talking machine is worse than an alarm clock."

"I'm going." Kachigan detoured long enough to grab a fresh collar band from his dresser top, stuffing it into the neck of his shirt as he trotted down the stairs. As he'd expected, the telephone bell was still emitting its shrill monotonous ring when he got to the bottom. For a moment Kachigan thought about not answering it at all, since he could probably spout word for word the lecture he was going to get, but he knew his father would eventually come down to get it if he didn't. He sighed and picked up the handset.

"Kachigan, where the *hell* have you been?"

The sheer annoyance in that gruff voice made Kachigan grin. He knew that Roger McGara read the papers every day, but there was always the possibility that the detective captain would assign one of his sublieutenants to bawl out the new employee. The fact that McGara himself was on the line meant Kachigan's list of possible murder suspects had hit a nerve. "Bathroom, Captain."

"Bathroom?"

"You know, that place where you sit covered with water for a while every morning?"

That got him a curse so violent, it sounded like McGara had snapped his teeth against the speaking bell. "Don't start playing smart with me, Kachigan. One phone call to Judge Detwiler, and I can have you tossed into jail with that drunken old anarchist you're supposed to be indicting."

"Is that what you called before"—Kachigan fished his pocket watch out and squinted at it in the cloudy morning light—"eight A.M. to tell me?"

McGara snorted. "Yeah, I can tell you're feeling your oats. You finally get a real murder case, and it turns out to be one where you can impress that overeducated girlfriend of yours with your dedication to your work. I got no problem with that, especially if all you're going to do is rattle a few cages down at Westinghouse. His payoffs are lousy, and never on time. But stop and use that brain you supposedly have for a minute, Kash. You *can't* take on the Pennsylvania Railroad!"

Kachigan busied himself buttoning his shirtsleeves. "Why not?"

"Because they're our number-one contributor!" Roger McGara's voice emerged from the handset bell in a roar only slightly muffled by the wires it had to travel through. "And because they also happen to own every judge and magistrate between here and Philadelphia. So even if you *do* find out they were behind this damned Westinghouse murder, you'll never be able to convict them of it."

"I don't need to convict them," Kachigan told his boss.

"All I need is enough evidence to get the charges against Abraham Maccoun dismissed."

There was a long, baffled silence. "Why the hell do you want to do that? Are you so limp between the legs that you'll do *anything* your girlfriend asks you to?"

Kachigan gritted his teeth. "I want to do it because Maccoun is innocent!"

"Of this Westinghouse murder, maybe," McGara conceded. "But a drunken old rabble-rouser like that is bound to be guilty of something. What'll it hurt to put him in the county jail and just let all the dust settle? Huh?"

Kachigan took in a deep breath. "Are you telling me I can't investigate this murder anymore, Captain?"

That got him the snarl he'd expected. "You made damn sure I couldn't do that, and you know it! Did you call the Pittsburgh papers yourself with all the details on Osborne's murder, or did Fat Art do it for you?"

"Taggart doesn't do anything off duty that doesn't involve beer, food, and sitting down." That wasn't true, but Kachigan didn't see any point in dragging his partner down into this mess along with him. "I called them."

"Then you're going to keep on calling them, to tell them about the nice progress you're making tracking down the anarchists—I repeat, Kachigan, *anarchists*—who were responsible for Osborne's death. Do you hear me?"

It was a good thing that telephone wires couldn't transmit pictures along with sound. If Roger McGara could have seen the expression Kachigan wore now, he'd have known just how carefully he'd been manipulated.

"Anarchists," Kachigan repeated, doing his best to sound dubious, defeated, and frustrated all at once. "Yeah, right. Anarchists."

McGara grunted. "Good boy. Hang in there, and we'll make a county detective out of you yet."

"Not if I can help it," Kachigan snapped before he could stop himself, and hung up on his boss's raucous laughter.

"You're sure Roger McGara said it was all right to do this?"

Kachigan gave his partner an exasperated glance. It had

taken him all morning just to haul Taggart out of bed and herd him through his morning routine of coffee, a dozen doughnuts, and the inevitable newspaper purchase before he would agree to board an eastbound local train. He'd kept right on buying newspapers and reading them while Kachigan had dragged him off at one railroad depot after another to question the station managers, ticket clerks, and trackmen about the bombs that had been exploding along their lines.

"You can ring him up if you don't believe me," he said as the train rumbled past the big, noisy roundhouse into Pitcairn. A white waltz of snowflakes flirted with their moving car, most of them melting as soon as they touched the window glass. "Just ask him what he ordered me to investigate this morning."

Taggart eyed him doubtfully. "After the fuss Ox Dettis made last night? Somehow, I don't think the answer's going to be the Pennsylvania Railroad. So why are we talking to every ticket clerk in this valley?"

"Because we're trying to find the ring of anarchists McGara wants to blame our murder on, of course."

"Oh. Of course." The train rolled to a stop in front of the Pitcairn railroad depot, and Kachigan made his way to the front of the car. Taggart followed him off obediently enough, but he let out a loud and plaintive bleat when Kachigan would have turned into the station. "Milo, for God's sake. Food first."

Kachigan frowned and pulled out his steel watch. He hadn't paid much attention to the time they'd spent gathering descriptions of the anarchist bombings. He'd been too busy writing down how much damage had been done to the tracks, the times and days that bombs exploded, and—this part always related with special relish—how many times a trackman had walked unknowingly past the site of a future explosion. But judging by his not-yet-restive stomach, he'd thought it was still only about eleven in the morning. His watch told him that his stomach was right.

"It's not lunchtime yet," he said.

Taggart managed to heave a sigh loud enough to be heard over the clanging of the riveters out in the railyard. "Not lunch, breakfast. This is when I normally get up. Just because you kicked me out of bed in the middle of the night doesn't mean I'm not still hungry.''

Knowing he wasn't going to win an argument about whether eight A.M. was the middle of the night, Kachigan chose a different tack. ''Those twelve doughnuts you ate this morning weren't breakfast?''

''Hell, no. Those were just something to sweeten the coffee.'' Taggart's own stomach chose that moment to rumble loud enough to be heard even over the clatter of traffic on Pitcairn's main street. ''Come on, Milo, take a break. If we eat now, I promise I won't stop you for lunch until at least three P.M.''

''All right.'' He glanced up the main street, seeing the glass storefronts of several restaurants and dairy bars tucked in between other businesses. ''Where do you want to go?''

''Don't worry, I know just the place.'' His partner led the way across the trestle bridge and down a side street to a small Chinese laundry with an eatery attached. Kachigan gave it a dubious look.

''Chinese for breakfast?''

''Better than greasy eggs and bacon,'' Taggart retorted, swinging the door open for him. ''Get the vegetable chop suey,'' he advised when Kachigan peered up at the unreadable menu scrawled on the chalkboard beside the lunch counter. ''Make your old man happy with you for a change.''

Kachigan sighed and dug in his pocket for quarters. ''All right, but if I don't like it, you're buying lunch tomorrow.''

''Does that mean you're buying today?''

''Why not?'' The one good thing about Chinese restaurants, he had noticed, was how little they charged. Taggart placed their orders with an elderly Chinese matron so tiny and wizened that she looked like an oddly gray-haired child, then went to claim two of the empty seats at the counter while Kachigan paid the bill.

''Okay, Milo,'' he said, when Kachigan had settled in beside him. ''Tell me what you're really doing.''

''Collecting information on anarchists,'' he said in amusement. "Or haven't you noticed me writing down everything those men told us?"

His partner snorted. "How could I not notice? It takes you nearly a minute per word. But what I want to know is *why* are you collecting it?"

Two mismatched mugs of tea got thumped down in front of them, straw-colored and smelling of flowers. Kachigan took a cautious sip and was startled by how much it reminded him of the tea his grandmother used to send them from Armenia. "Dettis told us that Lyell Osborne was an anarchist. I want to see if he actually had a reason for thinking that, or if he was just trying to stifle our investigation."

"So you're going to try and match up when those bombs went off with Osborne's schedule?" Taggart grabbed two wooden sticks from the cracked glass jar on the table and started rubbing them against each other as if he intended to start a fire from the shavings. "One big problem with that, Milo. You ever hear of a thing called a timer?"

Kachigan gave him an annoyed look, but the Chinese chef returned before he could reply. She slid a plate of barely wilted vegetables in front of him while Taggart got a heap of chicken parts covered in brownish goo. "Fork?" Kachigan asked, before she could disappear.

"Ah!" It could have been either an annoyed exclamation or a laugh, but either way it got him a dented fork pulled out from behind the counter. He speared it at random into his mixed greens and found himself chewing warm celery. The sauce on it tasted like vinegar, Worcestershire sauce, and sesame seeds combined: an odd combination, but not unpleasing to his Armenian tongue.

"Timers usually don't run for longer than twenty-four hours," he reminded Taggart. "If any of those bombs went off during times when Osborne was out of town—"

"We don't know that he *was* out of town."

"Oh, yes, we do." Kachigan put down his fork and extracted his evidence book from his coat, flipping back to what he'd written the night before. "I traded our information on Osborne's murder to the *Post* last night in exchange for the contents of their morgue file on him."

Taggart ripped chicken from its bone with an expert flick of his chopsticks. "Kind of risky, wasn't it? How did you know they'd even have a morgue file on him?"

"Inventor of the year," Kachigan reminded him. "Turns out he got the award watch back in mid-November, at the Electrical Engineers' annual convention in New York City. I'll have to check with Westinghouse's office files to be sure, but I figure he had to be out of the valley for at least four or five days around November seventeenth."

"And were there any bombs set on the railroad then?"

"Let's see. . . ." He flipped through the pages of notes that followed. "There was one on the sixteenth and another on either the twentieth or the twenty-first. Or maybe one bomb on each of those dates. The timing's possible for Osborne, but it's awfully tight."

Taggart grunted. "How about after Osborne died?"

"Good question." Between bites of cabbage and something that he hoped was dried mushroom, Kachigan turned pages back and forth, comparing dates from different sources. "No. But the last bomb anyone can remember went off on December eleventh. There haven't been any more after that."

"Except for Abraham Maccoun's alcohol bomb." Taggart sucked on another chicken bone, noisily. "What did they say the railroad bombs were made of?"

"Dynamite."

Taggart threw him an amused glance. "No lack of that around a railroad yard, is there? So the fact that Osborne didn't have any stashed in his ice chest doesn't exactly clear him."

"And it doesn't make him any more guilty than any other man in this valley," Kachigan retorted. More customers were coming in now, and the shout of orders and scrape of frying pans was rising to a lunchtime roar that nearly matched the din outside. "Let's say, for the sake of argument, that Osborne *was* a bomb-throwing anarchist. What I don't understand is why he would target the railroad for disruption. If it wasn't for all the air brakes the railroads buy from Westinghouse, half of those engineers in Wilmerding wouldn't be employed."

"If it wasn't for the railroad," said a voice on Kachigan's left, "George Westinghouse himself wouldn't be employed."

Kachigan swung around on his stool, startled. A swarthy Italian stranger gazed back at him in silence, confident he would be recognized. Kachigan was just opening his mouth to ask who he was when he finally saw the railroad-police guard's cap on the counter between them. This was the brothel customer who'd gone to fetch Ox Dettis last night.

"Why do you say that?" he asked instead. "Westinghouse is a brilliant inventor."

"And a lousy businessman." The guard's smile was a surprisingly good-humored flash of white teeth. "If it wasn't for the long-term contracts he negotiated with the railroads for brakes and signals, he'd have gone bankrupt long before now. Even a *paisan* like me knows you can't keep paying men all winter when you have no work for them to do. It may be good for the valley, but it's bad for your bank account."

"It's called 'generosity,' " Taggart said, reaching out with his chopsticks to steal a leftover piece of celery from Kachigan's plate. "But I don't suppose you'd know about that. The Pennsylvania Railroad's been called a lot of things, but 'generous' was never one of them."

Instead of angering the young Italian, that comment made his smile widen. "It's true, we don't pay men when there's no work to do. Fortunately for me, thieves still try to steal things no matter what the season is. And," he added calmly, "they still try to blow things up."

"Try to?" Kachigan frowned at him. "Does that mean they don't succeed?"

"Not anymore." The railroad guard sat back as the Chinese proprietor placed a bowl of what looked like steaming chicken soup in front of him, complete with papery dumplings. Kachigan caught a whiff of its familiar, comforting smell and made a note never to let Taggart order Chinese food for him again. "Not since a rail patrolman named Giovanni Ciocco was smart enough to figure out where the bombs were hiding."

Kachigan saw the gleam of laughter that accompanied the words. "Your name wouldn't happen to be Ciocco, would it?"

"It would," said his neighbor placidly. "And you're the Detective Kachigan they talked about in the newspaper this morning."

"Yes." He exchanged puzzled looks with Taggart while Ciocco spooned up more soup. After yesterday, the last thing he would have expected from one of Ox Dettis's employees was cooperation. Either the information they were being fed now was false, or this shrewd young Italian was operating on his own for some reason. "So where *were* the bombs hiding?"

"Under the switch-track plates." The answer came so promptly that Kachigan knew Ciocco must have planned all along to give it to him. He was growing more suspicious of this meeting by the minute. "A single stick of dynamite—just enough to demolish the switch and throw the train off the tracks. And the only thing showing was the trigger."

"Trigger?" It was Taggart's turn to frown at their informant. "You mean those bombs weren't set on timers?"

"No." Ciocco scooped up his last dumpling, then drank the rest of the soup straight from the bowl in true Mediterranean fashion. "Every one we disarmed had a fancy little pressure sensor attached to it. They only went off when there was a train actually on the tracks to derail—the pressure of a man stepping on them wasn't even enough." He sent them a mocking glance. "Tell me, Detective Kachigan—is it so stupid to conclude that some Westinghouse engineer had to be behind this?"

Kachigan grimaced, involuntarily reminded of the tiny switching devices that he'd seen on Lyell Osborne's worktable. The fact that Ox Dettis was trying to squelch his investigation didn't necessarily mean his accusations against Osborne were all smoke and no fire. In fact, if the railroad supervisor had acted on his suspicions the way Kachigan was starting to suspect he had, his subsequent actions made perfect sense. Fortunately, before he had to come up with a reply, Taggart intervened.

"Pretty amiable anarchists you've got out here in the valley, if they don't throw their bombs to create as much death and destruction as possible." The big detective leaned past Kachigan to poke a finger at Ciocco. "How do we know you're not making this all up, *paisan*?"

Instead of the slick reassurance or overzealous indignation Kachigan would have expected if Ciocco was lying, that question elicited an irritated growl. "Why should I make it up, eh? You think I got nothing better to do on my lunch hour than amuse county detectives with fairy tales?"

Kachigan shook his head. "Not if you're a good company man. But this story about triggers could be a red herring designed to take the heat off some union organizers at the yard." He saw the flicker of wariness that sparked alive in the guard's dark face, but couldn't be sure if it meant Ciocco was a unionizer or just afraid to be labeled one. "Train engineers could throw down a stick of dynamite and derail their trains without any trigger other than their throttle. As long as they had some convenient 'anarchists' to blame it on."

"They could also derail their trains with no dynamite at all and blame it on washed-out tracks. They all know where the bad places are—and that would be a hell of a lot safer than running the risk of your steam boiler cracking in a dynamite blast!"

"But accidents like that wouldn't convince the railroad to give you an eight-hour day," Kachigan pointed out. "Or make the yard into a closed union shop. Anarchist bombs might at least make them think about it."

Ciocco frowned. "We don't want a closed union shop."

"Yes, you do," Taggart said flatly. "Otherwise, Pitcairn would never have elected a socialist mayor last year. We may be county boys, Ciocco, but we aren't idiots."

"Yes, you are," the railroad guard retorted. "Do you really think the boss would believe any story about triggers without actually seeing one? I'm telling you, he took some of those bombs apart with his own hands just to see how they was set."

"Good. Then you still have the trigger mechanisms from them," Kachigan said in satisfaction. "Get Dettis to show us one, and we'll believe you."

He'd expected that outrageous request to be rejected, but he hadn't expected it to make the young Italian burst into such ringing laughter. All along the lunch counter, curious heads turned to peer at them.

"You want me to ask the boss to cooperate with Roger McGara's county police?" Ciocco stood up and spun a nickel down as tip. "Keep dreaming, Kachigan. You'd have better luck getting him to vote socialist in the next election."

"So." Taggart turned his collar out as they stepped back out into the darkening winter day. The pretty snowflakes had disappeared, replaced by sleet and a buffeting wind that carried the echo of the roundhouse riveters back in muffled rumbles from the hills behind Wall. "Was he lying?"

"About the triggers? I don't know." Clouds squatted low over the valley, pooling the coal smoke from railroad engines and houses alike into a cold, sulfur-sharp haze. It was a smell Kachigan always associated with Pittsburgh winters. "He was definitely lying about the yard wanting a union shop."

Taggart made a disgusted noise. "Big surprise. This valley's been rumbling for unions ever since Westinghouse set up shop here."

"So there's no love lost between him and the railroads?"

"I don't know that I'd say that." The deeper thunder of a passing freight train greeted them when they rejoined Pitcairn's main street, and Taggart lifted his voice to be heard over the combined din. "It's more of a love-hate relationship between them. The railroads love what George invents for them, not to mention the low prices he charges them for it."

"But they hate how well he takes care of his employees."

"Wouldn't you hate it if your best machinists kept quitting on you because the guy down the valley's offering them pensions?"

"Nothing's keeping the Pennsylvania Railroad from starting their own pension fund." Kachigan paused beside Pitcairn's multistory hotel as a trolley car added its rattle and spark to the noisy tumult. For a moment he stared after at it, irrationally convinced he'd seen Helen Sorby's familiar profile through the sleet-streaked glass. But when it stopped to unload its final passengers down the block, no familiar figure in a russet coat emerged. Wishful thinking, he decided.

His partner smacked him between the shoulder blades, hard enough to stagger him a little. "Ciocco's right, you *are* a dreamer," he yelled in his ear. "Come on, wake up! I've asked you twice if you still want to talk to the station clerks here."

"I didn't hear you," Kachigan said, honestly enough. He waited for another break in the afternoon traffic, then crossed the double set of iron trolley tracks. The short trestle bridge on the other side led over the straightened Turtle Creek and past a wood-framed fire department to the small Pitcairn depot. It didn't look old, but the soot and grime of countless passing trains had already darkened it to the color of slate. As he went up the steps of its veranda, he consulted his watch, then the printed train schedule that he'd picked up in East Pittsburgh. As he'd expected, the trains ran a lot less often after the homeward rush on Saturday afternoon.

"If we spend about thirty minutes talking to the men here, we can take the next local up to Trafford City," he shouted over his shoulder to Taggart. "Do you remember from the newspaper stories if any of the bombs went off further east than that?"

"Doesn't matter if they did." A ruthless hand fell on Kachigan's shoulder from behind and jerked him to an undignified halt. "Because it's not any of *your* business."

Kachigan swung around, reaching up to slap that grip away, but O. X. Dettis had already released him and stepped back. As he did, two broad-shouldered railroad guards closed in on either side, close enough to jostle Kachigan rudely between them. From the corner of his vision, he could see three other guards ring Taggart as well. As far as he could tell, his partner's only response was to look even more sleepy than usual.

He glanced back at Dettis and found the small red-faced man now glaring down at him from two steps up. The fact that he'd retreated to that vantage point before confronting them made Kachigan want to laugh, but he suspected that would only make the supervisor more annoyed with him. And more dangerous.

"What do you mean, it's not my business?" he asked instead, trying to sound deeply puzzled. *"You're* the one who told me Osborne was an anarchist. All I'm trying to do is prove that for the coroner's report."

"The hell you are!" Since he was now too far away to assault Kachigan physically, the only outlet for Dettis's rage was his roaring voice. The volume he achieved was startling, but then he'd probably had a lot of practice shouting over the sound of the yard. "You're trying to snoop around and find some dirt on the railroad to give the papers. You need to cover up the fact that you sprang your Italian girlfriend out of jail, on no evidence whatsoever, when she was probably one of the same damned anarchists who killed Osborne! How'd you like it if I went to the papers with that, huh?"

Kachigan couldn't suppress a jerk of surprise, although he managed to school his face to a blank enough expression that only the guards nearest him could have noticed. He opened his mouth to ask how Dettis had known about Helen Sorby, then realized where the information must have come from. His hatred of Roger McGara could hardly grow deeper, but for a moment it blazed so hot that he couldn't even speak.

"One problem with that theory, Ox," Taggart yelled back at him. "Last time I checked, Kachigan's girlfriend didn't have a Pennsylvania Railroad locomotive parked behind her house in East Pittsburgh. So I hardly think she could have been running the train that Osborne got seen falling off last Wednesday."

Dettis swung around to confront the other detective, and fortunately missed Kachigan's startled glance in the same direction. Unless angels had spoken to Taggart in a dream, there was no way his indolent partner could have gathered that information between the time he'd left him last night and when he'd hauled him out of bed this morning. But if he was bluffing, Art had managed to hit the target. Dettis's fleshy face darkened even further, to the brick-red shade of near apoplexy.

"That's a *lie*!" he roared. "There wasn't—for Christ's sake, that trestle is a Pittsburgh, Bessemer, and Lake Erie line! If Osborne got thrown off any train, it was one of theirs!"

"Not what my sources say," Taggart said, unruffled by the fury getting spit in his face. "And why would the Bessemer line want to cap off Osborne, anyway? He didn't set bombs under any of their tracks."

"You don't know—" Dettis broke off, glowering at both of them. "Goddammit, I *hate* county detectives. You're nothing but trouble, all of you, whether you're sucking up bribes or interfering with my yard." His impotent rage brought him dancing down the depot steps again. Before Kachigan even knew what the railroad boss intended, the two flanking guards had grabbed his arms and immobilized him for a jabbing punch into his torso. The impact drove his breath out and rocked him back on his heels, but Kachigan refused to give Dettis the satisfaction of struggling or even of breaking his stare.

"Get this straight, Kachigan." Veins enlarged on the older man's bald head, standing out in snaky relief against his blood-dark skin. "Those anarchist bombings took place on private railroad lines and damaged railroad property. Because of that, they fall into my jurisdiction to solve, not yours. If I hear from any more of my station telegraph operators that you're skulking around asking questions, I'm going to make sure that the people at Ellis Island send you back to whichever Arab country you came from. Is that clear?"

Kachigan gritted his teeth, steeling himself for the punch his next words would probably incite. "What about Lyell Osborne's murder? In case you forgot, that *is* in my jurisdiction and it's connected somehow to your bombings. I need to know how."

"No, you don't." Dettis scowled up at him. "All you need to know is that since Osborne died, the bombings have stopped. Anyone with the brains of a jackass could figure out how to close that case, but since you obviously—"

A crack of sound from up the valley, sharp as a thunderbolt striking through the thickening snow, sliced across the railroad boss's ranting voice and silenced it. The guard on Kachigan's left spun around, looking back at the noisy railyard behind them. His boss was staring that way, too, his red face suddenly wiped clean of enmity.

"Boiler crack?" he demanded.

Another of the guards shook his head. "No big steam clouds that I can see. Maybe something blew in the engine house—"

"No." Surprisingly, that voice belonged to Art Taggart. "You guys just heard the echo," he said, and jerked his chin toward the main street of Pitcairn, flooding now with spectators from every restaurant and store. "The explosion came from town."

"The power plant?" demanded Dettis, frowning. From beside the bridge, Kachigan could hear the frantic ringing of the volunteer fire station's bell, summoning its scattered members. Enough firemen were already on duty to begin hitching the big draft-horses to their pumper wagon. Others came running across the iron bridge, shedding coats and hats as they went.

"Fire's up on Brinton Avenue, Mr. Dettis," yelled an older man in a barber's white tunic, clearly knowing his duty to local authority. "Some kind of explosion, they say!"

"Some kind of explosion," Kachigan repeated, and yanked himself free of his guard's loosened grip. "Are you sure those anarchist bombs stopped when Osborne died, Ox?"

"Yes!" The railroad boss glared back at him. "This is none of your business—"

"Oh, yes, it is." Kachigan might not have Helen Sorby's ability to project her voice with effortless ease, but five years spent walking a beat had taught him how to outyell angry men when he needed to. "In case you hadn't noticed, Pitcairn is Allegheny County property, not railroad property. Anything that happens on the north side of the trolley tracks is in *my* jurisdiction."

9

BEING A SECRETARY, HELEN DECIDED, HAD A LOT more in common with being an indentured servant than she'd ever realized. In both cases, you had no control over where you were sent or who you could talk to. And in both cases, you seemed to have signed away your rights as a human being whether you realized it or not.

She hadn't been surprised to find Bonnie Howards's seat empty when she'd first returned to the main office. Most of the office seats were vacant while their occupants took advantage of their single Saturday water break to exchange gossip or make plans for their free afternoon. But to Helen's dismay, the chestnut-haired stenographer didn't sweep back in with the rest of the chattering crowd, even long after the bell had rung them to their seats. A tentative questioning of her other neighbors got her only a maddening chorus of disapproving looks and shushes. She gnawed at her lower lip, frustrated by the inherent limits of this ''undercover'' job. Every journalistic instinct in her insisted that Bonnie was the right thread to pull in this tangle of industrial espionage and murder. But how could she if she couldn't even find her?

A glance around the office, in desperate search of an excuse to ask a supervisor about Bonnie's whereabouts, yielded Helen no answers. Ironically enough, however, as soon as she sighed and turned her attention back to her work, inspiration struck.

Scooping up the sheaf of blank papers that was all she had left in her stack, she went in search of Miss Walroth.

"Yes?" The older woman glanced up from her ledger absently, as if she'd already forgotten who Helen was. "What is it?"

"I don't have any more work, ma'am. Dr. Grissaldi—um—took care of that last equipment list."

Walroth's smile warmed her face a little. "Probably by throwing it onto her desk, if I know her. Well, I think I can find something for you to finish out the afternoon." She fingered through one of the neat piles on her desk, then handed Helen another paper covered in scrawled writing and symbols. "Do you think you can translate that? It's a patent application."

Helen tried to eye it dubiously, although inside she was crowing. This was exactly the excuse she'd been angling for. "It looks pretty technical, ma'am. I'll do my best—but do you know if Bonnie's coming back soon? It would help if she could tell me some of the terms."

Walroth seemed to find the question entirely natural. "She's taking notes for a sales-staff meeting on the second floor. I expect she'll be back sometime before noon, but I don't know when. In the meantime, Miss Sorby, just leave blanks where you don't know the words. Someone else can fill them in later, if need be."

"Yes, ma'am," Helen said, but was unable to repress a sigh. Walroth smiled, as if that sound was one she heard all the time from her stenographers, and went back to her ledger.

After running the gauntlet of female disapproval back to her seat, Helen forced herself to settle to her new task, since she had to at least appear busy while she waited for Bonnie to reappear. The patent application wasn't in Westinghouse's handwriting, but it was nearly as illegible and so badly written that she couldn't be sure if the motor in question was designed for a domestic appliance or a battleship. All she knew was that the engineer whose scribbled handwriting she had to translate appeared to be under the impression that the word *cylindrical* should be spelled all with *i*'s and that *reservoir* contained one letter *r* instead of three.

Thirty minutes into this grueling task, her cheap rubber fountain pen added annoyance to irritation by sputtering to a stop. Helen heaved a sigh and looked around for an eyedropper and ink bottle she could use to refill it. None was visible along the stenographers' counter or on Miss Walroth's neat desktop, but she could see the dark gleam of a cut-glass inkwell through the glass panel of the door to Jenkins's inner office. The office manager himself was nowhere in sight.

A reckless impulse bubbled up in Helen, fed by frustration and the gnawing boredom of her secretarial work. She suspected that mere stenographers weren't supposed to enter that sanctum uninvited, especially to refill their fountain pens, but as the "new girl" in the company she could always plead ignorance if caught. And if no one seemed to notice, she could take the opportunity to open the desk drawer Bonnie had told her about and steal back her Waterman Ideal. She hadn't lied when she told Jenkins that it had been a present from her aunt, but it wasn't just for sentimental value that she cherished it. It was one of the brand-new fountain pens with an internal system of channels that let ink flow without dribbling or spurting when you first put pen to paper. The amount of money it had saved Helen in ink-free clothes alone was worth every penny of the extravagant price Aunt Pittypat had paid for it.

She collected a few sidelong glances from her fellow stenographers when she headed toward the office manager's door, and a few more from the typewriter operators she passed along the way, but since that same aisle led to the ladies' rest room, most of the looks were just the usual wrinkled noses at the disgusting color of her dress. A few of the adding-machine men did frown when she slipped into the manager's office, but since Helen had taken the precaution of carrying the sheaf of papers she had been working on and then placing them on the desk like a requested assignment, they all looked down at their work again. Helen breathed out a quiet sigh of relief and proceeded with the second part of her plan.

A quick scan of the rest of the main office through the window glass showed no other eyes turned in her direction. With fingers that shook despite herself, she uncorked the ink bottle with one hand and dipped in the eyedropper that had been placed with careful precision on the blotting paper beside it. With the other hand, hidden in the thankfully voluminous folds of her ruffle skirt, she pulled open the desk's top drawer.

Disappointment surged through her. The drawer was occupied by only a few tidy account books and a small pile of loose change, apparently kept for the office manager's lunch excursions. With a silent sigh, Helen slid the top drawer shut and wondered how she was going to manage bending over to open the rest. Maybe she should just wait until after work, as Bonnie had suggested.

The creak of a floorboard alerted her, but Helen sensibly didn't look up from the ink-filled eyedropper she was tapping droplets from. "I hope you don't mind, sir, but I couldn't see where else to get—"

Strong hands closed on her shoulders from behind, hard enough to make her cry out and lose her grip on the eyedropper. It dropped back into the bottle, splashing ink across Jenkins's neat desk in an indelible blue-black spray.

"I don't think so, Miss Sorby," said Alexander Erskine Greer's soap-smooth voice in her ear. "You may have been blocking the view from the front door with your—er—ruffles. But from out in the hall, I could see every move you made."

Helen took a stifled breath to make sure none of her body touched his. "I was just refilling my fountain pen—"

"And looking for a little advance on your first week's pay?" He ducked his head to lay one clean-carved cheek against hers. The smell of cigar smoke and expensive aftershave was so strong that Helen almost choked. "If you're that desperate for money, dear, there are other ways you can get it."

By writing a magazine exposé of your improper sexual advances in the office, for one thing, Helen thought savagely, but didn't let the words escape her tight-clamped lips. "I didn't take any money, Mr. Greer," she said instead. "You can look for yourself if you don't believe me."

"My pleasure."

It wasn't until he slid his hands down from her shoulders to her waist and then started to run them upward again that Helen realized what he'd taken her words to mean. The sheer arrogance of that stupidity broke the hold she had on her Italian temper. With a shout more of rage than of panic, Helen drove both elbows back and down in the way her brother, experienced in rough-and-tumbles, had taught her in their rowdy childhood. Greer staggered back from the blow, cursing, and the busy clatter out in the main office abruptly fell silent.

She swung around to glare up at the salesman, holding her cheap fountain pen like a knife. "I told you to leave me alone! Can't you get it through your thick head that I don't want to sleep with you?"

Those blunt words, easy enough for a radical socialist to say, were apparently an abomination coming from a secretary's mouth. She saw the flags of red that unfurled in Greer's clean-cut cheeks, but the rage in his eyes looked affronted rather than humiliated.

"Miss Sorby!" That was Jenkins's voice, sounding even more affronted. "What are you doing in my office?"

"Stealing your lunch money, Bill." Greer spoke before Helen could even gather her wits to reply, his voice confident and assured. "She was pretending to fill her fountain pen, but from out in the hall, I could see every move she made. I came in to stop her, of course."

"Of course you would, Mr. Greer. Thank you." Jenkins turned toward Helen, eyes narrowing in condemnation. "As for you—"

She snorted and threw her fountain pen down on his desk, not caring if its splatters added to the mess already there. "Don't waste your breath firing me," she advised. "Because I never really worked here."

That took some of the self-righteous hot air out of his sails. "What do you mean by that, young lady?"

Reckless rage was fueling her, Helen knew, but she couldn't resist letting these two supercilious males know just who they had managed to offend. "I mean that my real job is with *McClure's Magazine,* not Westinghouse. They sent me here to check out the working conditions for secretaries and factory girls." She swept a furious glance up at Alexander Erskine Greer. "And I really should thank you, because I'm sure they're going to love the story I'm going to write. I hope you'll both enjoy being the villains of the piece!''

"Miss Sorby!'' Jenkins at least had sense enough to look confounded. ''If this is true—but, indeed, all our actions were perfectly reasonable, given what we knew of you—''

''You mean to say, given what you assumed of me—'' Helen broke off, not because she'd reined in her temper but because she'd just seen a familiar chestnut-haired figure in a stylish dress hurry down the outer hall to the building's front doors. For some reason, Bonnie Howards was leaving half an hour early this Saturday. From the tense set of her hunched shoulders as she vanished through the door, and the fact that she'd promised to raid Jenkins's desk after lunch, Helen suspected this early departure wasn't made by choice. Instinctive alarm surged through her, swamping all other considerations.

''I'm leaving.'' She cut across the threats of legal action that Jenkins was now spluttering. ''When you finally realize that the fountain pen you confiscated didn't belong to any of your engineers, I'd appreciate if you'd send it back to me in care of *McClure's*. Good day, gentlemen.''

And without a backward look, she slammed her way through Jenkins's outer office door and headed for the building's exit. With any luck, her failure to go back for her coat would be taken as a grand gesture and not as the act of a reporter desperate to catch up to a crucial—and rapidly disappearing—source.

Outside, a cold slap of snow-laden wind made Helen catch her breath. When she'd made the decision to abandon her russet wool coat, she'd forgotten how flimsy an outfit she wore. In her usual wool jacket and serge skirt, she would have been chilly but not chilled to the bone. But Molly's cheap finery was already dampening with melted snow. With a rueful shiver, Helen hurried down the stairs to Commerce Avenue, hoping the exertion would ward off the worst of the cold.

By the time she reached the bottom, she could see Bonnie Howards's figure a block ahead, heading straight for the trolley station. Please don't let there be a trolley waiting, Helen prayed. Please, please, please.

Her prayers must have been too vaguely addressed to be

answered. Even as she reached the level sidewalk and picked up her skirts to lengthen her stride, she could hear the clang and spark of a streetcar arriving at the loop station. A misty curtain of snow blew off the roof of the tall hardware store on the next corner, cutting off her view for half a block. By the time she emerged from the haze, shivering and even damper than before, she could see the red light of the trolley climbing back up onto its iron bridge. And no one waiting at the station.

Fortunately, before Helen could lose her forward momentum, she heard the sizzle of a second trolley coming hard on the heels of the first. Either the one Bonnie boarded had been running late, or this one was headed down the East Pittsburgh Valley instead of up. No, Helen thought at it fiercely as she hurried to meet the arriving car. Don't you dare be going in the wrong direction!

This time, whatever saint watched over the movements of trains and trolleys heard her prayer and granted it. "Eighty-seven Ardmore," announced the trolley conductor, his Polish accent turning it almost into a song. "Adderly, Pitcairn, Trafford City. Miss, where's your coat?"

"I was in such a hurry I forgot it," Helen said breathlessly. She scrabbled in her skirt pocket for the nickel she needed to ride up valley. "I was trying to catch up with a friend, but I missed the trolley. Would you mind if I stood near the front of yours to see where my friend gets off?"

The conductor shook his head, but his mild blue eyes were amused. "You working girls today, the crazy things you do," he said, and set the electric motors back into gear. "Hey, miss, I don't care where you sit or what you do. Old Buckner's running so late in front of me that you're my only fare."

"Good." Helen tucked herself as close to his front driver's seat as she could, grateful to be out of the wind. The trolley lurched into motion, hauling itself up onto the iron bridge that spanned the Westinghouse Airbrake. Steam from the plant's exhaust pipes curled up around them, then got peeled away again by a blast of winter wind. For a moment, from the top of the span, Helen could see all the way up the valley to Wall Station. There were two brown-and-gray streetcars of the Ardmore line visible, a distant one trundling toward them from

Pitcairn and another much closer on their own line. Even as she watched, the second one stopped to discharge passengers on the far side of the valley.

"Do we have to stop if there's no one there to pick up?" she asked her own trolley driver as they coasted down the other side of the bridge. The other trolley was already moving on.

His exaggerated sigh blew up the corners of his blond mustache. "Miss, you want to get me fired for losing a fare? What if someone's waiting in one of the porches, out of the weather?"

"Then they miss the trolley," Helen said flatly. "The next one will be coming in a few minutes anyway." She reached into her pocket again, feeling the cool shapes of a few more nickels. "And I can give the company the fare you would have had."

This time his snort sounded much more real. "The company doesn't need it, miss. For a slight tip, though, I'll be glad to demonstrate just how fast these electric motors can go."

Helen peered through the snow-smeared front window, but she saw no sign of Bonnie Howards's distinctive curls among the black babushkas dispersing from the trolley stop. "It's a deal," she said, and dropped all her remaining coins into his hand.

The conductor grunted and pocketed the tip, but he waited until they'd rounded the curving ramp down from the bridge and rejoined the main line before he pressed all the way down on his throttle. From beneath the car's floor, the noise of the electric motors rose to a snarling whine. The result didn't exactly take Helen's breath away, but it did make the clatter of their wheels across the rail junctions speed up slightly. A stormy buffet of wind added to their momentum from behind.

"Snow coming in tonight," the conductor commented, as conversationally as if they hadn't been engaged in this odd streetcar chase. "Maybe a lot of it. My knee's been killing me all day." When Helen didn't reply to that, he went on with the ease of a man used to halftalking to himself to pass the time. "Good thing tomorrow's Sunday, eh? No one will have to kill themselves getting to work in all the snow."

"Except the railroad men," Helen retorted. "And they don't get paid any extra for doing it, either."

"Sure, they do," he said, his Polish accent deepening with amusement. "They pay themselves, miss, in tools and iron and ties for their houses. Railroad looks the other way."

"Do they?" she asked skeptically. Up the line, she could see the other trolley begin to slow for the Adderly stop and then speed up again. No one must have rung the bell, and evidently no one was waiting either. So much for being fired for losing a fare. "Why do they have railroad police, then?"

His grin exposed an immigrant's bad teeth. "To keep all the rest of us from helping ourselves, of course."

"Oh." It was their turn to clatter down to the Adderly stop, the sloping ground lending them an almost respectable pace. On the other side, however, the track climbed along a steep rock bluff, forced to elevate to stay out of the railroad yards below. The valley narrowed here, before it widened again to make room for the immense Pitcairn yards. Helen watched grimly while the trolley they were chasing disappeared over the top of the hill.

"Where's the first Pitcairn stop?" she asked.

"Anywhere our customers ask for," the conductor said placidly. "But usually not until past the brickyard. Be calm, miss. You'll catch up to your boyfriend, I promise."

"It's not—" Helen gave up, realizing that it was easier to leave him with his romantic illusions than try to explain the convoluted path that had brought her to chase coatless after Bonnie Howards. Sparks flew from the trolley's guide wire as they crested the bluff's highest point, swaying in the blast of wind. From there, a long and increasingly rapid descent brought them into the oddly lopsided borough of Pitcairn. Helen could see that the car before them had stopped at the town's main intersection, where it was discharging a steady stream of patrons and picking up others.

"Eh, that damn Buckner. See how he steals all my fares?"

"Yes." The other streetcar lurched back into motion, traveling up toward the steep end of town. Helen scanned both sides of the street as they approached, trying to spot Bonnie Howards's tall, trim figure amid the noontime rush. Her conductor friend obligingly slowed a little as they passed the previous trolley stop, but despite a shouted objection from one office worker waiting on the street, he didn't stop.

"Not many left on Buckner's car, miss. You sure your friend got on it?"

"I'm sure." Helen squinted at the trolley they were now only a block or two behind. To her relief, she thought she saw a glint of chestnut hair through the back window. A moment later, however, it was gone. Perhaps Bonnie had stood up and was moving down the aisle. "Is there one more stop in Pitcairn?"

"Sure, up by Brinton Avenue. You getting off there?"

"I think so." Helen stepped back toward the open trolley door, catching her breath at the cold wind that whistled through it. She leaned out anyway, watching the trolley in front of them throw off cascading sparks as it swerved from one track to another. When it jerked to a second stop, only a single figure emerged. To Helen's immense relief, it was the figure she had waited for.

Bonnie Howards didn't look left or right as she stepped down, since she was already on the residential side of the street. Instead, she looked up and began to climb the steep brick-lined street that led up from the trolley stop. Helen was so busy watching where the other stenographer went that it wasn't until she found herself looking straight up that sheer brick vista that she realized her own trolley wasn't slowing down.

"Hey!" Her yelp got only a mildly puzzled glance over the shoulder from her conductor friend. "That was my stop!"

"But I didn't see your boyfriend—" He hurriedly applied his brakes when Helen leaned farther out the door, bracing herself with both hands and looking for a suitable place to jump. "Hey, wait, miss, I'm stopping—"

She did wait, but only until the trolley had slowed enough to make her leap to the ground a safe one. By then, they were half a block past the brick street Bonnie had climbed. Helen tried to hurry back to it, but the slate sidewalk beneath her feet was treacherously slick with snow, turning what should have been running strides into an unsteady shuffle of cautious footsteps. By the time she had skidded around the telegraph office on the corner, Bonnie Howards had disappeared completely from view.

Muttering in Italian about her own absentmindedness, Helen picked up her skirts and started climbing the steep brick avenue after her. The less-traveled sidewalks here were glazed with even thicker ice, making her wonder how Bonnie had ascended so quickly. It wasn't until she saw the footprints in the rougher snow crust on the bricks that it occurred to her that she could improve her own time by walking there. *"Capo tosta!"* she said to herself in disgust, and stepped over the curb. The cold was starting to freeze up her wits along with her fingers and toes.

She'd suspected from the quick way Bonnie had disappeared that she'd turned down one of the side streets that intersected this hilly avenue. By the time she got to the first one, though, the block to the left was empty except for a fine haze of sleet. Helen groaned and climbed another block, only to find an equally empty stretch of dirt road leading off to the right. She slid to a frustrated stop, legs aching and breath rasping cold in her throat, and wondered where to go next. She could start banging on doors and ringing doorbells, she supposed—but the heat generated by her uphill run was already fading and dampness was seeping through Molly's flimsy dress at an alarming rate.

It wasn't any particular stroke of mental brilliance that came to her rescue—just a slow realization that snow was crunching beneath her feet every time she stamped them to keep warm. Her intent gaze swept the snow-dusted bricks of the sidestreets first and then came back to the slate sidewalk. The ghostly imprint of recent footprints cut a distinct trail through the shimmer of snow and ice, curving right toward the second door of the white frame duplex on the corner.

With a misty sigh of relief, Helen swung to follow Bonnie's trail. Through the snow and buffeting wind, she could hear the long whistle of a train from the railroad yards below, rising like an operatic solo above the cacophonous chorus of metal plates being welded and riveted. For some reason, the more familiar sound made her feel even colder. She tucked her aching fingers beneath her arms and hurried up the porch steps of the duplex, shivering hard now. With any luck, Bonnie would have the gas fire already lit by the time she opened the door.

Helen was never sure, later, if she'd actually knocked on the door those footprints led to, or if she'd just intended to. All she remembered was the flat thundercrack of the explosion splintering through the snow-muffled afternoon, and then the slam of unseen force that sent the door leaping out to meet her.

10

BEFORE OX DETTIS COULD DO MORE than sputter a curse, Kachigan had swung away from him, ducking around Taggart's unsuspecting guards and lengthening his stride to catch the fire company's wagon as it rounded onto the iron bridge. There was room left on the running board, and it only took a quick sprint and leap to haul himself onto it, even as the horses surged into a trot and the wagon bell began to ring. "Allegheny County police," he said to the row of startled faces that turned to stare at him. "I'm here to investigate the explosion."

If the firemen wondered how he'd known to show up in advance of this unexpected event, none of them was foolhardy enough to say so. "Hang on," the old man next to him advised, slapping his helmet more firmly onto his bald head. "It's going to be a slippy ride today."

Kachigan grabbed for the last leather strap that dangled from the wagon's side, hearing the slosh and splatter of water inside the capacious wooden barrel that served as its main reservoir. Moments later the pumper swerved onto Pitcairn's main street with a ferocious clatter of hooves and a stomach-wrenching skid of iron-rimmed wheels across the ice-slicked pavement. Spectators scattered out of its way, shouting and pointing up toward the steep end of town. Kachigan craned his head and squinted against the sleet-wet wind, ignoring the pain that the cold air hammered into his scarred cheek. No column of smoke seemed to be rising into the cloudy sky.

"What address are we headed for?" he shouted at the nearest fireman, barely hearing his own voice over the clanging bell, thundering hooves, and background din of the railyard.

"Somewhere up along Brinton, that's all I know. No one called it in, we just heard the blast."

The wagon rounded another corner, slicing recklessly across the path of an oncoming trolley. Kachigan heard the metallic squeal of its brakes cascade down in pitch as they passed and left it behind.

"Any railroad offices up there?"

That got him an ice-misted snort. "Hell, no!" said his neighbor scornfully. The fire wagon swerved again, this time onto a steep upward slope. "Not a railroad boss between here and Philadelphia that would trouble himself to climb a mountain like that to get to work every day. Especially not old Ox."

Kachigan revised his opinion of the town's feeling toward their local yard supervisor. "It's all houses, then?"

"What lots are even built on." The fireman yanked his chin strap tight again while the wagon swung onto the astonishingly steep brick road Kachigan had seen before and slowed to a groaning upward crawl. "There's not a lot of space before the hill drops off in through here."

"Yeah, I can see that." Kachigan braced himself and leaned out around the wagon's edge. A short stretch of dirt road labeled only with the letter K led off the steeper slant of the brick, with a thin scatter of houses crammed between it and the edge of a ravine. A cluster of onlookers in front of the white duplex at the corner marked it as their destination. The pumper wagon drew up with an unsteady, sliding lurch, and he could hear the thump as the driver hauled his brake lever to its tightest notch.

Kachigan followed the line of canvas-coated men around the wagon, wise enough to wait behind the milling group while they threw down hoses and unhooked axes from their clamps. He could see no smoke rising from the duplex, but the ominous oily smell of natural gas drifted out from the shattered front window and gaping door on the right. The handful of people huddled on the sidewalk in front of it, he could see now, were mostly women and a few children, either crying or talking in the high, excited voices of near hysteria.

"Okay if I question the witnesses?" Kachigan asked the oldest fireman. There didn't seem to be a fire chief present, and he looked as much in charge as anyone.

He got a preoccupied nod in return. "Tell 'em to stay out of our way until we get the gas turned off. Kozubal and Lawlor inside, Novotny and Pompa around back—let's go!"

They disappeared with a slithering hiss of hose against the snow-glazed street, leaving a single man behind to pull-start the motor that ran the pump. Kachigan followed them as far as the sidewalk, noticing that no flames or smoke seemed to be pouring from the open window. Among the gathered onlookers, he could see one woman and three children shivering in the cold, coatless and hatless. Those must be the inhabitants chased out by the blast. The others looked more like neighbors, come to watch and offer help.

"I'm Detective Kachigan, of the Allegheny County Detectives Bureau." He suspected it wasn't his identity that stopped their worried voices and swung their faces toward him so much as the authoritative male ring of his voice. "Did everyone get out of the building?"

"Out of our side, yes." The woman who hugged the children tight sounded tremulous, but it was shivers rather than shock that made her voice unsteady. Her Slavic face was pinched white with cold. "My husband's at work, it was just the kids and me. But I don't see the young lady who lived next door. That's where it happened, next door."

"Was she at home when you heard the blast?"

"I think so, yes. She only worked half days at Westinghouse on Saturdays. I could have sworn I heard the front door—"

The woman broke off, staring past Kachigan's shoulder. He swung around to see a flash of yellow oilcloth through the gaping door of the other duplex, and then the unmistakable bright pink ripple of a woman's dress. From their unsteady forward progress, Kachigan guessed the young neighbor lady was resisting evacuation for some reason, although all he could hear was the sound of muffled coughing. He took a step forward to help the firemen hustle her out, then paused when a hand tugged at him from behind.

"What's the matter?"

"That's not the girl who lives there!" the next-door neighbor said urgently. "Her hair's not red enough!"

"Who is it, then?"

That got him a baffled head shake. "I don't know, I've never seen her before."

Kachigan glanced back at the door just in time to see the struggling young woman hoisted bodily out onto the porch by an impatient fireman. Her dark hair spilled across her face in a disheveled straggle and her voice was still torn with coughing, but there was no mistaking the vehement passion in her Italian curse.

"I have," he said grimly, and went to grab Helen Sorby before she could push her way back into the gaping doorway.

"Let go!" She swung around, twisting frantically against his grip. "I have to—*Milo?*"

He gritted his teeth, torn between a desire to hug her and an even stronger desire to strangle her. "What in God's name are you doing here?"

"Trying to—rescue—" she gasped between coughs. "There's a—girl still inside—"

"Let the firemen get her." The suffocating stench of natural gas clung to her damp dress and wafted strongly out the door behind her. Kachigan didn't even try to lead her away—he simply swept her up in his arms before she could protest. For a miracle, she didn't struggle while he carried her back to the firemen's wagon. Probably because she was coughing too hard.

"Water," Kachigan said to the pump tender. "And a blanket, if you have one."

"I don't—need—" With a grimace at her own inability to speak, Helen gave up and let him set her down on the far side of the wagon, out of the worst of the wind. She shook her head at the dripping mug of water the pump man drew off his line, but accepted the blanket gratefully, dragging its folds around her with shaking fingers. In another moment her coughs had diminished enough to let her speak. True to form, her first words weren't a thank-you but an accusation.

"What are you doing here? Are you following me?"

Kachigan frowned down at her. "No, of course not. I was asking some questions down at the railroad depot when we heard the explosion." The reminder that Dettis would doubtless be showing up with his guards at any moment made his next words an order rather than a request. "Tell me what you were doing in that house."

"And what will you do in return?" she demanded.

"Not arrest you for this bombing!" he growled. "Which is the first thing the railroad's going to want me to do."

That got him a mulish look, but a chorus of shrieks and cries from the unseen onlookers interrupted before she could snap back. Kachigan glanced up at the pump tender, who could see the exploded building from his perch on top of the water barrel.

"What happened?"

"They're bringing out the girl who lived in the duplex." The grim tone to his voice warned Kachigan what he was going to say next. "Wrapped in a blanket."

Helen's dark eyes widened in the somber look he remembered from another fire site back on Breed Street. "Is she dead?"

"Afraid so." The fireman frowned at her when she began to push past Kachigan. "I wouldn't go around the wagon if I was you. There's—er—not too much left to see." He shifted his frown to Kachigan. "Whatever exploded in there, it looks like it must have been real close to her, right in front."

Helen winced. "Did she—do you think she . . ."

"Suffered much? Not by the looks of it. I doubt she even knew what hit her." His voice lowered in rough sympathy. "A friend of yours?"

Helen paused, then let out an odd little sigh. "No, just a girl I knew from work. But I think she could have been."

From down on the main road, Kachigan could hear the clatter of a carriage being driven at high speed. "Helen, tell me what happened, *now*," he said urgently. "It won't be safe to talk once the railroad police get here."

She eyed him in deep uncertainty. He wasn't sure what she

saw in his face that convinced her, but after a moment she sighed and gave in.

"Two days ago I took a stenographer's job at Westinghouse," she said abruptly. "To see what I could learn about Lyell Osborne. There was another new stenographer there, a girl named Bonnie Howards." She paused, apparently sorting through all the things she could tell him for the most important details. Or perhaps the least self-incriminating ones. "I found out by chance this morning that Bonnie is—was—Lyell Osborne's second cousin. I tried to catch her after work, but I missed the trolley she got on. So I took the next one and followed her here."

"Were you in the house when the bomb went off?" Kachigan asked.

Helen shook her head. "I'd just followed her tracks to the front door and started to knock. At least, I think I started to knock. That's when I heard the blast." She took a deep breath, nose wrinkling at the hydrocarbon smell that the wind was slowly blasting off of them. "Milo, are you sure it was a bomb? Couldn't it have been a gas explosion?"

As usual, her voice had been pitched loud enough for everyone around to hear. The pump tender glanced back down at them, shaking his helmeted head. "If that had been the gas exploding, miss, the whole house would be ashes by now. The explosion must have cracked a pipe, then blew out all its sparks with its own blast. I've seen dynamite do that, sometimes. All you have to do is—"

The rumble and squeal of the arriving carriage cut off whatever he'd been going to say. Rapid footsteps thudded toward them, even before the echoing thunder of the horse's hooves had died away. Kachigan glanced over his shoulder to see the scowling red-faced figure he'd expected. What he hadn't expected was the way O. X. Dettis's glare swung toward Helen, somehow identifying her as suspicious before a word had been spoken.

"Is that the girl who lived in the duplex that exploded?" he demanded, as if Helen couldn't be trusted to answer for herself. Kachigan could feel her stiffen in silent indignation.

"No. It's just a friend of hers from work." He gave his

former investigating partner a meaningful look, hoping she'd have the sense to heed his warning. Finding out that a reporter was investigating this case would undoubtedly light the fuse on the railroad boss's short temper. "The girl who lived in the duplex is dead."

Dettis grunted, looking grim but not particularly shaken. "Yeah? An accidental gas explosion, was it? I can smell the damn stuff everywhere."

"Actually, the firemen think"—a loudly cleared throat from above reminded Kachigan that Ox Dettis ruled this town and could continue to make life miserable for people in it long after he was sent back to policing brothels in Allegheny City— "that the cause can't be determined without further investigation," he finished smoothly. He could hear Helen's snort, but it turned into an unplanned cough so quickly that he hoped the railroad boss hadn't noticed.

"And who's going to carry out this investigation?" Dettis demanded. "The volunteer fire department?"

"No, us." A lazier, heavier tread rounded the edge of the wagon, and a moment later Taggart loomed behind Dettis, eyes slitted against the sleet that had beaded on his brows and beard. He must have walked all the way up from the railroad station. If he was surprised to see Helen Sorby bundled in a blanket beside Kachigan, his broad face showed no sign of it. "We investigate all the suspicious deaths in this county, Ox. You know that."

"Bullshit," Dettis said flatly. "You county boys only investigate the cases you're paid to investigate and then you just convict the people you're paid to convict. Well, I've already paid your boss to keep you the hell out of my town! Now get out, or I'll have you kicked out!"

For a moment the only sounds that followed that roared ultimatum were the frigid splatterings of sleet and the fretful snort and stamp of the gathered horses. Kachigan was still trying to decide how to respond when he heard Helen's unexpected voice.

"Do you *really* want me to tell my editors in New York that the Pennsylvania Railroad refused to allow a possible murder to be investigated?" She refused to meet Kachigan's glare, as if she knew quite well that what she was doing went against all his instincts. Her ringing voice had recovered enough from the gas fumes by now to echo off the adjacent houses, and carry with ease to the firemen and spectators on the far side of the wagon. "I can just imagine what the cartoonists and political commentators will make of *that* information."

The noise that emerged from O. X. Dettis was indescribable, half bubbling snarl and half choke of surprise. "You're a *reporter*?"

"*McClure's Magazine, Collier's,* and the *Saturday Evening Post.*" Kachigan suspected she'd tacked that last one on just in case the railroad boss was too illiterate to have heard of the first two. As far as he knew, the only thing Helen had ever published in the *Post* was a stinging letter to the editor about women's rights. "And any of them would be glad to pay me for a muckraking article this good. Of course," she added sweetly, "if you actually let the county detectives investigate, my story will probably deal with *their* corruption and incompetence rather than yours."

Dettis's fleshy face had darkened to a dangerous brick red, but to Kachigan's surprise, either Helen's double-edged threat or their silent audience of housewives and firemen seemed to cork the railroad supervisor's rage. With an inarticulate growl, he turned on his heel and stalked back to his private carriage. No one spoke until the iron squeal of carriage wheels against icy brick pavement had vanished downhill.

"I don't think Ox Dettis is a happy man right now," Taggart said placidly. "Nice to have you on our side, Miss Sorby."

"Is it?" She gave Kachigan a challenging look. "Aren't you going to kick me off this case now, the way he just tried to do to you?"

"No," he said, mostly for the pleasure of watching surprise blossom in her eyes. "For one thing, now that Dettis knows you're a reporter, I'm not letting you out of my sight until I hand you over to Thomas."

Helen frowned, no doubt impatient with that unwanted protection. "And for the other thing?"

"For the other thing," Kachigan said, "I'd like to know

what your friend Bonnie Howards looked like.'' He glanced through the high, spoked wheels of the fire wagon to the pathetically crumpled bundle inside the sleet-damp blanket. ''And you're the only one who knows that now.''

''Milo, did you hear me? I'm leaving.''

Kachigan glanced up, blinking in the uncertain light. With the gas turned off for safety, they'd been forced to scrounge among the neighbors on K Street for candles to examine the scene of the crime. The illumination had been bright enough at first, when they'd concentrated their search for clues in Bonnie Howards's bloodstained living room, but now that they'd scattered out to the other rooms of the rented house, shadows were dancing and sliding long fingers up the walls. The furnace was turned off as well, to keep water from spurting through shattered radiators, and even though Kachigan had covered the broken window with a tacked-up blanket and propped the door back against its frame, a constant cold draft shivered through the house. He was starting to envy Helen her blanket.

''What's the matter?'' he asked Taggart, keeping his fingers tucked into the sheaf of unpaid bills he'd found in the upstairs sitting room that Howards had apparently used as a study. The furniture here, as elsewhere in the little house, had the mismatched and bruised appearance of property that came with the rental. ''Do you have an appointment?''

''Yes, with my stomach!'' retorted his partner. ''I said I'd wait until three P.M. for lunch, not three A.M.''

''Well, how late is it?'' He'd been aware of the darkness gathering outside the sitting-room windows, but had put it down to the thickening snowstorm rather than the passage of time. A glance at his watch made him whistle. ''Half-past six already?''

Helen Sorby came down the second-floor hall, her blanket sweeping the floor behind her like a royal cape. Dust clung thick and gray to the hem of her pink dress, and cobwebs floated across her hair like a lacy veil. ''I need more candles,'' she said, holding out the guttered stump of the one she'd taken with her. ''I still have one more part of the attic to check.''

Taggart's heavy sigh said she was as crazy as Milo. "Aren't either of you hungry? It's suppertime."

"Supper?" Helen winced. "Oh, glory! Thomas wanted to take me out tonight—"

"To the Hotel Linden, for the steak special," Taggart finished. "We can still make it if we catch the next trolley."

She shook her head, so vehemently that Kachigan could feel the dust flying. "Not in this dress," she said flatly. "And anyway, I want to finish searching the rest of Bonnie's house, in case that railroad goon decides to come back later tonight."

"He's not a goon, he's an ox," Taggart said in amusement. "And he's probably home toasting his feet in front of the fire, just like we should be." When all that got him was a disgusted look and the abduction of his candle, he turned his plaintive expression back on his partner. "Milo, it's freezing in here and there's probably a foot of snow outside by now. Don't you think it would be best to get Miss Sorby home?"

Kachigan grunted, setting the bills aside and ruffling through the pile of blank telegraph forms and unopened letters that sat beside them. "Art, if you ever find a way to make Helen Sorby do what's best for her, be sure to tell me about it. In the meantime, why don't you go down to East Pittsburgh and have dinner with her brother? You can tell him I'll be bringing Helen home later tonight so he won't worry about her."

"You want me to bring you some food before I go?"

"No. I'm not hungry." The ignored letters all seemed to be from local merchants and department stores, demanding payment on various overdue accounts. In combination with the bills and notices from her irate landlord, the picture that was adding up of Bonnie Howards's financial situation didn't look good. He became aware that Taggart was still lingering in the doorway. "What's the matter now?"

"I don't like how this case is starting to smell," his partner said bluntly. "There's more going on here than a couple of crazy anarchists running around. If you're not careful, Milo, you might find yourself conked and pitched on a railroad trestle yourself."

"Don't worry, I'm not going to get on any Pennsylvania Railroad trains. We'll take the trolley home."

"Then you better be out of here by eight, because that's the last run the Eighty-seven Ardmore makes back to East Pittsburgh." Taggart turned up his collar and headed for the stairs. "See you tomorrow, Milo. And this time, don't show up a minute before noon!"

His footsteps thudded down the stairs, and a moment later Kachigan heard the thump and slide of the front door being pushed aside. There were no footsteps after that. The snow must already be deep enough to muffle them.

Another quarter hour passed, its silence broken only by muffled thuds from the side attic behind the wall and an occasional gust of wind carrying the sound of distant riveting through the broken windows below. Kachigan could feel his fingers getting colder, but it wasn't until he noticed the cloud of mist he was exhaling with each breath that it occurred to him he could simply gather all the dunning letters up and stuff them into his vest pocket, to be analyzed in a warmer and brighter location.

"Helen?" Picking up his candle, he went down the hall to the bedroom and found the door to it unexpectedly closed. He put a hand out to turn the knob, and heard a yelp from inside.

"Milo, wait! I'm cleaning up and changing my dress for one of Bonnie's—"

"Good idea." He leaned against the wall, pulling out his evidence book and sorting through the other items he'd tucked into it until he found the sketch Helen had made for him. Bonnie Howards's eyes laughed up at him from a strong and mischievous face. With the cascade of curls Helen assured him had been richly red in real life, she must have been quite striking. "What have you managed to find out?"

"That no one's been in that attic since 1898," Helen said in disgust. "And that Bonnie didn't have as many clothes as she should have."

"What?"

The door swung open to reveal a flushed but much cleaner Helen in a heavy wool skirt and jacket. It was clearly a size too large for her everywhere but in the waist, but in contrast to her previous confection of water-stained pink ruffles and bows, even Kachigan could see this outfit was cut in classic, expensively tailored lines. With her hair spread loose across her shoulders, it made her look like a child playing dress-up with her mother's clothes. The only thing that contradicted the image was her sober frown.

"There are no labels in any of Bonnie's clothes," she said simply. "They must have all been handmade by a seamstress, which costs more than a stenographer would make in a week."

Kachigan grunted. "Well, judging from the unpaid bills I found in the study, your friend Bonnie liked to live well beyond her means."

Helen's frown deepened, but it wasn't an angry look. "It's stranger than just that, though, Milo. If these were all of Bonnie's things, there should be spring and summer clothes as well as winter suits in her closet. But when I looked for something to wear, I noticed that everything she owns seems to be made of wool or fur-trimmed serge. It's as if she—"

"Wasn't planning to stay here long," he finished for her.

"Yes." Helen took a deep breath, then said in a guilty rush, "There's something else I know that I haven't told you. Bonnie might have—"

A violent banging from downstairs interrupted her, making Kachigan curse and spin around. Perhaps Taggart had been right about the dangers of this investigation. "Stay here," he snapped at Helen, then went down the stairs to the even colder shadows of the first floor. Snow swirled and flung itself through the gaping doorway, dropping a thin carpet across the foyer. A single pair of footprints tracked across it.

"Bessie!" It was a young and suddenly hopeful male voice, emerging from the small back kitchen. "Is that you?"

"I'm afraid not, sir." A tall figure loomed on the shadowed edge of his candle glow, and Kachigan lifted the taper to get a better view. "I'm Detective Milo Kachigan of the Allegheny County Detectives Bureau."

"Detective?" The intruder had a long and jutting face, probably pleasant enough under normal circumstances but cramped now with bewilderment and fear. "What happened? Is Bessie all right?" When Kachigan just gazed back at him in considering silence, he added defensively, "I have the right to ask about her, you know. She's my fiancée."

Kachigan cleared his throat, searching for words to convey

the bad news as gently as possible. It was an unpleasant task, but one he'd faced often enough as a patrolman to know by rote. "Sir, I'm very sorry to be the one to tell you, but the young lady who lived here was killed today by a suspicious explosion."

"*What?*" The young man's face froze, as if the blast of winter wind through the doorway had struck deep into his soul. "She's *dead*? No, that can't be true—" Movement on the stairs above them caught his eyes and for a moment Kachigan saw incredulous hope flash alive. Then Helen stepped down into the circle of their candlelight and that nascent joy died unborn. "Who are you?"

"Helen Sorby. I worked with Bonnie Howards down at Westinghouse." The quiet emphasis she put on the name, and the watchful way she eyed their visitor, told Kachigan she'd heard the name he'd called his fiancée. It might have been a pet name or a middle name she used only with close friends, but something deep in Kachigan's gut doubted that.

The young man's frown dug more deeply into his high forehead, as if he was starting to doubt the reality of this entire scene. "Who is Bonnie Howards, and why does it matter that you worked with her?" he asked. "The girl I'm looking for is a redhead, tall and pretty. And her name is Bessie Harris."

HELEN WASN'T SURE WHICH BOTHERED her more: the distraught look on the stranger's face or the knowledge that if she had managed to intercept Bonnie Howards back in Wilmerding, they might never have had to give him this bad news. If something hadn't happened back at Westinghouse to drive the other stenographer home early, or if Helen had managed to catch her at the trolley station and convinced her to confide whatever secrets she was guarding . . .

. . . then they would probably have come back to Bonnie's house together and both been dead now, the logical part of her brain reminded her, as it had been doing all night long. Helen sighed and consigned her unreasonably guilty conscience to the shelf of things to worry about later. All her unresolved differences with Milo Kachigan were already perched there. One more thing wouldn't matter.

She glanced over at Kachigan now and saw him unfolding the sketch she'd made on a torn scrap of shelf paper from the kitchen. "Is this your fiancée, sir?" he asked politely, and held it out to the young man.

"Yes." When he looked up again, the expression on his face was bleak. "She's really dead?"

"I'm afraid so." Kachigan inclined his head toward Helen. "Miss Sorby was worried about her today, so she followed her home from Westinghouse. The bomb went off just as she was about to knock on the door.''

"Death was instantaneous," Helen added. "Bonnie—or Bessie—probably never felt a thing."

"But these different names—" He shook his head, looking distraught again. "Why do you keep calling her Bonnie Howards?"

"Because that's the name she was employed under at Westinghouse," Kachigan replied. "It's also the name she used to rent this house, and to do business with the local stores. The question really is, why are *you* calling her Bessie Harris?"

"Because—" He paused, then sighed. "Because that's how she introduced herself to me when we first met. That's all."

"Mm." Kachigan pulled out his evidence book. "And your own name, sir, is—"

"Frank Robinson."

He wrote it down in his slow hand. "Address?"

"Five-sixteen Fairmont Avenue. That's in Trafford City."

Kachigan gave him an inquiring look. "The new town that George Westinghouse just built? Do you work for him then?"

"Yes, but not at the Trafford Foundry. I work as a machinist down at the Airbrake." Robinson ran a hand through his damp, thinning hair. "I was on my way home, and I thought I'd stop by to see if Bessie needed to have her walk shoveled. I knew something was wrong when I didn't see any lights," he added. "Bess liked to burn all the gas lamps at once. To keep the house bright and cheery, she said."

"Where and when did you meet Miss—er—Harris?"

The young man took a deep, steadying breath. "It was at a church dance here in Pitcairn. My sister likes to come to them, even though we belong to a different congregation up in Trafford. Bessie said she was there to meet people, because she'd just moved into the area."

"Do you know where she was from?" Helen asked, ignoring the frown she got from Kachigan for interrupting his interview.

Robinson shook his head. "Baltimore, I think she said, but she wasn't close to her family anymore. That's why she was planning to spend the Christmas holidays with us."

"Was it Baltimore that she moved from when she came to Pitcairn?" Kachigan asked.

"Oh, no." The young machinist sounded much more confident about this answer. "Bessie worked as a secretary in New York City for several years. But she was tired of the crowds and the traffic there, she said. So when her cousin found her a good position with the Westinghouse Company, she took it like a shot."

"Did she ever introduce you to her cousin?" Helen asked. This time, her interruption got her an admonitory rap on the ankle from Kachigan's booted foot, but she paid no more attention to that than she had to his scowl. "Or tell you his name?"

"Lyell Osborne. And she didn't have to introduce us, I already knew him from my work at Westinghouse. He is—he was—one of the best engineers in the company." Robinson's frown deepened. "Now he's dead, too. Do you think that's a coincidence?"

"That's why we're looking into your fiancée's death, Mr. Robinson," Kachigan said, with surprising gentleness. "We don't know enough yet to answer your question, but I hope to be able to soon."

Robinson nodded, taking a last somber look around the snowdrifted apartment as if memorizing it. "I'd better go home and break the news to my sister that there's going to be a funeral, not an engagement party. I suppose it will have to be tomorrow, even though it's Sunday. The day after that is Christ—" He broke off, his voice cracking as if it hurt too much to hear the words. "Do—do you know where Bessie's going to be laid out?"

Helen opened her mouth to say no, but Kachigan spoke first. "The firemen said they'd take her down to the undertaker on Broadway. I assume he'll make the arrangements."

"The one at the livery stable?" The young man scrubbed a hand across his face and steadied his voice. "I'll go down and talk to him before he leaves for the day. If you find any information about Bessie's—I mean, Bonnie's—people in her papers, detective, will you let me know? So I can contact them?"

"Of course." Kachigan tucked his evidence book away. "Would you like some company down to the undertaker?"

"No, thanks. I'd rather be alone." The young machinist paused in the open doorway, looking back with belated anger kindling in his eyes. "If someone did this to Bessie on purpose—you are going to investigate until you catch the one who did it, aren't you? And make sure her killer is punished?"

"That's exactly what I'm going to do." Kachigan's gaze slid from him to Helen meaningfully. "Because no matter what anybody tells you, that's my job."

"I never said you weren't doing your job," Helen insisted.

Kachigan snorted at her, but didn't bother lifting his chin out of his upturned collar. Snow blew and whirled around them, buffeted so hard by strong west winds that she was amazed any of it was actually sticking to the ground. At least ten inches had managed to, however, in the time they'd spent searching Bonnie Howards's house. It muffled the noise of the trains running in the railyards to an almost bearable rumble, but it also made the walk down the steep slate sidewalk of Brinton Avenue even more hazardous than it had been coming up.

"Of course you did," he said, rubbing at his cheek as if it ached. "Several times, in fact."

Helen frowned up at him. "No. I said that you weren't trying to free Abraham Maccoun. And you're still not doing that. That doesn't mean you're not doing your best to investigate these two murders."

"Right." Kachigan reached out to catch her elbow as she skidded on the treacherous layer of ice that lay beneath the snow. "And that's why you're not working with me, Miss Sorby."

She scowled and tucked her fingers deeper into the silken pockets of the expensive beaver coat she'd guiltily borrowed from Bonnie's closet. "Detective Kachigan, the reason I'm not working with you is because you don't want me to!"

"I never said—" He broke off at her scathing look and had the grace to look abashed. "All right, maybe I did. I just didn't expect you to take no for an answer."

Helen snorted again and pulled her elbow free as soon as they reached the flat white ribbon of Pitcairn's main street. At this time on a Saturday night, the pool halls and nickelodeons should have been bustling, but their colored electric signs reflected out onto undisturbed snow. Even the trolley tracks were snowed over, although the soft gullies carved in the snow above them showed that some of the cars had been running recently. The fierce industrial clamor of the roundhouse across the Turtle Creek had been muted by the falling snow—or perhaps the work had been interrupted by the storm—leaving occasional gusts of wind and the muffled rumbling of trains to fill the winter silence. The massive Pitcairn railyard threw gaslight up at the snow-gray night sky, lending it a diffuse blue-gold glow. It made walking through the storm almost pleasant, except for the chilly wetness that seeped though Helen's already-wet shoes.

"Let me tell you what Art Taggart and I have found out about this case so far," Kachigan suggested. Helen glanced at him in surprise, but his gaze seemed to be fixed on the distant smudge of a trolley coming down the line. She couldn't decide if that meant he was self-conscious or scheming. "Then you can tell me what you found out down at Westinghouse."

She opened her mouth, although she didn't know if it was to argue or agree. As it happened, she never had the chance to decide. The door of the nearest pool hall slammed open as they reached it, and what she thought was a drunken pool player reeled out toward them, arms flailing. It wasn't until she heard the fierce Armenian curse and saw how the "drunk" had twisted Kachigan's arm up behind him that she realized he was armed with a long-barreled pistol and had it wedged into the detective's back.

"No screaming," the attacker warned Helen, when she opened her mouth to take a deeper breath. "No one in Pitcairn can help you tonight. The only ones out patrolling are us."

The cap the railroad policeman wore told her who the "us" must be. With a grimace, Helen obeyed his gestured command to walk ahead of Kachigan, hating the fact that she couldn't coordinate glances with the detective. Some drumming instinct warned her that their best chance of escape was now.

"What does the Pennsylvania Railroad want with us?" she demanded, hoping her annoying questions would distract their guard long enough for Kachigan to make a move. "We haven't done anything to you." When all that got her was a wordless grunt, Helen cast around for something else to say. "We didn't find any proof today that the railroad killed Bonnie Howards, if that's what you're worried about. In fact, we didn't really find out anything about her at all."

"Lady, shut up." Unfortunately, the railroad guard sounded more bored than annoyed. "I don't know who you are and I don't care what you did today. All I know is that Mr. Dettis wants to see you. Now cross the street and head for the depot, or your boyfriend here is going to have one less lung."

Helen bit her lip and scanned the silent street ahead of them for any sign of help. The trolley hadn't come any closer in the entire time they'd been walking—it must have gotten itself stuck in the snow. And although she could see a few dark figures emerging from the other pool halls and nickelodeons down Broadway, it only took one look to tell her those were railroad guards, too. Dettis must have stationed them along the main street to intercept them.

"Do it, Helen," Kachigan said quietly. "There's too many of them to get past."

She sighed and swung to cut across the empty street, heading toward the bright gaslights of the railroad depot. For a moment she toyed with the idea of throwing herself off the low iron trestle that bridged the Turtle Creek, but a glance down showed her dark dirty water only partially skimmed with ice. A quick shiver ended that plan. In any case, Helen had no guarantee that she was the person Dettis wanted. Instead of being distracted by her disappearance, the railroad guard might just as well have said good riddance and let her float downstream like Ophelia.

Another handful of guards emerged from the railroad depot when they approached it, closing in around them with the precision of trained bodyguards. Impersonal hands fell on Helen from either side, chaining her arms and sweeping her up the icy steps at a brisker pace than she would have chosen. There didn't seem to be anyone waiting at the train platform, despite the fact that muffled church chimes from the hill-slope town behind them were only just ringing eight P.M. Helen wondered if the thickening snowstorm was to blame or if Ox Dettis had simply chased away all potential witnesses to this abduction.

She'd hoped that their wardens would take them into the gleaming depot itself, where bloodstains would have ruined the polished wood floors and marble counters. To her dismay, however, they were merely hustled over to the edge of the platform and held there. A moment later she saw the misty gleam of a locomotive burn through the veil of snow, and heard its approaching roar separate out from the roar of wind blasting down the valley. She glanced sideways at Kachigan and saw that his face had tightened into bleak and forbidding lines.

"Milo—"

He shook his head, but it wasn't in answer to her unspoken question about escape. "Now do you see why I didn't want you working with me on this case?" His words were barely audible through the combined shriek of storm wind and whistle of air brakes. "Bernard Flinn knew what he was doing when he made me a county detective. He said I'd probably get myself killed within a year, without any help from him."

Helen winced as the locomotive tore past them, so close that she could feel the slap of icy air. She would never have stood this close if the guards hadn't stationed her here. "Killing us won't get Dettis clear of this," she insisted, as much to convince herself as to shake Kachigan from his gloom. "Taggart knows everything you do and Thomas knows everything I do—"

"Except Dettis doesn't know that Thomas exists." Kachigan threw her a grim look. "And I don't think he'd believe us now, even if we told him. As for Taggart . . ." He shook his head, watching a battered passenger car pull to a stop beside them. It was sandblasted free of any identifying emblems or car numbers, as if it had been slated for repair in the roundhouse. No lights were on inside it, but Helen doubted it was empty. "I'm not sure Art would find the energy to do anything about our deaths, no matter how much he knew. That's just not how you survive in the detective bureau, Helen."

She bit into her lower lip, hard enough this time to start a throb of pain, but didn't quite manage to quell the nervous churning of her stomach. The train jerked and hissed to a stop, and before she could move, her flanking guards lifted her and swung her bodily into it. Kachigan came next, hurled in so hard that he slammed them both into the unseen back of a passenger seat.

Helen gasped and clung to the torn leather, trying to keep her balance as the train lurched into motion again. She felt Kachigan brace a hand on the back of the seat and then vault over it, turning to lift her across a moment later. They edged their way out into the center aisle, the light through the windows fading as the train pulled out of the station again. Helen yelped as she banged into another seat in the darkness. This one had been pulled from its bolts and left wedged between two others, she supposed in preparation for being replaced.

"Stop right there." A match flared alight in the darkness at the other end of the car, making the tip of a cigar glow sullen red. A moment later Helen smelled the acrid odor of cheap tobacco. She squinted through the shadowy interior, trying to force her eyes to adjust to the dimness. Enough snow-scattered light still reflected from the Pitcairn railroad yards to show her the stocky silhouette of Ox Dettis, outlined against the distant coal-fired glow of the locomotive. He seemed to be alone, but the shouted conversation between the front and back platforms of their car told her that at least some of the railroad policemen had boarded with them. Apparently, their boss didn't feel their presence was needed inside the car to keep his prisoners under control. Either that, or he didn't trust them not to blackmail him later.

"What do you want, Ox?" Despite Kachigan's wary words, his voice sounded less bleak and more alive to Helen. He must have made the same deduction she had, that two of them versus one arrogant railroad boss was an equation that could be solved in their favor. "A deal?"

Dettis's bark of laughter was more scornful than amused. "If you're offering one, Kachigan, it's only to save your skin."

"Seems like a valid enough reason to me," the detective

said dryly. While he was talking Helen could feel him leaning against the metal-framed seat that blocked their path to the railroad boss, apparently testing its stability. It wobbled just enough to make Helen scowl up at him. If he tried to use it as a base for launching a leap at Dettis's throat, she suspected it would skid right out from under him.

Dettis shook his head, blowing a cloud of pale smoke out into the frigid air. "Not good enough," he said bluntly. "Big Roge McGara told me you can't be trusted to play the game, Kachigan, not unless there's a trumped-up indictment hanging over your head. And I just don't have the time right now to frame you. It's a lot easier to make you disappear."

Helen scowled across at him. "What about me?" she asked, sharply enough to drag Dettis's attention to her. Perhaps that would give Kachigan the chance to find another way across the barrier. "You don't even know who I am! Aren't you worried that making me disappear might get you in a lot more trouble than it solves?"

He took a step closer, peering at her through the dimness. "Who's going to miss you?" he demanded. "Are you married?"

"No." She was offended by the relieved grunt that elicited, as if only a husband would be enraged enough by his loss of property to take action. "But I have a rich and doting aunt who could bribe any of your railroad guards to tell her what happens here tonight."

"Yeah, right. And my uncle's Teddy Roosevelt."

She took a deep breath, but the train car jostled across a switch track and swerved left before she could snap back. She felt Kachigan's hand lock around her elbow and haul her with him in an exaggerated lurch, as if they'd both lost their balance. The move left them hanging on to the side of the car, right beside a cracked and drafty window. Helen wondered if Kachigan hoped to break it and jump out before Dettis could stop them. If so, she knew she was going to wind up coatless again. There was no way the thick beaver coat that she'd borrowed from Bonnie Howards would fit through the narrow railcar window.

"Miss Sorby's not lying, Ox." The flat and defeated note

in Kachigan's voice alarmed Helen, until she felt his fingers close tight around her elbow, loosen, and then close tight again. She didn't nod or even glance at him in reply, but with her free hand began to slowly untie the satin closures on her coat. She had to pause halfway when the lights of Trafford City's small railroad station unexpectedly illuminated the battered car interior, but as soon as they rolled past it and were steeped in snowy darkness again, she loosened the rest. The image of Dettis's face, creased in angry lines and as fire red as his cigar tip, stayed with her even after the railroad boss was plunged back into shadow. "And even if she was, do you think the reporters at the *Post* are going to conveniently forget about this Westinghouse murder? Or not know who to blame it on if two more severed bodies show up along the tracks?"

"Which is exactly why your bodies aren't going to show up along the tracks," Dettis retorted. "I don't know who killed that Westinghouse anarchist, but they must have been idiots. Even a two-bit thug knows that after you roll a guy, you should throw him somewhere no one will ever look. Like at the bottom of the little railroad pond we put down this spur—"

Helen had felt Kachigan's muscles tense halfway through that threatening speech, but she never had a chance to find out what he was planning. The car rolled into the towering shadow of a railroad cut, dark walls of shale hung thick with snow-covered waterfalls of ice on either side. An instant later, for the second time that day, she heard the heart-wrenching thunder of explosion. Except this time, it came from directly beneath the train.

The blast tore through the train car, making the old metal screech and buckle in its wake. Helen cried out as the world tipped and spun and swept her footing out from beneath her, but her voice was lost in the din made by the locomotive crashing down off the tracks. She clung desperately to the tattered railroad seat, kicking her feet at the one now below her until she found purchase in its exposed springs. Taller than she was, Kachigan had already wedged himself in and was battering single-mindedly at the window above their heads while the derailed train continued to skid sideways along the tracks. She never heard his shout, but the quicksilver flash of cracks spreading through the pane warned her to turn her face away. Glass rained down in a shattered cascade, bouncing off her turned-up collar and unbound hair. Helen was abruptly thankful that she hadn't taken the time to pin it up.

"Come on." The train had stopped moving, and she could finally hear Kachigan's voice again over the ominous crackle and hiss of the spilled locomotive. She shed her beaver coat with one quick shrug, then let Kachigan put both hands around her waist and boost her up through their escape window, which had now become a narrow skylight. "Can you make it out?"

"Yes." Helen braced her hands against the cold metal struts between windows and pushed herself up until she could kneel first on one knee, then on both. Shouts of alarm from down the tracks told her that despite the bomb's intervention, they weren't going to have much time to get away. She slid back to the metal side panel of the car, not trusting her weight to one of the other ancient windows, then glanced down the shale-rimmed gorge while she waited for Kachigan to haul himself out after her. No one on the train itself seemed to be paying much attention, but a swinging glow of oil lanterns was coming up the track fast.

"Milo, trackmen."

"I see them." He kicked himself free of the window frame, then vaulted down over the edge of the car. Helen scrambled to the edge and slid off after him, fully prepared for a long drop to uncertain footing on the railroad bed. The fall ended sooner than she'd expected, in the grasp of two strong arms. What made Helen giggle, though, was the way Kachigan grunted and stumbled back a step under her weight, then let her drop abruptly down into the snow.

"That wasn't very romantic," she informed him breathlessly. "You should have just let me fall."

"Shut up," he said between his teeth. "And run."

The fact that he didn't waste time arguing with her doused Helen's mirth fast. She grabbed up her borrowed wool skirts in both hands, irritated by their dragging length, and followed him down the railroad tracks into the looming darkness of the deep cut. Snow swirled and danced in strange patterns around them, and the sound of their muffled footsteps echoed back and forth in what sounded to Helen like miniature explosions. She heard shouts behind them, but with snow blurring the words together, she couldn't tell if they were from puzzled rescuers or furious railroad guards. It didn't seem prudent to stop and make sure.

"Where—are we—going?" she asked Kachigan, gasping with the effort of plowing through the wet and heavy snow. Even staying in the track that he had broken ahead of her, she slipped and slid with each stride she took. Despite the blowing wind, Helen found she was glad to be free of her beaver coat.

"Anywhere—away from—the tracks." He sounded breathless, too, but then he was breaking the path for both of them. "As soon as—this damned gorge ends—"

They rounded a curve, leaving the crackle of the locomotive behind them, but the railroad cut showed no sign of ending. Helen spared a glance back over her shoulder and was dismayed to see a pair of oil lamps still bobbing in their wake, although she couldn't hear the sound of footsteps. It occurred to her that with the trail they were leaving in the snow, it wouldn't be hard to trace them no matter how far ahead of the pursuers they got.

"Milo, they're—tracking us!"

"I know." He reached back and grabbed her wrist, making her lose half her grip on her skirts. Their heavy drag against the snow was more than made up for by the increased speed of being towed, so Helen didn't protest. "Come on, we're going up."

"Up?" She threw an incredulous look at the rock face nearest them, and saw that it was breaking away into more natural ledges and shelves as the man-made cut widened into the stream-carved valley it had originally been. Kachigan ignored her protest, leading her at an angle across what must have been a talus pile, then scrabbling up a steeper face and pulling her after him. Helen teetered, then caught her balance on a jagged icicle as big as she was. She followed him down the ledge, finding that the snow actually helped her footing by giving her shoes a firm surface to dig into. Another angled scramble brought them up to a higher ledge, but this one ended another forty feet down the cliff. A steep gully led upward from it.

"Milo, I can't—"

"Yes, you can." He swung her ahead of him ruthlessly. "But they won't. When we get to the top, we're home free. *Go!*"

She went on hands and knees, scrambling up and then sliding back in frustrating showers of loose rock and snow. After two such setbacks, she found she could dig her hands more easily into the crevices and cracks along the shaly sides of the gully, using one after another to pull herself up. Pretend it's a ladder, she told herself, trying to ignore the knot of fear churning inside her the higher up they went. Don't stop, don't look up to see how steep it gets above. Don't look down. . . .

She did once, but only because she heard the crack and rattle of Kachigan setting off a miniature avalanche. To her immense relief, all she saw was rocks tumbling and falling down toward the surprisingly dim glow of the oil lights. The detective clung stubborn as a barnacle to the rocks below her feet. "Keep going," he said through gritted teeth. "Keep climbing!"

A shot of gunfire cracked through the snowy silence before she could reply. Helen gasped and went up the rest of the gully in a frantic scramble of clinging hands and flailing feet, the sound of her ragged heartbeat in her ears nearly drowning the thunder of more gunshots. She only knew that her climb had ended when she unexpectedly ran out of handholds. For one terrifying moment she thought she would pitch backward and fall, but a gust of wind swept up out of the gorge and smacked her hard between the shoulder blades. She toppled forward instead and recklessly caught hold of the brambles that poked out of the snow with her bare fingers, using them to pull herself up to the hilltop.

She rolled out of the way as soon as her feet were out of the gully, making room for Kachigan to join her. When his dark head didn't immediately appear, all Helen could think about was the flurry of gunshots she had heard. She scrambled back toward the edge of the cliff, just in time to be bowled over by his final upward lunge. They fell into the snow together, the sound of their tearing gasps so much the same that Helen couldn't be sure whose was whose.

"Where were you?" she demanded, into the damp shoulder of his overcoat. "Are you all right?"

Kachigan managed to snort, although it sounded rather breathless. "My own damn fault. I looked down—and saw the guy with the gun—fall trying get away from those rocks I knocked down." A weak chuckle shook through him. "All those shots were straight up in the air."

"And it made you laugh?" Helen levered herself up on her elbows to scowl down at him. "You had to stop climbing because you were laughing so hard?"

"If you could have seen how fast you were moving—"

She stopped him by flinging a handful of snow in his face and got hugged in return, so hard her aching lungs protested. They lay locked together for a long moment, with the snow falling thick and soft around them. The gorge below was re-assuringly silent. It wasn't until a contrary gust of wind blew snow down the back of Helen's wool suit and made her shiver that Kachigan cursed and scrambled to his feet.

"Helen, I'm sorry. I forgot you didn't have a coat—"

"I'm warm enough, except for my feet." She followed him obediently up the slanting hillside that rose from the top of the cliff they'd climbed. The brambles turned to forest a few feet in, but enough clearing of dead wood and selective cutting had been done to make travel through it easy. The wind had already shaken most of the snow off the limbs, leaving little to fall on them when they did have to push past branches. "It looks like someone lives near here."

"A bunch of someones live near here." Kachigan paused at the snowdrifted crest of the hill to let her catch up. On the descending side, a scatter of brightly lit windows sketched the outline of another hillside town below them, this one less steep and much less crowded than Pitcairn.

"Trafford City," Kachigan said in satisfaction. "And if I'm not mistaken, that big building in the middle is a hotel."

Helen peered through the snow at the colored glow of electric lights, shivering. Now that her flush of exertion had faded, she was beginning to notice the icy dampness soaking up her stockings from her shoes. "Do you think it's safe to go there? Isn't it the first place Dettis will think to look for us?"

"It may be the first place he thinks to look," Kachigan agreed. "But it's the last place he'll actually go. All his pay-offs to Big Roge McGara can't protect him here."

"Why?"

The detective pointed at the enormous new foundry whose tall chimneys threw a ruby glow up into the snow-filled sky. "Because this is George Westinghouse's town, not the railroad's. And because we just crossed over into Westmoreland County."

"ONE ROOM," KACHIGAN SAID. "ONE night."

There was a way that desk clerks in fancier hotels had of indicating disapproval without moving more than a fraction of their facial muscles. In the Trafford Inn, with its polished mahogany appointments and dark Oriental carpets, the reaction he got was a quarter inch of eyebrow lift and the slightest of glances at his bare ring finger. Not a comment about his scratched hands and muddy coat, much less a pointed look at the disheveled and coatless female he'd brought in with him. Kachigan began to wonder if he had enough money in his wallet to cover the bill.

"One room, sir?"

"That's right." He knew from experience that trying to explain away or excuse your questionable behavior only made matters worse. It was better to keep your mouth shut and just let people believe whatever they wanted. And right now he had no intention of leaving Helen Sorby alone unless it was in a locked room to which he held the only key. "Are any available?"

The desk clerk paused, but the total absence of guests in his foyer didn't give him much wiggle room. "We have several, sir," he said. "Do you have a preference?"

"Top floor, lots of heat." Helen had gone to stand shivering by the marble-topped fireplace as soon as they'd come in out of the storm. Her absence made it easier for Kachigan to register, but it also worried him enough to keep his dealings with the desk clerk curt. She'd never admit it, but he suspected his radical socialist was about ready to drop from exhaustion.

"How much?"

"Dollar-fifty." The older man took his money, watched him sign *Mr. and Mrs. Sorby,* and handed over his key, all the while exuding silent desk-clerk disapproval. "Room three-oh-five, left at the top of the stairs. Any bags?"

"No." He didn't bother trying to explain that, either. Instead, he pocketed the key and went to fetch Helen from her fire. Water had puddled on the tile hearth beneath her sodden shoes and droplets of melted snow glittered in her tangled dark hair.

"Did they have rooms?"

"Mm-hmm." He slid a hand beneath her elbow, just in case she needed steadying up the stairs. "I got us one."

That earned him a swift upward glance, but not the indignant protest he expected. "Then you're *not* sure Dettis won't come looking for us," she said perceptively.

"I'm sure *he* won't. I'm just not sure that means we're going to be safe." He turned the key in the lock. "Roger McGara's not exactly delighted with me right now. And I wouldn't put it past him to make a little excursion over the county line."

"But—" Helen paused in the doorway, eyeing the single brass bed and overstuffed sofa with a suddenly doubtful expression, as if what she was doing had just sunk into her cold-numbed wits. Kachigan didn't waste time trying to reassure her. Instead, he crossed to the low blue flame of the gas fireplace and twisted the valve that turned it into a generously hissing wall of golden heat. It drew Helen like a magnet to collapse sighing on the hearth.

"I'm going to go get us some supper," he said, before she could protest. Ever since they'd entered Trafford City, his stomach had been reminding him that he hadn't eaten since eleven this morning. "Don't go out to the bathroom or let anyone in until I'm back."

She nodded without even looking up from unlacing her shoes. Fifteen minutes later, when he returned with thick ham sandwiches dripping their smoky juice through the brown paper they'd been wrapped in, he found her asleep on the hearth with one shoe off and the other half-untied.

"Helen?" He shrugged out of his coat and came to kneel beside her, but she didn't wake until he started to tug at the stubborn wet knots of her shoelace. She blinked at him for a moment, then made a noise that could only be described as an inquiring yawn. He smiled and pulled her shoe off. "Ham sandwiches," he said in answer to that wordless question. "And coffee."

"Oh, good." She leaned forward to ease one waxed paper cup out of the bag he'd set beside them, not even noticing when he began pulling off her sodden stockings. Bits of broken shale scattered as he wrung the water out. He set them beside the fireplace to dry, then started to rub the warmth back into her feet. Helen gave him a startled look over her coffee cup.

"What do you think you're doing?"

"Making sure you don't fall back to sleep," he retorted. It was true enough, even if it wasn't the reason behind his massage. Helen Sorby had slender and elegant feet, as nice to look at as the rest of her, but right now they were alarmingly cold. "You can't tell me who Bonnie Howards is while you're snoring."

"I don't snore," she informed him, quite untruthfully, and reached for a ham sandwich. "I thought you were going to tell me everything you and Taggart had found out first."

"That was before our investigation of Bonnie Howards's death almost got us killed."

Her grimace acknowledged his point, and her resigned sigh said she agreed with it despite herself. One of the things he liked best about Helen Sorby was that she never let her opinions overrule her reason. "I met Bonnie two days ago when I started working undercover at Westinghouse," she said, without further ado. "At first, I thought she was just another of the stenographers in the main office. Then this morning, I found out that her Cousin Lyell got her the job about month or so ago, which is when all the trouble started." She saw his puzzled frown. "Inventions and patents were stolen. Important plans went missing. Leo—you know who Leo is?"

"The Swiss lady engineer who shared an office with Osborne?"

"Yes. She thinks someone is trying to ruin Westinghouse."

"They wouldn't have to try very hard," Kachigan pointed out. "He overextends himself every winter by keeping men on the payroll when he doesn't have work. Did Leo think Bonnie Howards was the troublemaker?"

"She wasn't sure. But since I knew Bonnie had been with Osborne the night he died—"

"*What?*"

Helen glanced up from her half-eaten sandwich, looking a little guilty but mostly pleased with herself. "When we didn't find any trace of him in East Pittsburgh that night, I decided to look elsewhere. And since my tenants at Essene House appear to know every barman and tavern keeper in the Westinghouse Valley on a first-name basis, I drew a picture of Osborne and gave it to them."

"And you *believe* what one of them told you?"

In retaliation for that dubious question, Helen jerked her bare feet out of his grasp and tucked them beneath the hem of her wool skirt. "My tenants are poor struggling immigrants, Milo, not known criminals. At least, not anymore. The girl who learned about Osborne could have been a secretary or a factory girl if she hadn't been orphaned too young to do anything but walk the street!"

Kachigan sighed. "I should have left you cold and hungry," he said, reaching for his own sandwich. "You were easier to pump information out of then."

"Well, you're the one who keeps interrupting me," she said in exasperation. "If you really wanted to keep me talking, you would bring over a pillow from the sofa and make me comfortable."

He groaned and set the sandwich down untasted. "Are you always this demanding in the evenings?"

"No," Helen Sorby said in a tart voice. "Only when I've been bombed, abducted, and chased up a cliff at gunpoint."

"Good. I'd hate to have do this more than once a month."

That got him the smile he was fishing for, the one that lit her entire face with amusement. "It *was* only a month ago that we were getting shot at by Bernard K. Flinn, wasn't it? Somehow, it seems a lot longer."

"I know," Kachigan said. The flare of bitterness and regret in his voice surprised even him, and spilled a cold, awkward silence across the firelit hotel room. He scraped the cushions off the couch and brought them back to rearrange in a comfortable semicircle around the tiled hearth, but it didn't reestablish the warmth that had been there a few moments before. Helen's smile had vanished without a trace, leaving her face even more somber than before.

Kachigan cleared his throat, but what came out wasn't the follow-up investigative question he'd intended. "Helen, I'm sorry."

That kindled a familiar rumpled scowl. "Sorry for what?" she asked ominously. "Letting me investigate this case?"

"No. Sorry for—" He broke off, overwhelmed by the mountain of things that stood in need of apology. Sorry for not being smart enough to stay clean in the detective's bureau, he wanted to say. Sorry for not being able to dig myself out of that mire of corruption the way I wanted to before I came back into your life. And most of all, sorry that my damned pride and arrogance kept you at arm's length, and endangered your life.

"For being such a damned idiot," he said at last. It seemed a comprehensive enough summary. "I never meant you to get hurt."

He'd been referring to the bomb blast that had caught her on Bonnie Howards's threshold, but that didn't quite seem to explain the furious look she turned on him. "Oh, didn't you? Well, maybe you should have thought about that *before* you decided to disappear for three weeks!" Helen's voice rose to the scalding shout that only the strongest emotions could boil out of her. "What was I supposed to think that meant? That you had more important things to do, like shake down whorehouses and gambling joints for illegal payoffs?"

Kachigan's own temper leaped to meet hers, lit all too easily from the angry coals that had smoldered in his gut ever since his arrest. His scarred cheek ached with the effort of gritting his teeth to keep from shouting back. "That's just how I knew you'd react when you read about me in the papers," he said bitterly. "Is it any wonder I didn't want to see you?"

"But I *didn't*—" Helen broke off and glared at him, apparently too furious even for words.

"Think I was corrupt?" Kachigan finished. His laugh hurt his throat so much he knew it couldn't have been a pleasant sound. "You've certainly said it often enough the past few days. And you never say anything you don't mean, Helen."

"That's because of the way you've been acting lately!" she flung back. "I knew in November that you would *never* have taken those bribes. If you'd come to see me the day after the indictment, I'd have shown you the article I wrote accusing the county police of framing anyone sent to clean up their ranks!"

Kachigan gave her a disbelieving frown. "You never published it anywhere."

"That's because you never came by to tell me your side of the story! I'm a reporter, I can't make up facts." Helen's scowl deepened. "But instead, I had to read the newspapers to make sure you were still alive and hadn't skipped out of town just like my—"

She broke off with a passionate Italian curse, but not before Kachigan heard the stab of long-buried hurt in her voice. His anger crashed into self-disgust. Before he could think of all the reasons he shouldn't do it, he reached out and caught her still-cold hands in his.

"I'm not like your ex-husband," he said fiercely, ignoring her attempt to pull away. "If you knew how many times I caught myself walking down your street—but, Helen, I wanted to come to you with *proof* that Roger McGara had set me up, not just my word against his. Enough proof to blow that damned indictment to bits and pieces. Every day I thought I'd get it, except every day it still wasn't enough—and then before I knew it, I was in East Pittsburgh looking at you through the bars of a lockup cell."

Her fingers turned inside his grip to cling to his with surprising strength. *"Idiot!"* she said, but the anger was already seeping out of her voice. "Couldn't you at least have rung me up and told me what you were waiting for? Or dropped a postcard in the mail? Three weeks should have been about enough time for you to write a line or two—"

He stopped that affectionate insult by the simple expedient of lifting the hands he held and kissing them. The audible catch of Helen's breath made him smile, but when he glanced up at her dark eyes, he could see them burdened by an uncomfortable awareness of the hotel bed behind them. With a sigh, Kachigan released her hands and returned to the safer confines of their murder case.

"Tell me what your resident crib girl found out," he said, and picked up his sandwich. "I promise I'll believe it."

"Her name's Molly," Helen told him. "And she found two—er—crib-girl friends of hers who recalled seeing Osborne at a bar in Pitcairn the night he died. He was with a very well-dressed lady, they said, but they weren't sure whether it was his sister or his girlfriend. I think it was Bonnie."

"Who may have been his girlfriend instead of his cousin." Kachigan weighed her curious look, then told her about the silk chemise that he and Taggart had found in Osborne's bathroom. By the time he was done, Helen was shaking her head, but it was in bewilderment not shocked denial.

"If Bonnie came here as Lyell Osborne's girlfriend, what was she doing engaged to Frank Robinson? Trying to make Osborne jealous?"

"Under a completely different name? I doubt it." Kachigan frowned. "Judging from the unpaid bills I found in her rental house, Bonnie wasn't very responsible about money. If I didn't know she was tied in with this Westinghouse murder, I'd have said she was just a garden-variety confidence artist, moving from town to town and making her living by pretending to get engaged to as many well-off young men as she could."

"Like my ex-husband, you mean," Helen said. Kachigan threw her a startled glance, but although her voice was still bitter, it had lost the prickly defensiveness she usually exuded whenever that particular subject came up. "You think she got

Lyell Osborne to say she was his cousin, just to get her the job at Westinghouse?''

''Why not?'' He chewed on his cold ham sandwich, thinking over the timing. ''Robinson said Howards used to live in New York City. We know Osborne was there in mid-November to pick up his Inventor of the Year award—''

''Oh, do we?''

He ignored the interruption. ''Let's say she picked him up there and talked him into bringing her back to Pittsburgh. He gets her a nice discreet place to live across the valley from his house, lands her a job at his own company, takes her out once in a while for a night on the town—''

''And on one such night takes her to the railroad depot, where he gets picked up by a private railroad car with a Westinghouse insignia on the back while she goes home.'' Helen busied herself with shedding her wool suit jacket to avoid his scowl. It wasn't easy, but Kachigan didn't let the high-necked lace blouse she was wearing distract him from his exasperation.

''Thanks for telling me about that unimportant little detail now,'' he growled at her. ''Is that something else your crib girl found out?''

''Yes. And I *was* going to tell you, until you interrupted me again with that silk-chemise story!''

''Huh.'' He polished off the last of his sandwich and eyed the dismembered remains of hers. ''Anything else I've rudely kept you from being able to tell me?''

Helen leaned back against the pile of sofa cushions, stretching her bare feet out toward the fire with a sigh. ''I don't think so. And yes, you can have the rest of my sandwich.''

Kachigan pulled the paper across, not trusting the untidy layers to stay in one piece if he picked them up. ''Did Bonnie seem to be romantically involved with any other men down at Westinghouse? Did you ever see her leave with anyone?''

''No. She did banter with one of the salesmen once, a young man named Alexander Erskine Greer, and he called her his love. But since he's the type that flirts with anything in skirts, I don't think it meant much.''

Kachigan frowned. ''How do you know that?''

"Because she laughed at him after we'd gone outside."

He sighed at her obtuseness, wrapping the sandwich paper up and tossing it into the fire before he remembered it was gas, not wood. The paper blackened and curled itself around the pipe that fed the burners. "I meant, how do you know he flirts with anything in skirts?"

Helen opened her eyes long enough to frown at him. "That's beside the point. The real question is, if Bonnie was just a confidence artist, why was she killed by an anarchist bomb? And why was Lyell Osborne thrown off a Westinghouse train car?"

"I don't know." Kachigan took off his own jacket and yanked his clinging, wet collar free of his shirt. The pile of sofa cushions he had thrown behind them was doing a good job of reflecting the gas heat, creating a circle of almost uncomfortable warmth around the fireplace. Since Helen's eyes had closed again, he went ahead and shed his wool vest, too, letting his damp shirt bake in the heat. "I don't suppose George Westinghouse is such a moral stickler that he'd kill one of his engineers just for dating the wrong girl."

"Not the engineer in charge of his Brazilian hydroelectric plant," she said sleepily. "That would be shooting himself right in the foot. The project's going to be set back for months, and they might even have to pay a penalty for being late."

He grunted. "All right, then, let's assume Osborne was killed to get George Westinghouse in trouble. Why would O. X. Dettis claim Osborne was behind the anarchist railroad bombings?"

"What?" It was Helen's turn to slew around and glare at him. "Thank you, Detective Kachigan, for sharing that unimportant information with me! What anarchist railroad bombings?"

"I assumed you already knew about them," Kachigan said, honestly enough. "You seem to know everything else I do, if not more."

"Stop buttering me up with compliments and talk," Helen commanded. "What bombs have gone off? No one in East Pittsburgh said anything about them."

He snorted. "And that's exactly the way Ox Dettis wants

it. None of the big papers ran any stories—you have to talk to the trackmen to find out exactly when and where they occurred.''

"Was anyone killed?"

"No. The bombs were set along the tracks, under switch plates. They derailed locomotives, damaged the tracks, cost the railroad a lot of wasted time and money. That's all.''

Helen's eyes widened. "Is that why the train derailed tonight? That explosion was an anarchist bomb?"

"That's my guess. I'm betting that line doesn't get used much. Who knows when the bomb could have been planted.''

He let her lean back against the cushions and mull that over for a while, careful not to point out that her new position had put her comfortably shoulder to shoulder with him. "What proof did Dettis have that Lyell Osborne was the one behind these bombings?'' she asked at last. "He's the last person I'd suspect.''

"Apparently, Dettis thinks all those foreign and female engineers down at Westinghouse are anarchists.''

"Oh, great proof.''

"Yeah, that's what I thought," Kachigan agreed. "But then a railroad police guard told me he found complicated triggering devices rigged to some unexploded bombs. He might have been lying—but I saw the same kind of gadgets on Osborne's worktable at home.''

"And according to the letter I read, the patent that was stolen from Osborne was for some sort of spring trigger.'' Helen fell quiet again, but he could tell from the tense rise and fall of her breath that she wasn't dozing off this time. A rich waft of floral perfume drifted up from her skirt as it dried in the heat. It must have been Bonnie Howards's, since he'd never known Helen to wear more than a little jasmine-scented dusting powder. "Milo, you don't really think Osborne was bombing the railroad, do you? Because if he was, and Dettis knew it—''

"Then he had every reason to send Osborne on a short walk down a long railroad trestle," he finished, frowning. "What's wrong with that theory? The way Dettis tried to silence us tonight implies he has something to hide.''

"But then why would Dettis go to the trouble of planting a bomb in Bonnie Howards's house? The last thing you'd think he'd want is all the fuss and attention of a pretty young girl getting killed by an anarchist bomb. The big-city papers certainly aren't going to look the other way on *that* story! Why didn't he just pick her up the way he did with us and with Osborne?"

Kachigan opened his mouth to reply, but the hotel-room door thundered under an impatient fist before he could say anything. He scrambled to his feet and scanned the room, looking for something he could use as a weapon. Helen came to stand beside him, her hair falling across her face in a disregarded tangle.

"There's nothing here we can use to fight with, is there?" she asked, beneath the clamor.

"There's the telephone." Kachigan gave her a push toward the handset that had been placed with modern efficiency on the nightstand beside the bed. That would also put her out of the line of potential fire. "Tell the desk clerk to call the police at the Westinghouse foundry—tell them this is a company problem. I'll try to distract whoever's out there."

One thing he'd noticed about Helen Sorby before—she could argue with you about social issues until the cows came home, but she wasted no time in a crisis. He heard the pad of her bare feet across the wood floor, until another spate of knocking drowned it out. With a deep breath, Kachigan positioned himself against the wall beside the door. There was no sense being in the line of fire himself, if he could help it.

"Give it up, McGara," he yelled through the heavy wood door panels. "This is a Westmoreland county. You're not going to get us out of here without a fight."

"That's why I knew you'd be here." The voice that replied was muffled, but the placid tone would have told him it wasn't his boss even if the Italian accent hadn't. "Don't worry, I'm by myself. Look through the peephole if you don't believe me."

Kachigan leaned away from the wall, eyeing the hotel door in surprise. He was looking for the kind of crudely drilled hole that most brothel doors came equipped with, so it took him a minute to notice the elegant glass lens set in its fancy brass case. A quick duck and glance through it showed him a dark Italian face, rounded out of its usual proportions by the magnifying lens but still wearing a distinctive blue railroad policeman's cap. He frowned and straightened again.

"How do I know Dettis isn't hiding around the corner, Ciocco?"

That got him an amused grunt. "You don't see any fire or smoke coming down the hall, eh? How could he be here?"

"Milo." Helen had cupped her hand over the speaking bell of the telephone. "The clerk wants to know exactly what this company problem is before he rings up the foundry. He says there's no one in the hotel tonight except for us and a neighbor who comes in all the time to use the hotel's safe-deposit box."

Kachigan frowned and considered his options. "Ask the clerk what his neighbor's name is."

She relayed the question, then looked up. "John Ciocco, he says. He lives on Sixth Street here in Trafford."

"Then tell him not to call the police." Kachigan took a deep breath, then reached out and slid the dead bolt, cracking the door open wide enough to see down the hall past Ciocco. Empty silence echoed through the hotel's top floor, the kind of unbreathing silence that even the most disciplined policemen couldn't fake. "All right," he said. "Come in."

"*Grazie.*" The young railroad guard came through the doorway politely enough, although the clink of something heavy and metallic in his coat pockets made Kachigan bar him from taking more than step inside. His friendly smile widened when he saw Helen beside the bed. "Ah, the young lady from the burned house in Pitcairn. I think you forgot this."

He held out the gleaming length of beaver he had tucked under one arm, but to Kachigan's relief, Helen made no move to come and take it. Instead, she gave him a suspicious glance. "Where did you get that from?" she demanded.

"From the wrecked car down on the B.Y. Line." Ciocco tossed the coat onto an arm of the denuded couch, still smiling. "You *were* the one Dettis took for a ride down there tonight, weren't you?"

Kachigan scowled at him. "Yes, we were. But you weren't."

"How could I be?" Giovanni Ciocco looked mildly surprised. "Dettis didn't decide to put the net out to catch you until after four P.M. With the trolleys running so late in this snow, it took me a good hour just to come home, much less get out to the cut ahead of you. And I had to make sure the snow had plenty of chance to cover my tracks after I set the bomb. Otherwise, Dettis would have traced me right back to Sixth Street."

"*You're* the one who's been setting these railroad bombs?" Kachigan asked in surprise.

"Oh, no. Not at all." Ciocco fanned his hands out in a gesture of self-disparaging modesty. "Just the one tonight, so you could escape. Worked good, eh?"

"It worked perfectly." Helen came across the room to join them, although Kachigan noticed that she was still wary enough to stay out of arm's reach. "But why on earth did you do it?"

Ciocco shrugged. "Maybe because I don't like Ox Dettis dumping dead people in our skating pond," he said flippantly. "Maybe because I don't think it's smart to tangle with county detectives, even the ones their bosses don't like. Or maybe I want a pension, and I'm gambling that you can get me in at Westinghouse if I help you. Take your pick."

Kachigan gauged the balance of intelligence, maturity, and humor in the young Italian's face. "It couldn't just be because you don't like killing people, could it?"

Ciocco's full-throated laugh echoed in the hotel's silent halls. "Sure, that, too," he agreed. "That was why I left the old country. Too many favors to do, too many big men fighting over too little money, and then the *omerta*—you know what that means?"

Kachigan shook his head. "Silence," Helen translated, before Ciocco could. She added another phrase in Italian, of which Kachigan could only make out the word *Siciliano*. It sounded like a question.

The young man laughed and nodded. "*Si, da Siracusa. E lui?*"

"Mezzo Calabrese."

"Then you know how it is." Ciocco switched back to English, and returned his gaze to Kachigan. "That's what I came to America to get away from. Not to be part of, legal or illegal. All right?"

Kachigan looked a question at Helen Sorby and got back a decisive nod. Apparently, her instincts concurred with his. "All right," he said, and stepped back to let the young Italian in. "So, what did you take out of the safe-deposit box to show us?"

That got him a whistle and a lifted eyebrow. "Good thing you're almost as smart as you think you are, Detective Kachigan. Otherwise you'd be getting yourself in trouble all the time."

"I could say the same about you," Kachigan retorted.

"True enough." Ciocco reached a hand into his pocket and eased out a tight little metal package, all coiled springs and meticulously soldered wire. "You said you wanted to see this, and since I happened to have a spare . . ."

Kachigan took it from him and turned it over to examine the intricate mechanism of levers and springs. "Is it like the ones you saw in Osborne's house?" Helen asked, standing on tiptoe to look over his shoulder.

"Almost exactly." The only parts that didn't look familiar were the bronzed metal plate to which it all attached and the long wires that must have been clipped from the explosives. "Where did you find this?"

"Down near the water tower in Pitcairn. I think the bomber hoped to knock it over with the blast." Ciocco gave him an inquiring look. "Was it definitely made by that dead engineer?"

"Yes," Kachigan said flatly.

Helen frowned up at him. "Then everything Dettis told you about Osborne is true. He must be the one who killed him."

"No," Ciocco said, just as flatly. He shrugged at their startled looks. "I can't be sure, of course. But I was on duty Wednesday, and I can tell you for sure, we never put out a net for Osborne, the way we put one out for you tonight."

"Maybe Dettis didn't want any of the guards to know about the murder," Helen said.

"But why not? He feels no hesitation asking us to kidnap a county policeman, eh? Why keep an anarchist secret? Especially one he could use to embarrass old Westinghouse." He shook his head, looking very doubtful. "If I know Ox Dettis, he would have nailed that dead engineer up on our flagpole and painted a big sign on his body, saying 'This is George Westinghouse's fault.' He wouldn't have thrown him off another railroad's line in the middle of the night."

"Then why did he try to kill us tonight?" Kachigan demanded. "Just to keep the riffraff out of Pitcairn?"

Ciocco shook his head again, more definitely this time. "No, he's afraid of something you might find out. But all he told us, when he ordered us to put the net out for you tonight, was that you were poking your noses into something he'd paid Roger McGara to leave alone." He shot an inquiring glance at Kachigan. "You don't know what that could be, do you?"

"Knowing my boss, any of a thousand different things," Kachigan said dryly. "And it's no use asking him. He probably already *has* forgotten about it. And even if he hasn't, he'd be more likely to shoot us than help us." Kachigan weighed the trigger device in his hand for a moment, then glanced back at their newfound ally. "You mind if I keep this?"

"One condition." Ciocco pointed a finger at him. "You promise to get me a job on George Westinghouse's police force when you clear this whole mess up and win his undying gratitude, eh?"

The question was only half-joking. Kachigan lifted an eyebrow at the young railroad guard, a little surprised by this unfounded confidence. "Assuming a lot, aren't you? How do you know I won't hash up this investigation, and make George Westinghouse just as mad at me as Ox Dettis is?"

Ciocco's good-humored smile lit his angular face. "Do you know how hard it was to get even the railroad police to take a *paesan* like me instead of an Irish or German boy? I figure any Armenian smart enough and tough enough to make county detective couldn't be that much of an idiot. So, you promise?"

"We promise," Helen said, before Kachigan could find his

voice. "Do you promise to be careful around Ox Dettis? If he really thinks his anarchist bomber is dead, he's going to start wondering where tonight's bomb came from."

"I doubt it," Ciocco said, buttoning his coat. "Dettis knows that B.Y. line never gets used in the winter, that's why he took you up it. When I went down the tracks to help them tonight, he was already cursing us for not checking that switch plate weeks ago." He paused with a hand on the doorknob. "You're the ones who need to be careful. Don't take the train out of here tomorrow, or even the Ardmore trolley. Dettis will have men stationed on both of them."

"Don't worry," Helen assured him. "We're not going in that direction."

Kachigan frowned at her, but held his tongue until he'd seen Ciocco back out into the quiet hallway and shot the dead-bolt lock home. "What direction *are* we going in tomorrow?" he asked.

"East." Helen swung toward the telephone, bare feet padding confidently back across the floor. "I think there's a Westmoreland County trolley line that runs from here out to Greensburg. If I tell Thomas to wire money ahead, we can get two train tickets at the station there for New York City."

"New York City?" Kachigan wasn't sure which surprised him more, the unexpected destination or the leap of sheer pleasure he'd felt at her unspoken assumption that they would travel there together. "Isn't that a little far to go just to detour around Ox Dettis?"

"It's not a detour." Helen glanced over her shoulder, the receiver already in one hand and the other flexed on the switch hook ready to tap for the connection. "If Osborne really made those triggers and set those bombs, then he and Bonnie may both have been known anarchists. New York City is where we have the best chance of finding that out."

"Why's that? Are there anarchists on every street corner?"

"No, but there's one in charge of a new magazine that every anarchist is going to be reading soon." Helen gave him a smile that made Giovanni Ciocco's look lukewarm. "If there's a pocket of anarchist activity anywhere in this county, trust me, Emma Goldman knows about it."

13

HELEN WOKE THE NEXT MORNING FEELing as if a fairy godmother with a very odd sense of humor had cast a spell over the day. The creak of weight on her bed and the warmth of a man's hand on her bare shoulder had startled her awake, but the annoyingly tight tangle that she always made of her blankets just as quickly told that she'd slept alone. She twisted the bedclothes even tighter by hauling them up to her chin as she rolled over, and saw Milo Kachigan's smile widen.

"It's all right," he said, as if he could read her mind. "I spent the night on the couch, remember."

"And do you have a crick in your neck now?" They'd had a lengthy argument over who would fit best where before they'd retired the previous night. Spell or no spell, Helen liked being proven right.

"No, because I fell off halfway through the night and decided to stay on the floor." Kachigan's smile seemed brighter than usual, but Helen couldn't decide if that was due to the radiant dazzle of winter sunshine through the window, or just the contrast from his noticeable shadow of beard. "I'm going out to get coffee and a shave, if I can find a barber open on a Sunday morning. Is there anything you need me to bring back besides breakfast?"

"Safety pins and hairpins," Helen said promptly. She was

tired of sweeping dust off the floor with the hem of Bonnie's wool skirt, and she seemed to have lost every hairpin she owned somewhere along the way yesterday. She pushed a hand through her tangled hair and grimaced, feeling bits of shale cascade onto her pillow. "And a hairbrush or a comb. I must look like the wreck of the *Hesperus*."

"You look like an angel." A corner of Milo Kachigan's mouth kicked up in amusement at her disbelieving look. "An untidy angel," he amended, and while she was still deciding whether to argue that, he bent over and dropped an unexpected kiss onto her cheek. Helen's breath caught in her throat. That touch of lips had lasted far too long and ended up much too close to her mouth to be considered a polite morning greeting. The weight on her bed lifted abruptly. "Be dressed when I get back," Kachigan advised, and left the room.

For once, she'd done as she was told without argument, but the sense of being caught in some eccentric fairy's spell hadn't broken with his clean-shaven return a half hour later. They ate sweet rolls and drank coffee, discussed travel arrangements while Helen pinned up her hair and adjusted her skirt hem, checked out under the desk clerk's disapproving eye, then walked arm in arm down the scraped but icy sidewalk to the Trafford trolley station. Through it all, what surprised Helen most was how completely normal and comfortable this forced intimacy seemed. Her first marriage had been a whirl of romantic delight shattered overnight into bitter disillusion. This felt more like—well, more like friendship.

At least it did until she glanced up from the Sunday paper she'd bought before boarding the eastbound express train at Greensburg, and caught Milo Kachigan watching her instead of the snow-covered scenery. He didn't say anything, but his eyes seemed to have turned a darker shade of blue than usual. Helen shivered and retreated to the infinitely safer world of Pittsburgh mayoral politics.

"I can't wait until the election in February. With Guthrie running, I think we finally might have a chance to elect a progressive candidate."

"Helen—" Kachigan broke off, his gaze sliding off to the snowy mountains the train was slowly chugging through.

"What makes you think Emma Goldman's going to be in her office today?" he asked at last. Helen didn't think that was what he'd originally planned to say, but she didn't protest the change in subject. "It's not just Sunday, you know. It's Christmas Eve."

"Miss Goldman is Jewish." She turned a page, ignoring the unfairly slanted coverage that the conservative *Times* was giving to Mayor Hayes. "And I know she's not traveling, because I got a letter from her a week ago, asking me to do a quick editorial on immigration rights. She said that the first issue of *Mother Earth* was going to come out late, because she'd lost her assistant editor."

"To another magazine?"

"To jail," Helen said, and gave Kachigan a mischievous look. "She was arrested by Anthony Comstock for handing out leaflets on birth control in Times Square."

She'd expected that to fracture the fairy spell of peace and harmony that had wrapped itself around them, but all it did was make his eyes crinkle. "You do know the most interesting people," he said, and leaned back in his seat, tipping the cheap bowler hat he'd bought that morning over his eyes to shade out the winter sun. "Wake me up when we get to New York City."

But by the time their train finally pulled into the Grand Central Depot, hours later, it was Helen who had to be shaken awake. She lifted her head with a start, hearing the odd echoing whistle of arrival you only got in large covered rail terminals. "Are we there?"

"Mm-hmm." Kachigan handed over her beaver coat and began folding up her scattered newspapers as the train hissed to a stop. Helen rubbed at the itching imprint of wool tweed on her cheek and realized she'd been sleeping with her head on his shoulder. Fortunately, the detective was smart enough to make no comment on that.

"Do I need to pawn my watch for cab fare, or can we walk to Emma Goldman's office from here?"

"We can walk. It's just down Madison Avenue." It felt odd to be getting off a train in New York City without any luggage to heft or an absentminded aunt to shepherd through the teeming crowds. Helen tucked her hand under Kachigan's arm and let him lead her off the train. His gaze lifted almost at once to the huge arching barrel vault of glass overhead. It was grimed black with smoke from a thousand trains and liberally streaked with pigeon droppings. "Pennsylvania Station back home is nicer than this," he said in surprise. "Don't they ever clean this place?"

"No, because they're supposed to be building a new one. They started planning for it in 1903, but I've yet to see them break ground. It probably won't get done until 1913." She looked around for the Madison Avenue exit and tugged him toward it. "Is this your first trip to New York City?"

"Unless you count my mum being three months pregnant with me when she and Pap came over on the boat." He followed her willingly enough through the crowd of boisterous students and soldiers returning home for the holidays. "You come here often?"

"Not as often as I should. Aunt Pittypat likes to make a shopping trip every fall, and I usually come along to have lunch with one or two of my editors. I should come up in the spring, too, but I never seem to have the time. And it's amazing how well you can keep in touch with just the post and the telegraph offices."

"The wonders of the modern age. Live in one city, work in another." Kachigan followed her through the open side doors, as filthy as the rest of the old building, and out into the late-afternoon bustle of the city. New York didn't seem to have gotten the snow that Pittsburgh had yesterday, but a light glaze of hoarfrost still covered the shaded sides of its tall buildings, while ice glittered on wrought-iron fences and the bare branches of a few ornamental trees. The sun was low in the western sky, slanting a shaft of light across Madison Avenue at every busy intersection. "Which way now?"

"South." Helen led him past the fancy Victorian hotels that ringed the train station, toward the more businesslike block of ten-and twelve-story office buildings with their bustling ground-level stores. Despite the late hour, most of the stores were aglow with holiday decorations and still open to shoppers. In fact, the city seemed intent on preparing for Christmas

right up until the stroke of midnight. She let Kachigan forge
a path for them through the streaming crowd to the building
that she'd pointed at. Its space of sidewalk was less hectic than
the rest, tenanted with a Christian Science reading room on
one side and a darkened office of the American Express carriage company on the other. Helen headed for the foyer entrance tucked between them.

"We're here to see Miss Goldman, of *Mother Earth*," she
told the black man reading Marx behind the reception desk.
He nodded, as if that made perfect sense on a late Sunday
afternoon, and waved them toward the elevator without taking
his eyes from the page. Helen deliberately slid the wrought-
iron grille open before Kachigan could do it for her, ignoring
the exasperated look she got. Fairy spells couldn't last forever.

"Do you know what floor we need?"

"The third." She let him punch the button and pull the
doors closed, now that she'd made her point, but she didn't
slide her hand back through his arm. Emma Goldman didn't
dislike men, but Helen had once heard her say that she saw
no need for women to hang on them like a brace of dead
ducks. The elevator lurched and grumbled its way up two
floors, then jerked to a stop three inches below the third. Helen
swung the metal doors open and once again ignored Kachigan's proffered hand, lifting her too-long coat to step up under
her own power.

The familiar glass-paned office door was open, although the
usual sound of fervent voices wasn't racketing out of it on this
visit. Helen paused in the doorway and frowned. The front
office generally shared by the magazine's young and unpaid
staff, including its founding editor, was completely empty.

"Miss Goldman?" she called, letting her voice ring loud in
the silence.

Something dropped with a thud back in the layout room,
and rapid footsteps echoed through the silence. A moment later
Emma Goldman appeared from the hallway, her elegant black
walking dress covered with clipped odds and ends of paper
from laying out copy and her attractive face frowning behind
its round spectacles.

"Miss Sorby! I thought I recognized your voice." Observant dark eyes swung from Helen to her companion. "Who is your gentleman friend? He looks like a policeman."

"That's because he *is* a policeman." Helen smiled at Kachigan's startled look. People always underestimated Emma Goldman, guessing from her polished appearance and throaty voice that she was a brainless socialite instead of a brilliant social reformer. "He and I are investigating another murder case in Pittsburgh, like the one I wrote about in my last *Collier's* article."

"Ah, the unveiled Armenian detective!" Goldman came forward with surprisingly masculine strides to shake Kachigan's hand. He must have given her back as firm a handclasp as he got, judging from her satisfied grunt. Helen took a deep breath and held her own hand out next, to be wrung by one of the strongest grips she'd ever encountered. Fortunately, she was prepared for it and managed not to wince.

"I hope you didn't drop by just to chat," Emma Goldman said, stepping back and giving them a shrewd look over the top of her glasses. "I need to finish this copy proof by midnight and all my elves have gone out to have what they euphemistically like to call Christmas cheer."

"We'd like you to take a look at our murder victims and some of the suspects, ma'am." Kachigan reached into his coat pocket for his evidence book. Helen had whiled away part of their long train ride by sketching not only Osborne and Howards in those rough pages, but also Dettis, Ciocco, Sparenberg, Greer, and Grissaldi. "We know all their names but we're not sure of their—um—political affiliations."

Emma Goldman gave Helen a piercing look. "You have reason to believe they might be anarchists?"

"We don't have definite proof," she said. "But at least one of our murder suspects seems to think so."

"Ah." Goldman bent her head closely over the book, silently scrutinizing the page on which Helen had sketched Lyell Osborne's face. "This man I've never seen before. What is his name?"

"Lyell Osborne," Kachigan said. "He's an electrical engineer with Westinghouse."

"The Westinghouse Electric Company?" Goldman glanced

up alertly. "That is the one headquartered in—oh, what is that odd name? Wilmerding?"

"Yes."

She nodded as if that made sense, but her second glance down at Osborne's portrait was as blank as the first. "I'm afraid I don't know him or his politics," she said, shaking her head. "If he was an anarchist, he wasn't one involved with any of the groups I know."

Kachigan flipped a page to Bonnie Howards. "Was she?"

"An anarchist?" Emma Goldman's eyebrows lifted in quick surprise. "I should say not! That girl doesn't have a political bone in her body!"

Helen pulled in a startled breath. "You know her?"

"Of course." Goldman pinned her with an unexpected frown. "Don't you, Miss Sorby?"

"No."

"Then we're going to have to get you up to New York City to attend professional luncheons more often," the magazine editor declared. "My dear girl, this is one of your most famous fellow journalists. Surely you've heard of Ada Blanche Deems?"

"*What?*" Helen's disbelieving yelp echoed in the empty front office. "Not the investigative journalist from the *New York Herald*? The one who exposed the use of child labor in the cigar sweatshops here in Manhattan last summer?"

"Precisely the one." Goldman tapped a finger on the sketch in the evidence book. "A redhead, right? Tall and busty, with a taste for expensive perfume?"

"Yes." Helen glanced down at the sketch herself, feeling stunned and strangely guilty. "I can't believe I met her and I never knew. . . ."

Goldman snorted. "Well, you can safely discount her as a suspect now, Miss Sorby. Ada would much rather uncover a murder than commit one."

"Perhaps that's what she did," Kachigan said grimly. "Because she's not a suspect, ma'am. She's our second victim."

"Did you believe her?" Kachigan yelled over the subterranean roar of the subway passing beneath their grated corner. They were waiting for the horse-drawn traffic to clear on Seventh Avenue so they could cross and make their way toward Herald Square.

"Believe who?" she shouted back, blowing on her fingers to warm them. Icy winds were scouring the man-made canyons formed by the towering ten-and twenty-story office buildings now that the sun had set. "Ada Deems or Emma Goldman?"

"Goldman." Kachigan spotted a break in the traffic caused by the slow plod of a teamster's wagon and reached out to snag her cold hand, dragging her across the street. He stopped just as abruptly on the other side, when the sweet-scented smoke of a sidewalk chestnut roaster billowed out to engulf them. A nickel flashed in the gaslight, and a moment later Helen was cupping her fingers carefully around a hot paper bag. "She said that none of the people you drew in my evidence book were *active* anarchists. Did you think that means she didn't truly know them?"

Helen opened her mouth to say yes, then paused to reconsider. Emma Goldman's confident voice had never wavered, but there had been an odd expression on her face while she'd glanced through those sketches, not so much of deceit as of internal debate. "No," she said at last. "I think she did know one of them. I'm just not sure which one."

Kachigan grunted and held a hand out. Helen eyed it for a puzzled moment before it occurred to her that he hadn't bought the roasted chestnuts just to keep her fingers warm. She dug out a plump one and dropped it onto his palm.

"Then why didn't she just say so?" Kachigan peeled off the chestnut's thin shell, releasing a drift of sweet aroma into the frigid air. Helen's empty stomach let out a jealous growl. They hadn't eaten anything since their luncheon of club sandwiches on the dining car somewhere in the mountains behind Harrisburg. "She can't be worried that I'll arrest them just for having radical politics."

"Why can't she?" Helen asked curiously.

"Because I'm here with you." The detective shook off the last of the chestnut's papery shell, then handed it back to Helen uneaten. She glanced up in surprise and saw the hidden smile that crinkled the corners of his eyes. Her own traitorous lips curved upward in response before she could stop them. "And we're obviously working together on this case. Aren't we?"

"Yes." Helen had a feeling she was agreeing to more than just an observation about Emma Goldman, but she didn't care. She exchanged the peeled chestnut for another one in its charred shell, then bit into its dry, smoky sweetness. "Maybe she knew one of our suspects, but couldn't tell us how she knew them without revealing secrets that weren't hers to tell. Or maybe one of them used to be an anarchist, but isn't any longer. Miss Goldman's careful about who she involves in her activities ever since a government official got fired just for saying he admired her stand on women's rights."

Kachigan grunted and ate the next chestnut himself. Helen handed him the rest to peel now that her hands were warm again. They were walking along the quieter, residential sidewalks of Thirty-seventh Street, where the crowds had thinned down to an exhausted and homeward-bound trickle. Even from here, though, she could see the gaslit glow of Broadway and hear the echo of bells and holiday music being played by a Salvation Army band on a street corner up ahead.

"How about what Miss Goldman said, about Osborne and Howards—I mean, Deems—not being anarchists. Do you believe that?"

"Yes," Helen said promptly. "She might withhold some information, but she'd never tell an outright lie."

"That's what I thought." Kachigan caught her arm and swung her closer to the brownstone housefronts as a millionaire's fancy carriage rolled past, plumed horses trotting high and throwing out a splatter of mud with patrician nonchalance. "So if Dettis was wrong about Osborne setting those bombs along the tracks, who did do it?"

Helen had been thinking about that ever since they'd left the offices of *Mother Earth*. "The person who stole the trigger design from Westinghouse," she said promptly. "In order to make trouble between him and the Pennsylvania Railroad."

Kachigan gave her a sardonic look as he turned the corner onto Broadway. "That assumes that whoever stole the trigger device wasn't working for the Pennsylvania Railroad in the first place."

She frowned up at him. "Why would they bomb their own lines and locomotives? Just to make Westinghouse Electric look like a nest of anarchists?"

"That does seem a little extreme," he admitted. "And Ciocco did say he was sure Dettis wasn't the one who killed Osborne. But then who did?"

"The person who stole the trigger design from Westinghouse," she said again, impatiently. "Osborne designed that device, Milo. If he found out who stole it from the company, don't you think he'd be likely to confront that person?"

"And force whoever it was to shut him up?" Kachigan nodded thoughtfully. "But then what about Howards? Why was she killed?"

"That depends on what she was sent there to investigate." They had reached Herald Square by then, lit by the bright glow of electric lights in the *New York Herald*'s printing room. It occupied all of the triangular plaza's east side, a vast space open on all sides at the base to let the heat and roar of the presses roll out into the winter night. The closed-in higher floors, where the writing, editing; and layouts got done, were darkened in some places but still glowed brightly in others. "Somewhere in there is a managing editor who can tell us that," Helen said resolutely. "All we have to do is find him."

But what they found, when they walked unchallenged up the building's echoing metal stairs and penetrated the bowels of its city room, was a scatter of reporters tapping two-fingered at their typewriting machines and three grimy press boys flipping cards in the alcove that looked as if it should belong to someone important. "Fortune's gone," said the eldest without even looking up from the game. "Sorry."

For one baffled moment Helen thought he was announcing the status of his gambling debt, but a glance at the nameplate on the desk enlightened her. "Is Mr. Fortune the managing editor?" she asked.

"Yeah." He flipped a ragged red jack down on the floor, to the jeers and hisses of his fellow players. "Come back tomorrow, if you wanna see him. Christmas edition's already to bed."

Helen exchanged frustrated glances with Milo Kachigan.

"Is there any way we can track him down tonight?" the detective asked. "It's about a reporter of his who's been murdered."

That brought all three ink-smudged faces up to stare at him, with the intensity of young men who want to be crack reporters themselves someday. "You a policeman?" asked the eldest, after one shrewd look. "Working on the case?"

"Mm-hmm."

He flexed a card between his fingers, frowning. "Tell me who the reporter was," he said at last. "And I'll tell you where Fortune went for supper. Deal?"

Kachigan gave Helen an inquiring look. She gave him back a vehement head shake, knowing there was no guarantee that the press boy wouldn't run that information straight across town to a rival paper. Being scooped like that would make the managing editor furious with them, and that wouldn't suit her plans at all.

"Sorry, no deal." Kachigan fished out another pair of nickels and tossed them on top of the cards. "How about if I just make your game a little more interesting tonight?"

That got him grins from the two younger boys, although the eldest just looked thwarted and annoyed. "Try Katz's deli, down on Houston Street," one advised. "All the editors eat there on holiday nights."

"Thanks." Helen tugged Kachigan away before he could open his mouth to ask directions and reveal his lack of familiarity with the city. If they realized he was from anywhere farther away than Scarsdale, it wouldn't take the newsboys long to connect him with one of their roving reporters. "I know where that is," she said in response to his irritated look. "And it's too far to walk, so we don't need to know how to get there. We can take a cab."

"Not unless we stop and pawn my watch first," he reminded her.

"I have money." She still had the lunch dollar she hadn't used yesterday. It should be enough to get them to Houston, if not back again. "Come on."

He followed her down to the street obediently, and proved himself adept enough at hailing a New York hansom to win

Helen's admiration. "Katz's Delicatessen, on Houston Street," she told the driver. It must have been a common enough destination in Herald Square—he rattled off the fare and made change for her dollar without ever looking more than half-awake. But he sent his cab horse into a smart enough trot when he was done. Helen sighed and relaxed back into the single seat, content for the moment to watch the passing storefronts with their mix of gaslit and electrical illuminations and their glittering holiday decorations. She didn't even feel moved to give Kachigan more than an obligatory frown when he draped an arm across her shoulders. His warmth felt too good in the open cab to slide away from, and his smiling eyes told her he knew it.

"What are we going to do after we talk to this editor of yours?" he asked. "Sleep on a park bench, or try to find an open settlement house to take us in for the night?"

She winced at the reminder of her abandoned duties in East Pittsburgh. "We're going to get on the express train back to Pittsburgh, that's what we're going to do," she said firmly. "There's one that leaves at ten P.M. and arrives at eight in the morning. It shouldn't be too crowded on Christmas Eve—we can sleep across the cheap seats."

"What's the rush? There's not going to be anybody at Westinghouse to interview tomorrow."

"No, but there's going to be one extremely annoyed aunt on the South Side," Helen informed him. "Pittypat spends the entire month of December preparing for Christmas, Milo. If I miss it, she'll disinherit me." She eyed him curiously. "Won't your dad want you at home, too?"

He shook his head, but he was smiling. "Different calendar. Our Christmas comes two weeks later than yours. My sister probably hasn't even started cooking yet."

"Oh, good," she said without thinking. "Then we can have *two* dinners this year."

That earned her a laugh and a hug that made heat pour into her cheeks despite the icy night wind. "You'll like our holiday food," Kachigan promised. "Sophia makes the best dolma and manty you ever tasted."

"What's that?" Helen asked.

"Stuffed grape leaves and meat dumplings." The cab pulled up in front of a brightly lit but unassuming storefront. No fancy electric lights burned its name through dingy windows, but the constant stream of people in and out of its narrow doors told Helen why the newsmen traveled all this way. She hopped out of the cab before Kachigan could help her down, still embarrassed about the brazen way she'd invited herself to his family's holiday celebration.

When she began to push into the delicatessen's dining room, with its long battered wooden tables, a young boy caught her by the arm and held her back. "Ticket," he said sternly, and waved what looked like a church raffle card under her nose. "You need it to buy, lady."

"Sorry." Helen didn't bother to try explaining that they hadn't come with enough money to buy the food her empty stomach would have liked. She waited for Kachigan to get his own ticket, trying to ignore the smells of corned brisket and roasting sausages that drifted from behind the long service counter. Instead, she glanced across the sea of people eating their sandwiches and pickles and the little dense squares of dough whose name she could never remember, and realized she had no idea what the *Herald*'s managing editor even looked like.

Kachigan solved that problem, by the simple expedient of raising his voice to a beat patrolman's hailing shout. "Fortune here, from the *New York Herald*?"

A tall and loose-boned man, much older and much better dressed than Helen had expected, looked up from a nearby table. The complete lack of interest or reaction from his fellow diners told Helen that summonses like this must be a common occurrence among this crowd of newspapermen and women. "I'm Fortune," he said, and put down his thick pile of pastrami with its minimal framing of bread. "You from another paper?"

"No, from the Allegheny County Detectives Bureau." Kachigan steered Helen through the waiting queues of customers, commandeering two chairs from a nearby table to let them sit across from the silver-haired *Herald* editor. "I have some bad news for you, Mr. Fortune. Ada Blanche Deems—"

"Keep your voice down!" Fortune hissed, before he could even finish the sentence. "Do you want to send ten reporters out of here tonight with garbled stories about her being dead?"

That unexpected comment appeared to rob Kachigan of the power of speech. Helen took a deep breath and stepped into the silent gap. "How did you know—" She saw Fortune's frown swing across to her and lowered her voice to an even slighter whisper. "How did you know she was dead?"

"Is she?" he asked grimly.

"Yes."

The newspaper editor cursed and stared down at his sandwich as if he had no memory of how it had gotten into his well-manicured hands. "I didn't know it, I was just afraid of it. Ada telegraphed her bylines in religiously, especially when she was on an undercover assignment. When day after day went by without a single telegram, I feared the worst."

Helen frowned and opened her mouth, intending to inform the editor that Ada Blanche Deems had died only the previous afternoon. A silent but painful stamp on her toes stopped the words. "Can you tell me what Miss Deems's assignment in Pittsburgh was, Mr. Fortune?" Kachigan asked, pulling out his evidence book. "And confirm that this was her?"

Fortune barely glanced at the picture Helen had drawn, as if Ada's vivacious face was too painful to look at now. "Yes, that's her," he said, frowning. "Can I see your badge, detective? I'd like to know who I'm talking to before I spill my guts out."

Kachigan fished out the brass shield from his pocket and let the newspaper editor scrutinize it. "Milo Kachigan." Fortune's frown deepened. "Why do I know that name?"

"Because I wrote about him in *Collier's*." Helen prudently tucked her feet under the rungs of her chair so they couldn't be trampled again. "It was the cover story last month."

"You're Helen Sorby?" Fortune subjected her to even more stringent scrutiny than he'd given Kachigan's badge. "Did you know Ada in Pittsburgh?"

"Not under her real name," Helen said ruefully. "We worked together as stenographers at Westinghouse. I was there undercover myself, investigating the murder of an electrical engineer," she added, ignoring Kachigan's irritated look.

That elicited a surprisingly bitter laugh from the *Herald* editor. "Christ almighty," he said, shaking his head. "I was just telling a couple of reporters yesterday that these damned undercover assignments were getting so out of hand, we'd have reporters bumping into each other pretty soon. Damned if it didn't happen."

Helen opened her mouth to ask a question. This time, Kachigan silenced her by the simple expedient of dropping a hand onto her knee. Since his squeeze was much too brotherly and painful to be construed as anything but admonition, all she did in return was dislodge it. In any case, he was asking the question she'd intended to ask. "What was Ada Deems investigating at Westinghouse, Mr. Fortune?"

The editor paused to eye Helen, as if she had been the one asking the question. "Industrial espionage," he said at last. "She had a cousin who worked at Westinghouse, and he told her he knew there was a spy in the company selling trade secrets around the world. He just didn't know who it was." Fortune shrugged. "I didn't think it was a great story, but Ada wanted to help her cousin out. And she had a knack of writing good copy, no matter what the subject matter was. Damn, I'm going to miss her."

That was the opening Helen had been waiting for. She took a deep breath and leaned across the table. "Would you be willing to consider me as a temporary replacement, Mr. Fortune? To finish this story and find out exactly why Ada died?"

"No," Kachigan said before the newspaperman could reply. "You are not going back to Westinghouse Electric and that's final. If you try to, I'll blow your cover."

Helen glared at him, but since she'd already blown her own cover by losing her temper so gloriously the previous day, she didn't try to argue with him about the freedom of the press. "All I'm offering to do is write a story about the spying at Westinghouse and how it resulted in Ada's murder," she said instead. "I'm sure *Collier's* or *McClure's* would be glad to buy it from me, but I thought it would be most appropriate for the *Herald* to publish it along with Ada's obituary."

"I agree," Fortune said briskly. "On one condition: none

of your political moralizing, Miss Sorby. Ada always said it was your worst flaw as a writer.''

''I don't—'' She felt more than heard Kachigan start to laugh, and this time it was her foot that came down hard on his. ''Mr. Fortune, sometimes the political ramifications of the events I write about are overwhelming!''

''Then they're also self-evident,'' the editor retorted. ''The *Herald* isn't a socialist paper, Miss Sorby, and I'm not going to let you turn it into one. You'll write about the facts of this case and let the moral speak for itself. Agreed?''

''Agreed,'' she said reluctantly.

''Good.'' He pushed his cold sandwich aside and grabbed up the deli tickets they'd dropped on the table. ''Then let's get ourselves some sweet-potato knishes and talk terms.''

TWENTY-FOUR HOURS LATER KACHIGAN still couldn't decide if the trip to New York had been a success or a fiasco. It wasn't just the lingering stiffness and aching eyes from a vain attempt to sleep on the overnight train back to Pittsburgh. It wasn't the fierce scolding he'd gotten from his father about being gone without explanation for two days, or the fact that he hadn't been able to locate Art Taggart since he'd come home despite hourly telephone calls to his partner's East Pittsburgh flat. And it wasn't even the risk involved in the newspaper assignment that Helen Sorby had so recklessly offered to complete for Ada Blanche Deems. He knew his stubborn investigating partner well enough by now to be resigned to the fact that she couldn't be dragged off a criminal case whether she was being paid to write about it or not.

All of which brought Kachigan right back to the conclusion he hadn't wanted to face. What was bothering him wasn't any of the doubts or dangers associated with this murder investigation. It was the uncomfortable knowledge that in the past two days, he and Helen Sorby had skated daringly close to the edge of real intimacy. And then backed away again.

They were sitting down now to a six-course Christmas dinner, a mixed feast of Irish and Italian dishes that filled Pat MacGregor's haughty Victorian dining room with the surprisingly earthy smells of potatoes, garlic, and fish. Helen's aunt had married into Scottish banking money, but according to her disrespectful nephew Thomas, she never let that stand in the way of a good meal. In working-class Irish fashion, Pittypat insisted on personally handing around the platters of meat and spooning out generous helpings of her many side dishes, while her elderly maid and several remarkably overfed cats stood by and watched in silent disapproval. Helen was on her feet, too, laughing and pouring dark red wine for Milo's father without even a wrinkle of her prohibitionist nose. She moved around to fill her brother's glass as well, then gave Kachigan a surprised look when he put his hand across his.

"Milo, you don't have to drink water at Christmas just to please Aunt Pat." Although Helen seemed to be her usual forthright self, the way her gaze slid past his without ever quite meeting it told him she was feeling the same awkwardness he was. "Thomas convinced her years ago that prohibition doesn't apply to holidays."

"I'm not doing it for your aunt," he said, although that wasn't entirely true. He knew Pat MacGregor had never quite decided if she approved of him associating with her niece, and he doubted their unchaperoned trip to New York City had done much to reassure her. The least he could do was not violate her nondrinking principles in her own house. "I'm doing it because I've got to go back to work tonight."

As he'd expected, that made Helen frown and set the wine decanter down with a thump. "What work? You didn't tell me about any new developments in our case."

"Helen, the freedom of the press doesn't require the police to divulge every detail of their work to you," her brother said sharply.

She opened her mouth to argue with him, but Istvan forestalled him with an inquiring grunt of his own. "What work you do on American Christmas, Milosh?" he asked in the halting English he always used around the Sorby family, as a sign of respect. "No places open to go ask questions, eh? So where you go?"

"Out to East Pittsburgh, to break into Art Taggart's flat," he said, and resigned himself to the reaction that would get.

Surprisingly, it was Pittypat and not Helen who responded. "Surely, it isn't legal to break into someone's home, even if you're a county detective?" she asked, peering at him across a small mountain of mashed potatoes. Helen's aunt was a plump and soft-faced matron with an earnest innocence that fifty years of struggle, success, and social activism somehow hadn't managed to wipe out. "Won't you get into trouble for it?"

"Only if Taggart is in there and objects."

"He may object," Thomas said around a mouthful of bread. "But I can guarantee he won't be in there."

"Why not?"

"Because he's staying over at Essene House with me." Thomas saw the startled look that Kachigan and Helen both turned on him, and shrugged. "Sorry, I was going to tell you, but in all the rush of picking you up at the train station and bringing you here, I forgot. He said Big Roge McGara had threatened to hang him up by his thumbs. I couldn't turn him away."

"Of course not." Helen took the final platter from her aunt and dished a healthy portion of oil-and-garlic spaghetti onto her already loaded plate, then pushed an indignant peach-colored cat off her seat and sat down. It looked as if she were planning to make up for all the meals she'd missed over the last few days, Kachigan thought in amusement. "I'm sure the fact that Taggart plays a mean hand of poker was just an added bonus."

Thomas grinned. "Hey, I needed someone to help keep the tenants in line while you were off having fun in New York City. And we had a room free with Maccoun in jail." He passed the platter of spaghetti along to Kachigan. "If you want to talk to him, Milo, just ring up Ardmore 5-6-2-3."

"*After* supper," his father said sternly, when Kachigan started to get up. "You don't insult Mrs. McGregor by walking away from her dinner table."

"*Thank* you, Mr. Kachigan," Pittypat said with an unexpected smile dancing in her eyes. "It is so nice to see I'm not the only one on the South Side afflicted with utterly manner-less children. Children who cannot be bothered to inform their only surviving aunt when they have been shot at and forced to flee for their lives,'' she added for good measure.

Helen threw her brother an exasperated look. ''I don't know what Thomas told you, Aunt Pat, but we weren't fleeing for our lives. We went to New York to find out who our East Pittsburgh murder victims really were.''

''So you claim.'' Thomas pointed a fork across the table at her. ''I think you just went to eat sweet-potato knishes. Why didn't you think to bring me one back? You know I love them.''

''Because we didn't have enough money between us to hire a cab back to Grand Central Depot,'' his twin sister retorted. ''If it hadn't been for my new editor giving us a ride as far as Herald Square, we'd still be in New York City, starving and sleeping on street corners.''

''Just as long as they were *separate* street corners, dearest,'' Pat MacGregor said, with the earnest gravity that Kachigan was starting to suspect hid a sense of humor as well developed as her nephew's. Thomas burst into laughter, and even Istvan Kachigan grunted his appreciation of that sally. Another twinkle appeared over the bowl of mashed potatoes, confirming Milo's hunch. Pittypat's next words showed that she also shared at least some of her niece's quick intelligence. ''Does this mean you're writing articles for the *New York Herald* now, Helen?''

''Special correspondent from Pittsburgh,'' she admitted, and smiled at her aunt's proud patter of applause. ''Thanks, Aunt Pittypat. But all that means is that I write for them occasionally, to save them the cost of sending a reporter if there's something happening here they want to cover.''

''How on earth are you supposed to send them copy?'' Thomas asked, frowning. ''Even special-delivery mail must be too slow for a paper with daily deadlines.''

''It is. I have to telegraph in my reports.'' She saw his appalled look and laughed. ''Don't worry, I don't have to pay for it. They have a special account with Western Union and the other telegraph lines. If it's an emergency story, they'll actually hire a line just for me to use.'' For the first time since she'd sat down, her dark gaze actually connected across the table with Kachigan's. "That reminds me—why didn't you want my editor to know when Ada Blanche Deems was killed? The fact that he never got a telegram from her while she was alive—"

"Means someone must have been intercepting them," he finished for her. "Probably at the telegraph office she was sending them from, in Pitcairn. In which case, the most likely culprit—"

"Would be Ox Dettis," Helen finished in turn, impatiently. "What's wrong with Mr. Fortune knowing that? I'm going to write about it eventually. No matter who our actual murderer is, the Pennsylvania Railroad is guilty of obstructing justice—"

"And buying enough influence to silence all the local papers." Kachigan lifted his voice to override her protest. "What makes you think the New York papers are going to be any more immune to railroad money than the Pittsburgh papers are? For all you know, Fortune was getting those telegrams from Deems and throwing them right into his wastebasket."

As he'd expected, that made Helen Sorby's face kindle with instant indignation. "Milo, you *can't* accuse the editor of the *New York Herald* of trying to cover up the murder of his star reporter! Why on earth would he have hired me to look into this case if the railroad had paid him to shush it all up?"

"Maybe to set you up for the same fate." Kachigan wasn't sure he really believed that, but he had to admit that even a fierce scowl was better than the awkward avoidance he'd been getting from Helen Sorby. "Fortune certainly didn't seem very surprised to hear about Deems's death, did he?"

"That was because—" She broke off, not because of the repeated chime of a discreet doorbell but because her aunt had deliberately lifted a silver sugar pot and let it crash down onto its silver tray. "What?"

"We are about to have visitors," Pat McGregor informed her. "And as delightful as you two may find it to discuss this murder case with each other in ear-shattering shouts, I really do not think anyone else needs to be subjected to your method of investigation."

The usual olive tint of Helen Sorby's skin turned to dusky

rose, and Kachigan felt his own face heat and tighten with embarrassment. Pittypat gave them a satisfied nod, as if their chagrined silence had been precisely the effect she'd been aiming for, then looked up as her gray-haired maid returned from the front hall alone.

"Our visitor wouldn't come in?" she asked in concern. "I hope the shouts and crashes didn't frighten him off?"

"No, ma'am. He had other telegrams to deliver." The maid smacked an enormous white cat with the paper she held to chase him off the side table, then handed the crumpled missive to her mistress while she went back to her job of guarding the desserts from other feline raiders. Kachigan made a mental note not to have any of the custard pie.

"Bad Snowflake," Pat MacGregor said sternly to the cat, which had sought refuge on her lap. "Snowflake knows he's not allowed on the sideboard."

"Snowflake is deaf," said her impatient niece. "Aunt Pittypat, read your telegram. It must be important, if someone sent it on Christmas Day."

"Oh, dear, that's true. I hope it's not bad news about Cousin Gillan." Pittypat unfolded the telegram and scanned it, then dropped it on the table with a sigh of relief. "Oh, good. It's not for me at all."

"Did it come here by mistake?" Thomas inquired.

"No, dear. It's for your sister."

"What?" Helen snatched up the flimsy paper and read it at much more length than her aunt had. When she was done, she glanced up at Kachigan with a dumbfounded expression, then held the telegram out across the table to him without a word. He took it with a feeling of foreboding, almost afraid to find out what could render Helen Sorby speechless.

EXTREMELY DISTURBED ABOUT ALLEGATIONS OF MURDER AND MALFEASANCE IN EAST PITTSBURGH, the telegram read. HAVE MISS SORBY AND MR. KACHIGAN MEET ME AT HEADQUARTERS TOMORROW, NINE SHARP. ALL CONCERNS WILL BE ADDRESSED.

The name at the bottom was GEORGE WESTINGHOUSE.

"Aunt Pat!" Helen's voice hovered somewhere between a threat and a wail. "What have you done?"

Pat MacGregor looked up from feeding the white cat a shred of ham. "Dearest, you can't expect me to stand by while your life is threatened and do nothing!" she protested. "I knew Mr. Westinghouse would share my concerns. That's why I telegraphed him last night at his country home in the Berkshires."

Kachigan cleared his throat. "How long have you known the Westinghouses socially, Mrs. MacGregor?"

"Ever since George started banking with my husband," she replied. "I can't remember what year that was anymore, but his electric company was just a small warehouse in Garrison Alley then, full of strange gadgets and excited young engineers. He's a marvelous man, don't you think?"

"I wouldn't know, I never met him." Helen managed to look amused and frustrated at once. "Aunt Pat, do you have any idea how much trouble we've gone to trying to find out what's going on down at the Westinghouse Company? Why didn't you tell me that you knew George Westinghouse personally?"

"Dearest, you never asked! How *could* I know what you've been doing? All you ever told me was that you were going to write an undercover article on the conditions of the women workers in the electric factory. I didn't think you'd want Mr. Westinghouse to know about *that*."

"No," Helen admitted.

"So you're not angry with me for sending that telegram?" Pittypat's hazel gaze moved from Helen to Kachigan. "I haven't interfered in one of your clever little traps?"

Kachigan sighed and shook his head. "So far, Mrs. McGregor, all the traps in this case have been set by our murderer." He glanced down at the telegram in his hand, his eyes narrowing in sudden thought. "Of course, now that we have George Westinghouse on our side—"

Thomas pushed back his chair and headed for the sideboard's array of desserts. "I'm not going to dress up like Helen and play bait again," he warned over his shoulder. "My side still hurts from the last time we tried that."

"Don't worry," Kachigan said, both to Thomas and his own father, who had followed enough of the conversation to be staring at his son with intent fire-blue eyes. "None of us is going to play bait this time."

"But you can't have a trap without some bait," Helen Sorby argued. "Who do you propose to use to lure our murderer out? George Westinghouse himself?"

"Not in person," he said, and smiled at her puzzled look. "Given what our murderer seems to be interested in, I think the only thing we'll need to reel him in is one of Westinghouse's electrical gadgets."

George Westinghouse reminded Kachigan of a silver-backed gorilla he'd seen once in a traveling circus. Like the ape, the famous inventor was heavy-chested and long-armed, and he had the same shy tendency to throw quick glances from under his bushy eyebrows, avoiding any prolonged stare. Kachigan didn't take those sidelong looks personally. Westinghouse was known for his modesty—he had a legendary aversion to being photographed and refused to allow any city or town in Pittsburgh to be named for him. The reason Kachigan had always heard was that the mention of his surname in conjunction with the crime and mayhem of a city would embarrass Westinghouse too much. Having now seen the inventor's reticence at first hand, however, Kachigan thought the real answer was much simpler. George Westinghouse just couldn't bear the thought of that much attention focused on himself.

They'd arrived promptly for their appointment at the Westinghouse castle, and were met once again at the door by the discreetly hovering John McCaplin. Instead of leading them up to the well-furnished office Kachigan had expected, however, he took them out of the building entirely and down into the bowels of the air-brake plant itself, into what looked like a small and cramped metal turner's workshop. The bright, expensive glow of its various futuristic electric lightbulbs would have told them that it was the "old man's den," however, even if the hand-painted sign someone had tacked over the door hadn't labeled it in exactly those affectionate terms.

George Westinghouse had greeted them politely but with a minimum of eye contact, then proceeded to jot notes along the margins of his blueprint while they told him everything they knew. Kachigan wasn't sure if the notes were on the murders or on the newest gadget taking shape under the inventor's pencil. Either way, however, there was no question Westinghouse was paying attention. Before Helen could even finish describing their most recent discoveries in New York, a swift but fierce glare silenced her.

"You are not going to turn this into a melodramatic story for the *New York Herald,* young lady. If that's what you came here to do, you can march out right now, no matter whose niece you happen to be."

Helen looked stymied, but only for a moment. "I don't make up my news stories, sir. And you can't stop me from writing that the first murder victim was an electrical engineer who worked in Wilmerding, because that's a fact I can prove in court. Everyone will know what company he worked for, whether I mention your name or not."

"If you don't want to find yourself in a press melodrama, Mr. Westinghouse, the best thing you can do is help us figure out which of your employees is the culprit," Kachigan added. "That way it will be his name that gets splashed across the newspaper headlines, not yours."

The inventor grunted. "It's hard to believe that any of my engineers would do something as underhanded as steal a patent. . . ."

"Or throw a fellow engineer off a train?" Helen inquired. "You're not dealing with an employee filching a little money from the till, Mr. Westinghouse. I think you've got a professional company spy and saboteur hiding in your ranks."

"More made-up melodrama, Miss Sorby?"

She glared at him, undeterred by the fact that he wasn't looking back. "Sir, I didn't make up the bomb that killed Ada Blanche Deems, or the ones that have exploded up and down the tracks in this valley! I didn't make up Lyell Osborne's mutilated corpse. You can ignore all those unpleasant things if you want to, but it's not going to make the spy in your ranks go away. And it's not going to save your company from going bankrupt and putting thousands of men out of work!"

Kachigan saw the jerk of frown under Westinghouse's steel-gray mustache and knew that at least some of Helen's fierce words had sunk in. He took up the thread of the argument when she paused to take a breath. "Sir, what you're doing with your labor force in this valley—eight-hour days, time off for sickness, pension plans for skilled workers—is making other companies around the city very nervous. It's not outside the realm of possibility that someone among them would try to stop you."

"Hmmph." This time, Westinghouse's sidelong look was challenging. "So, just how are you planning to catch this saboteur of yours?"

"We think the best way to lure him would be with another lucrative invention," he said bluntly. "We can leave it in some apparently unguarded spot and see who comes to take the bait."

He could see that Westinghouse looked unconvinced. From the corner of the room where he'd tucked himself in discreet secretarial silence, John McCaplin cleared his throat. "I think that's an excellent idea, sir," he said. "We can leave the invention in your office at the castle, and station a guard in the adjoining conference room—"

Westinghouse gave his private secretary a surprised look. Either he was unaccustomed to getting opinions from him, or like Kachigan, he'd forgotten McCaplin was even there. "We could, I suppose," he said, after a minute. "But you know how much it cost us to lose the patent on Osborne's pressure trigger, John. Can we really afford to risk another invention like that?"

"Um . . . no sir." McCaplin's flash of enthusiasm faded back into his usual secretarial reserve. "Sorry, sir."

"But we *wouldn't* lose it, Mr. Westinghouse," Helen said, giving McCaplin an irritated look. "It'll just be the worm on the hook that lets us reel in the fish."

"Sometimes the fish gets away with that worm," Westinghouse reminded her gruffly. "At least, when I go fishing, he does."

Helen exchanged frustrated looks with Kachigan. "What if we were to use something else beside an invention, then?" he asked, thinking his way through the change in plans even as he outlined it. "Something that could lure our murderer but that he could get away with and still do no harm to the company.''

''Such as?''

Kachigan paused, still unsure of the answer to that. To his surprise and relief, Helen picked up the thread of his proposal as smoothly as if they'd planned it ahead of time. ''Such as the plans that Lyell Osborne drew up for your new hydroelectric plant in Brazil. If the saboteur really wants to destroy your company, stealing those plans would be the best way to do it.''

Both Westinghouse and McCaplin threw startled looks at her. ''But we don't have the Brazilian plans,'' the older man said, frowning. ''Leo says she couldn't find them anywhere in Lyell's desk or files.''

''Does our murderer have to know that?'' Kachigan asked, when Helen seemed stuck on that objection. ''Couldn't we spread the news around the office that Osborne's plans have been located, and just show them a set of rolled blueprints from some other project?''

Westinghouse nodded, looking half-convinced. ''But to make it a believable story, we'd have to say where we found them. And if this—this saboteur of yours has already looked for them in whatever place we say, he'll know we're lying.''

''No, he won't,'' Helen retorted. ''All we have to say is that Osborne hid the plans somewhere on Leo's side of the office. Who would ever think to look in that mess? Or have the time to search it properly?''

Westinghouse let out a series of gorilla deep grunts that kindled into a reluctant roar of laughter. ''True enough, Miss Sorby, true enough. I've known Leo to lose things there and not find them until years afterward.''

''So you'll let us set the trap?'' Kachigan asked.

''On one condition.'' Westinghouse aimed a sidelong scowl at Helen. ''My personal name—or any unnamed reference to me—must not appear anywhere in your newspaper story, Miss Sorby.''

She frowned at him for a long moment and Kachigan had to stifle an urge to kick her ankle to make her agree. ''Not even in association with your new pension plan?'' she asked at last. "You don't want the world to know you were the one who suggested giving your men a company-paid retirement instead of a turkey?"

"How did you know—" Westinghouse caught himself, shaking his head. "I can see why the *New York Herald* decided to hire you, Miss Sorby. You're a damned fine reporter. But the only one I need to have my good deeds reported to is the Lord above, and I don't think He reads the *Herald*."

That drew a reluctant smile from her. "Very well. I'll attribute the decision to 'officials high-placed in the Westinghouse Companies.' Is that vague enough for you?"

"It will suffice." Westinghouse rolled his half-finished blueprint up with a decisive snap and handed it to McCaplin. "There, John. Go and tell Leo to pretend she just found the Brazilian plans in her office—"

"No," said Kachigan and Helen simultaneously.

The old man blinked at them, startled for once into a direct glance. "What's wrong with that?"

"The fewer people who know about this plan, the better," Kachigan told him.

"But surely you don't distrust Leo! She's been with me since 1878. . . ."

"If we knew who to mistrust," Helen said impatiently, "we wouldn't need to set this trap in the first place."

"And whoever our culprit is, he's not stupid," Kachigan added. "If even one person acts in an unnatural fashion, he'll be warned not to take the bait."

Westinghouse grimaced. "Then maybe I should just stay hidden down here all day—"

"That might be best." Kachigan glanced back at McCaplin, noticing that the private secretary somehow had the ability to efface himself even when he was standing in the middle of the room. "Do you think you can act naturally enough to tell Miss Grissaldi that you found the Brazilian plans in her office early this morning? If she asks, you can say that Osborne left a note for Mr. Westinghouse telling him the exact location."

Quick intelligence and amusement flashed to life again in the younger man's eyes. "I think I can manage that, sir. After all, Dr. Grissaldi won't expect me to know any of the specific details about the blueprints, as another engineer might."

"She also won't expect you to dance for joy and sing about the project being saved," Westinghouse said gruffly. "But don't be surprised if *she* does, John."

"Sir, nothing Leo does surprises me." McCaplin's smile was as discreet and polished as all his other manners. "And that will certainly have the desired effect of spreading the word about the plans resurfacing."

"You'll have to tell Leo that Mr. Westinghouse wants to approve the plans before she starts working on them," Helen warned him. "Otherwise she'll tear them out of your hands and the game will be up."

"Good point," Westinghouse agreed. "And then where do we set your trap, Mr. Kachigan?"

He'd been thinking over the timing and placement of the bait while they'd been talking. "With your permission, sir, I think the suggestion of your office would be best." He looked back at McCaplin. "During the day, you'll have to guard them yourself. At night, I'll come in with my partner, Art Taggart, and take over." He saw his other investigating partner scowl and hastily added, "And on the weekends, Miss Sorby and her brother can relieve us."

All that accomplished was to make George Westinghouse scowl at him instead of Helen. "How long do you think this trap is going to sit before our mouse nibbles the cheese?"

"I don't know, sir. Is there a time limit?"

He snorted. "How long do you think it takes me to look over blueprints, Mr. Kachigan? And I can't stay puttering down here forever, much as I might like to." The inventor shot a sheepish look at his secretary. "I've got meetings scheduled all week with bankers and investors, not to mention a bunch of planning sessions with my engineers. And Friday is the last full working day of the year."

Westinghouse said it as if the significance should be obvious, but a look at Helen Sorby's puzzled face didn't enlighten Kachigan. "Is that important?"

"Of course it's important! It's the day I hand out gold watches to my retiring Airbrake workers, and announce that they'll be the first of my men to get pensions." He gave Helen

Sorby a sardonic sidelong glance. "I expect the press will want to be there in the office to cover it."

She opened her mouth to answer him, but two gentle raps on the workshop's door interrupted her. "Mr. Westinghouse, that mold you wanted to adjust came back from the foundry this morning," said a deferential voice. "I've got it out in the yard, cleaned and ready to work on."

"All right, Frank. I'll be right out." Westinghouse stood up, reaching for his coat. "My assistant calls. Are we done here, ladies and gentlemen?"

"I think so." Kachigan helped Helen put on her borrowed beaver coat, wondering why she suddenly looked so uncomfortable in it. "Will five P.M. be a good time to take over guard duty from you, McCaplin?"

"Make it a little later," the secretary suggested. "That way the crowds of workers will all be gone. I don't mind staying late."

"Good enough." For some reason, Helen had suddenly been afflicted with an unusual attack of fussing with her muff. Westinghouse waited politely for a moment, then sighed and went out through the door McCaplin had held open for her. A moment later they heard his deep voice talking to someone in the yard. The sound dwindled into the surrounding din of the busy air-brake plant.

"Is something wrong, Miss Sorby?" McCaplin inquired, after another moment of waiting.

"I can't seem to find my gloves—oh, there they are. I was afraid I'd dropped them." Helen's eyes stayed fixed on her muff, a sure sign to Kachigan that she was lying through her teeth. "I'm sorry for holding you up. We can go now."

"Can we?" Kachigan tucked her arm through his, pulling her close enough to earn an indignant glare. He ignored it, letting McCaplin go ahead of them and dropping his mouth to hiss, "What's wrong?" in her ear as soon as the secretary's back was turned.

Helen shook her head, evidently not trusting her too-loud voice enough to answer. Whatever she'd noticed in the Air-brake, she clearly wanted to put distance between herself and it now. Kachigan had to take the stairs up to Station Street

two at a time to keep up with her. "Trolley to catch," he said
over his shoulder to John McCaplin, and left the secretary
blinking at the edge of the Westinghouse Castle lawn.

Helen made it halfway down the block before she erupted.
To Kachigan's surprise, what came out was a breathless sigh
of relief. "Thank God, I don't think he noticed us—"

"Who?" he demanded. "Westinghouse?"

"No, of course not." She gave him an impatient look.
"Didn't you recognize his voice back there, when he called
through the door?"

"Recognize whose voice . . . ?" Kachigan's own voice
trailed off as a tardy memory sparked awake in his brain. So
much had happened since that snowy night in Pitcairn, he
hadn't even recognized the name when he'd heard it. "Oh,
my God. Westinghouse's shop assistant is Frank Robinson!"

"That's right. And the last thing I wanted him to see was
me in Bonnie's coat." Helen glanced down at the silky beaver
fur and winced. "Well, at least now we know why she was
dating him. He must have been the one Lyell Osborne suspected of stealing the company's secrets."

15

PATIENCE HAD NEVER BEEN ONE OF HE-
len's outstanding virtues, but she tended
to be especially deficient in it during the
winter holidays. As a child, she'd chafed
at the days that separated Thanksgiving
from Christmas, Christmas from New Year's Day, wishing all
those joyful feasts could somehow be made to come together
in a bunch for maximum enjoyment. Later, after her parents
had died of typhoid and the holidays had become things to
endure rather than enjoy, her impatience turned in a different
direction. From them on she had wished that the holiday season could somehow be hurried through to its end so she could
return to the normal, daily life that didn't remind her so much
of what she'd lost. But this year, for the first time in nearly a
decade, Helen couldn't remember feeling that particular sense
of urgency.

Instead, all she remembered feeling was irritation at Milo
Kachigan: first for disappearing after his unexplained arrest,
then for reappearing only to clash with her over Abraham
Maccoun's imprisonment and the investigation into Lyell Osborne's murder. Despite their day trip to New York, a space
of time that in retrospect seemed more than ever to have been
wrapped in some inexplicable fairy spell, Helen found herself
on the day after Christmas more irritated with the county detective than ever. It was just like him to set a perfect trap for

their murderer and exclude her from it from the start.

"I thought you said we were going to be there on the weekends," her brother protested, cutting short her diatribe on the subject over their Tuesday supper. "What's wrong with that?"

"What's wrong with it is that it's four days from now!" she said, aggrieved. "And if this trap's going to spring at all, it'll happen soon. George Westinghouse said himself that it shouldn't take him long to look over those electric-plant plans, if that were what he was really doing. Our spy has to know that, too. He'll make his move tonight or tomorrow, watch and see."

Thomas reached for the last slice of apple strudel. Art Taggart had contributed the dessert to the settlement-house luncheon that day, in repayment for the sanctuary they'd granted him. He'd continued munching on it for the rest of the afternoon, looking remarkably sleepy and at ease for a man under a death threat. The only reason any was left at all was because Kachigan had arrived to haul his partner off for guard duty at five that afternoon, leaving Helen to glower after them in stymied silence.

"Why don't you go back to work at Westinghouse tomorrow if you want to be on hand for the finale?" Thomas asked, wiping crumbs from his beard. "You've only missed one day from work, and you can honestly say that was for traveling back from your Christmas holidays."

"No, I can't," Helen said gloomily. "Before I left work on Saturday, I had an argument with the office manager."

"Of course you did." Her twin brother rolled his eyes. "What was it about?"

"The fact that he confiscated my personal fountain pen and accused me of stealing it." Relict indignation bubbled up inside her at that memory. "Thomas, it's *disgusting* how secretaries are treated in a big company like that! As if they weren't even human, just mindless machines that couldn't be trusted to know their own names, much less lead worthwhile lives outside of work!"

He gave her a perceptive look. "I can see you're going to write an article about that."

"Yes, I am." Helen tapped her fork absently on her empty

bowl, then realized she had drawn the attention of her entire tableful of tenants without meaning to. Seeing their row of expectant eyes, she hurriedly cast about for something to announce. "I want to thank you all for your help in tracking down the man who was found dead in our backyard. Thanks to you, we now know exactly who he was and what he was doing on the night he died."

Molly grinned back at her, clearly knowing that the credit was mostly hers. "What about that lady who blew up in Pitcairn last week, ma'am?" she asked. "Was she a murder victim, too?"

"Yes, she was," Helen confirmed. "Her name was Ada Blanche Deems, and she was a newspaper reporter from New York City."

To her surprise, that news bought her a chorus of disbelieving hoots and whistles from around the table. "I wouldn't be too sure about that, ma'am," said the older Buchak boy around his after-dinner toothpick. "I heard that particular skirt was nothin' but a flimflam girl."

"She made her living by getting engaged to a passel of fools up and down the valley," added his younger and slightly more literate brother. "It said so in the *Westinghouse Valley News*."

"What?" Helen demanded.

"Here, I'll show you." Molly Slade jumped up from the table, still butterfly quick despite her bulging belly. She came flitting back from the foyer with a newspaper held at arm's length from her green satin dress. Despite the muddy footprints left by someone's drying boots, the headline of OBITUARIES was still readable. "See there, ma'am."

Helen frowned over the smeared typeface for a while. "Well?" her brother demanded from across the table. "Can you read it?"

" 'A young woman residing in Pitcairn died yesterday of burns suffered during a gas-grate explosion—' " Helen broke off, shaking her head. "That's a lie right there. Ada was killed by a bomb, not an accidental explosion. 'Strangely, it wasn't until after her death that she was discovered to have been engaged to two completely different men. Frank Robinson, of Trafford City, first identified her as his fiancée, Bessie Harris'—that's true enough—'while Alexander Erskine Greer of Wilmerding identified her as Miss Bonnie Howards, a co-worker and also his affianced bride.' '' Helen glanced up at her brother with a frown. "That can't be right, either. She never said a word to me about being engaged to Alexander Greer. Do you think he could be lying?"

Thomas snorted. "Oh, sure. Who wouldn't want to be known all over the valley as the fiancé of a flimflam girl?"

"Then Greer must have been another of the men Lyell Osborne suspected of stealing his trigger device. Ada would *never* have gone out with him otherwise."

There must have been enough repugnance in her voice to catch even her oblivious brother's attention. "What did Greer do to you?" he asked, frowning.

"Annoyed me," Helen said shortly, and returned to the obituary before he could ask any more questions. " 'There is some reason to believe that the young woman's place of birth may have been Baltimore, although other friends believed her to have lived more recently in New York City. An officer of the Pennsylvania Railroad police in Pitcairn identified her as the well-known confidence artist Ada Blanche Deems—' '' Helen's voice scaled upward so fiercely that the Buchaks both cursed and Molly nearly fell off her chair. "*Affangole!* Ox Dettis *was* reading all her telegrams!"

Annoyingly, her twin brother's only reaction to that news was to grin and tsk at her in imitation of their easily offended aunt. "Helen, dearest, *such* language—"

"Thomas, this isn't funny." Helen glared at him. "Don't you see, this makes it more likely than ever that Dettis is the one who had Ada and Osborne killed?"

"So? You had already suspected him, hadn't you?" Thomas absentmindedly began to gather up the dirty dishes, although that was supposed to be the Buchaks' assigned task. "Now all you'll need to do is to catch him red-handed in Kachigan's trap."

"*Capo tosta!*" She threw the newspaper across the table, startling the Buchaks into hurried action. Helen barely noticed, since what she had been aiming at was her brother's obtuse head. The rest of the tenants, alarmed by the vehemence in her voice whether or not they understood the words, beat a hasty retreat for the back parlor. "How are we supposed to do that when Dettis doesn't even know those plans exist?"

Thomas frowned at her across the empty table. "You don't think he has an inside man working somewhere at Westinghouse?"

"He might have ten of them, for all we know, but there's no way we can be sure he'll hear what we want him to hear about this—" She broke off, her eyes narrowing in swift calculation. "Unless I'm the one who tells him," she finished with determination.

"Oh, no." Thomas's frown grew blacker. "Helen, there is no way I'm going to let you go talk to a man who almost got you killed last Saturday. We'd *both* wind up dead, because even if Aunt Pittypat didn't kill me for it, I'm damned sure Kachigan would."

Helen laughed and shook her head. "No, Thomas, this is perfect! I don't have to see Dettis at all—I just need to send one of the tenants up to the Pitcairn telegraph office with a dispatch addressed to the *Herald,* telling them that the crucial plans for the hydroelectric plant have been found." She gave him a look of dancing amusement. "And that they'll be shipped out to the Brazilian field office first thing tomorrow!"

Her brother might be unobservant, but he wasn't a complete dunce. "You want to force Dettis to tip his hand tonight," he said after only a few seconds of thought. "Why?"

"So I can be there to report on it, of course." Helen pulled her battered old steel fountain pen out of her pocket and began composing her telegram on the unrolled brown grocery paper that served them for a tablecloth. "Now all we need to do is think up an excuse to join Milo at the castle."

"There's always food," Thomas pointed out, practical as ever. "They're going to get hungry staying up all night, unless Kachigan lets Taggart talk him into buying some supper on their way to Wilmerding."

"Just because they were facing a twelve-hour shift of guard duty?" Helen snorted. "Don't be silly, Thomas. Start wrapping the leftovers."

•   •   •

Food or no food, Kachigan wasn't pleased to see her.

"How did you get in here?" he demanded in a whisper that somehow managed to lose none of its ferocity for being so soundless. The small third-floor conference room that adjoined Westinghouse's private office was swathed in silence as thick as its velvet drapes and Oriental carpet. Helen could even hear the ticking of the Westinghouse tower clock, all the way from the opposite end of the building.

"Ladies'-room window." She was careful to make her own voice a murmur, but she still heard Taggart shush her from the other end of the room. "Thomas boosted me up," she added, this time mouthing the words rather than saying them. "I came through the secretaries' office and up the backstairs."

Kachigan's scowl didn't diminish. "Did anyone see you?"

She shook her head and held out a grocery bag full of bread and pasta fagioli in mute apology. "Supper," she said simply.

He opened his mouth, doubtless to say he didn't want any, but the noisy growl of his stomach contradicted him. The detective grimaced and took the bag from her, opening it to release a redolent scent of simmered potatoes, beans, and pasta. In the intense silence, Helen heard Taggart's sigh of relief all the way across the room. Heavy footsteps came to join them.

"Bless you, Miss Sorby." His lazy gray eyes glittered at her in the darkness. The only light was the distant glow of an electric bulb in its green shade, apparently always left burning on Westinghouse's desk. "How'd you guess we hadn't eaten?"

"Milo never does."

Taggart's grunt of laughter managed to be even quieter than her answer, although the rustle of paper he made taking out the top loaf of bread made Kachigan scowl again. "Where's the soup?"

"Inside the bread loaves. I had Thomas hollow them out, because I was afraid china bowls would clink."

That got her an admiring look from the detective. "Smart girl you've got there, Milo."

"Too smart," said his partner grimly. "All right, Helen. What have you done?"

She threw him a guilty look, startled by his perceptiveness.

"Just stopped long enough to steal my good fountain pen back from the office manager's desk. He can't complain, he never had the right to take it—"

It was Kachigan's turn to shush her indignant voice, this time by the simple expedient of stepping closer and clapping a silent hand across her lips. "You wouldn't have come tonight unless you knew for sure that those blueprints were going to be stolen," he hissed in her ear. "How did you manage that?"

Helen grimaced against his palm, resisting the urge to bite it, and instead startled a grunt out of him by slipping a hand into his coat. She felt the quickened beat of his heart under her questing fingers before she found the inner pocket and extracted his evidence book. Kachigan's burst of exhaled breath stirred her hair, but Helen was too busy uncapping her newly-retrieved fountain pen and looking for a blank page to notice what emotion he was stifling.

Telegram, she scribbled with the blessedly smooth gold nib. *Sent Pitcairn office, for Dettis to read. Blueprints to go Brazil tomorrow.*

He must have understood the jerky words, for she could feel the quick rise and fall of comprehension in his breath. "You're sure he'll catch it?"

Helen nodded and reached into her own coat pocket this time, bringing out the damp scrap she had torn from the *Westinghouse Valley Times.* Kachigan squinted at the obituary in the uncertain light. He must have made enough out of it to agree with her. His hand fell away from her mouth and he stepped back, reaching for the second loaf of bread inside her bag.

"All right, you can stay."

"Thanks." Helen shed her beaver coat in a silken swish of sound. She'd worn her oldest and softest cotton dress beneath it, not wanting any rustle of stiff cloth to warn their quarry. The creak of a floorboard overhead caught her abrupt attention, but it was followed by the puzzling sound of repeated tapping rather than moving footsteps. It wasn't until she heard the distant crackle of electricity that she realized it was the noise of an engineer working late in the office overhead.

"How late does the building stay open?" she asked Kachigan, sitting on the couch beside him as he dug into his pasta fagioli. Taggart had already gone back to his post beside the half-opened door to Westinghouse's private office.

"To anyone on staff, as late as they want." Kachigan tore off a thin piece of bread crust and used it to scoop up the thick soup, as expertly as if it were one of his flat Armenian bread rounds. Helen didn't see any point in telling him that she had brought spoons. "The outside guard has standing orders to let them in, night or day. I guess inventions can't always wait for regular work hours."

"So our culprit could already be in the building?"

He nodded. "Unless it's Dettis himself. He'll have to break in."

"Or take out the guard."

"Mm."

Helen fell silent, thinking over all the possibilities. The tower clock ticked steadily through the silence, annoying her with its ability to speak freely when she couldn't. After a moment she opened Kachigan's evidence book again, turning to the back of the page she'd already covered with her slanting hand.

Main suspects, she wrote. And then after that: *Dettis, Robinson, Greer.*

Kachigan made no noise when she showed the page to him, but he leaned close enough to tap a finger beside the third name. "Why him and not any of the engineers?" he asked, his voice barely more than a breath in her ear.

In answer, Helen waved the obituary in front of him again. *Engaged to Ada,* she wrote in the evidence book under both Greer and Robinson's name. Under Dettis's, she put *read telegrams, wants us dead.*

Kachigan set his half-empty bread bowl aside and took the fountain pen from her. *Machined Osborne's first trigger,* he wrote under Robinson's name, with his usual painstaking care. Helen lifted an eyebrow at that. While she'd spent the rest of her day reestablishing her command of Essene Settlement House, he must have been questioning Airbrake workers. Under Dettis, he wrote *had triggers from defused bombs.*

Helen nodded and took back the pen. *Made bad contract for G.W. in Brazil,* she added under Greer's name.

"That's all evidence," Kachigan said softly in her ear. "What about motive?"

Helen frowned. Dettis was easiest—she wrote *labor problems* and put an exclamation point after it. For Greer, she put *ambitious and unprincipled,* but Robinson made her pause. From the little she'd seen of the grief-stricken machinist, he seemed nothing if not sincere. *Blackmail,* she wrote, with a question mark. *Bribery?* And then after a moment of wild speculation, *anarchy?*

The fountain pen was rudely jerked from her hand before she could continue. Helen lifted her face to protest, but Kachigan's attention was no longer focused on her. With a minimum of silent motion, he was now poised and staring at the connecting door to Westinghouse's office. Helen couldn't hear anything, but through the portion deliberately left ajar, she could see that the electric glow of the desk lamp had brightened noticeably, as if someone had adjusted the shade. A moment later she heard the scrape of a drawer being pulled open and felt her pulse start to beat up in her throat.

Kachigan left her side in surprising silence, somehow managing not only to muffle his footsteps but also avoid creaking the floorboards under his feet. A moment later his slim shadow darkened the glow from the door. Taggart's larger silhouette, already within range of the private office, never moved, but Helen could see the alertness that stiffened his broad shoulders and lifted his head.

"Now," Kachigan said quietly.

The slam of the connecting door, loud as a gunshot in the silence, made Helen jump and scream in reflexive surprise. Fortunately, the sound was lost in an uproar of shouts, thumps, and then the crash of bodies falling to the floor. She leaped to her own feet and ran to the open door, although caution and a vivid memory of her brother's scuffles with his neighborhood gang kept her positioned well to one side in case one of the combatants hurtled through.

She couldn't see much—the desk lamp had apparently been one of the first casualties—but she could hear the ragged gasping of someone whose breath has been knocked out of them, momentarily drowned out by the solid clank of metal handcuffs being locked around someone else's wrists. Helen frowned and ran an exploratory hand across the wood-paneled wall she was clinging to. When she found nothing, she edged farther into the marble-linteled doorway and checked the wall on the other side. This time her search was rewarded with the cold jut of a thin metal toggle between her fingers. She clicked it to the opposite setting, and a bluish glow of electricity sprang to life in the overhead fixtures.

The first thing she saw was Milo Kachigan, leaning against the expensively curved glass windows that fronted Westinghouse's private office and looking annoyed rather than pained by the trickle of blood dripping off his chin. The shards of spherical glass around his feet informed Helen that the shattered vacuum bulb from the desk lamp hadn't met its fate passively. And Kachigan wasn't the only victim it had claimed. A curse from the other side of the desk drew her startled gaze to a face that could have adorned an Arrow collar advertisement, if it hadn't been for the handful of razor-sharp cuts now incised into one clean-cut cheek.

"Greer!"

The Westinghouse salesman gave her a ferocious scowl. "What are *you* doing here?" he demanded, looking more put out by her presence than by the massive iron handcuffs Taggart had just finished locking around his wrists. "Is this some kind of ambush for a muckraking newspaper story?"

"This is—" Kachigan had to stop to drag another breath into his compressed lungs before he could muster enough air to finish the sentence. "This is an arrest, Mr. Greer."

"For what?" The young man's natural arrogance was seeping back into him at about the same rate as the detective's breath. "I have the right to be in this building—"

"But not in this office," Art Taggart said, sounding amused. "And you definitely don't have the right to be rummaging around in your boss's desk drawers at nine o'clock at night."

Greer favored them with what he probably considered a charming manly smile. "Yeah, so I stretched the rules a little. But hell, I'm the one who's got to go back and convince the

Brazilian government to wait an extra six months for our hydroelectric plant instead of jumping ship to Edison. I don't know how the goddamned engineers think I'm supposed to do that when they won't even let me look at the plans before they ship them down to the field office—"

Helen's breath caught in her throat. "You thought—I mean, you knew that the Brazilian plans were being sent away tomorrow?"

A little of Greer's self-confident smugness slipped away, leaving his face better looking in its absence. "Well, it wasn't any big secret. Was it?"

Kachigan's gaze met Helen's across the width of the turret office, mutual comprehension sparking between them swift and electric as the current running through a filament. His nod at her may have been due to lingering breathlessness, but she thought it more likely acknowledged the fact that the trap they'd just caught Alexander Erskine Greer in was the one she had designed herself.

"Actually, Mr. Greer," she said sweetly, "it *was* a secret. Only one man knew—or thought he knew—when those plans were being sent away. And if Ox Dettis told you, that means that you must be working for him."

Kachigan straightened away from the wall, still oblivious to the blood that had trickled down his neck to stain his collar. "What's the going rate for company spies these days, Greer? Shares of railroad stock or just a straight commission on stolen patents?"

There was a long moment of silence, during which Helen could see the expression on Greer's face change from bluster to surprise to mulish defiance. As far as she could tell, guilt never even touched the edges of it. "None of your business," he snarled at last, all pretense of charm fading from voice and face. "You can't arrest me for something you can't prove!"

"Is that right?" Kachigan directed a sardonic look past Greer at his partner. "And here I thought a county detective could arrest anyone he wanted for no reason at all, providing he hadn't been paid not to."

Taggart gave him back a thin slice of smile. "Nice to see you finally figured out the system, Milo. McGara will be proud." He gave a jerk on Greer's joined wrist cuffs. "Come on, you. Let's go downtown."

Helen bit down hard on her lower lip and darted back into the conference room to get her coat, restraining the automatic jerk of protest that any illegal action kicked alive in her. Even a dedicated social reformer could tell when pressure was being applied to crack through a suspect's bluff and bluster. Unfortunately, she wasn't sure Alexander Erskine Greer had much hidden under his Arrow-collar exterior except stupidity.

The salesman proved her right by making the castle's fancy wrought-iron elevator cage echo all the way to the first floor with curses that would have done a teamster proud, followed by sullen adolescent silence as they passed through the revolving wood-framed door and out into the bitterly cold night. The snow from two days before still blanketed Wilmerding's buildings and lawns, although it now wore an ash-gray cloak of train soot and smoke from the air-brake plant. Helen felt her feet crunch on the icy crust of dirt and frost, and deliberately let herself lag three paces behind the captured man so that if she slipped, she couldn't create an opportunity for him to escape. For once, Kachigan didn't even try to take her arm and steady her. Instead, he took a position on Greer's other side, flanking the salesman to ensure that he couldn't cut and run. There were far too many trains rumbling up and down the valley to make his recapture certain. Or even safe.

"You sure you want to spend the rest of your life in jail, Alex?" Kachigan asked while they walked past the darkened storefronts of Commerce Street. "No more whiskey, no more cigars, no more women . . ."

"Quit wasting your breath, Milo," Taggart said, swinging onto Station Street and heading for the dim glow of the empty trolley station. "Let's just take this jackass down to the county jail and let Big Roge put the thumbscrews on him tomorrow to get confessions for your murders."

"Murders?" In the snow-brightened reflection of the Air-brake lights, Helen could see Greer's eyes suddenly widen with real anxiety. "You're going to blame Osborne's death on *me*?"

It wasn't the fear in his voice that caught Helen's attention as much as the sheer, self-centered disbelief. Greer had seemed resigned enough about being caught stealing for Ox Dettis, but he clearly hadn't expected his corporate crime to lead to a far more serious accusation. That was due to stupidity on his part, she thought. Or, hard as it was to accept it, perhaps real innocence.

"Osborne *and* Deems." Kachigan pushed his prisoner up onto the trolley platform, then ticked the points off on his fingers while they waited for the next car to arrive. "You had the motive to kill them, to keep Westinghouse from finding out about your little side-job with the railroad. And Dettis gave you the means—an old Westinghouse car to fool Lyell Osborne into boarding, an unexploded anarchist bomb to set in your two-timing fiancée's fireplace—"

"No!" Greer protested. "I never even knew she was dead until I saw the funeral notice! And as for Osborne—" He shook his head so vehemently that his fair hair whipped around in mussed disarray. "That wasn't me. That wasn't even Dettis!"

"A likely story," Helen said in disdain.

"No, Miss Sorby. An unlikely one." A silhouette came up the iron stairs that connected the elevated trolley station with the train depot in the valley below. Even in the shadowed winter night, Helen could see the sullen brick-red cast of that bald profile. "But if you'll follow me back down to my private car, I think I can convince you that it's still true."

"Do we have a choice, Ox?" Kachigan asked, in a voice that had turned almost as cold as the wind blasting down the valley.

A gun barrel lifted, reflecting back the overhead glow of gaslight. With a mixture of anger and resignation, Helen saw that it was aiming directly toward her.

"Afraid not," said O. X. Dettis.

16

IF THE GUN HAD BEEN POINTED AT ANYbody else, Kachigan would have tried jumping Dettis then and there. But it was trained unwaveringly at Helen Sorby, and even if she'd been willing to risk being shot at, Kachigan didn't think he could summon the resolution to attack. Even now, the cold clench of fear in his gut kept distracting him, although the logical part of his mind insisted this was the best time to attack. Once they got onto that train car, Dettis would hold all the cards—and this time, there wouldn't be a stick of dynamite lurking under a switch plate somewhere down the line to rescue them.

"Milo, I'm sorry." Helen sounded far more disgusted with herself than afraid. For some reason, that made his own fear diminish. "You were right not to want me here tonight."

Dettis let out an unexpected honk of laughter. "Mark the date on your calendar, Kachigan. That's the last time you'll ever hear a woman apologize to you." A distant clatter and spark drifted across from the far end of the trestle bridge, spurring the railroad boss to cross the trolley platform. His gait was marred by a noticeable limp, one Kachigan didn't remember him having. Their last encounter had apparently left Ox Dettis with more than just a bad taste in his mouth. "Come on, Miss Sorby. You show the boys the way down to the train station." He took her arm, not politely but in a businesslike grip above the elbow, just like the one Kachigan had on Greer. "I think they'll be smart enough to follow us, don't you?"

She scowled at him, but knew better than to argue with a loaded gun. Kachigan exchanged frustrated glances with Taggart, then shoved Alexander Erskine Greer after his covert employer. "Come on, let's go."

Despite his cuffed hands and bloody cheek, the Westinghouse salesman gave him another of his annoyingly smug smiles. The combination of stupidity and arrogance in that magazine-pretty face made the shard of metal buried in Kachigan's cheek ache with pain from his gritted teeth. "Not as smart as you thought you were, huh, detective?"

"Still smarter than you," Taggart said, and shoved him ruthlessly down the iron steps ahead of them. From then on, Greer was too busy trying to keep his balance to spout any more irritating comments. Under the cover of his panicked, clattering footsteps, the big man asked, "Want to make a grab at the train door?"

Kachigan shook his head. "Not unless Helen tries to break away and it looks like Dettis will shoot her." His brain was thrumming with ideas again, now that the mindless clamp of fear had lifted. "We should be able to use the emergency air brake—"

"All aboard," Dettis said, stopping at the back door of another private railroad car. This one, however, gleamed with polished chrome fittings and a freshly painted Pennsylvania Railroad insignia on the back. Only a single railroad guard stood beside it on the platform, and Kachigan frowned at that seeming carelessness. Given the fact that they'd escaped him once before, he wouldn't have expected Ox Dettis to treat them so cavalierly.

Helen must have noticed it, too. She paused on the gaslit platform, glancing back over her shoulder with an obvious question in her dark eyes. Before Kachigan could shake his head at her, however, Dettis had swept one arm around her waist and hefted her bodily up the three steps and into the private car. Despite his short stature and balding red head, the railroad boss must have had the strength of the animal he was nicknamed after. Kachigan knew how strong Helen was, and that she'd been resisting that transfer the whole time.

"Come on," he said grimly to Taggart, and shoved Greer toward the waiting train. Wisps of steam were already rising from the train bed in the cold winter night, the usual sign that the locomotive was firing up its boilers and getting ready to depart. He saw the platform guard give a hand signal to the engineer even before he'd pushed Greer onto the steps, and the small train started with a jerk while Kachigan was waiting to climb in after him. He shoved Greer up with a ruthless hand and swung himself aboard, hearing the heavy thunder of Taggart's shoes on the platform behind him. He turned and held out a hand to the other detective, hauling him onto the bottom step with a grunt of effort.

"About time you boys boarded," Ox Dettis mocked, when they finally climbed the steps to the lavishly upholstered sitting room that made up half of the train car. Electric lights threw a magnificent glow over the leather seats and brocade curtains, the polished mahogany trim and brass fixtures. "You should learn to listen to your conductor."

"Where are you taking us this time?" Helen Sorby demanded fiercely. To Kachigan's relief, he saw that she had managed to pull free of Dettis's grip and was sitting as far from him as she could get, although the railroad boss's pistol still casually pointed in her direction. The gap between them left plenty of room for Kachigan to block a bullet with his body. Or even better, with Alexander Erskine Greer's body. "Are you going to throw us in the Turtle Creek this time?"

"Only if you keep asking me annoying questions." Dettis switched his glare to Kachigan. "Stop staring at me with that blood drooled down your face, county boy. You look like a rabid dog. Go sit down with your girlfriend while Fat Art takes those handcuffs off my boy Alex."

Greer's smile was a little one-sided now from the blood that had dried on his cut face, but it still managed to look infuriatingly smug. "Thanks, Mr. Dettis. I knew you wouldn't let me down."

The railroad boss grunted and pocketed his gun, limping around the car's small bar to pour himself a drink. Kachigan frowned and went to sit beside Helen, more puzzled than ever

by this careless behavior. There wasn't a single guard stationed
inside the car, and even though Greer was now rubbing at his
freed wrists, he doubted the salesman's masculine arrogance
would actually translate into much use during a fight. Taggart
had gone to lean in the opposite corner, his lazy stance belying
the questioning glint of his gray eyes when they met Kachigan's. And even though a small cold hand had crept into his
under the cover of Helen's borrowed beaver coat, the expression on her strong-boned face looked far more bewildered than
anxious.

"So why did you—" She gave Kachigan an indignant look
when he squeezed her fingers, but broke off obediently
enough. From behind the bar, Dettis tossed back his shot of
whiskey and snorted at them in amusement. Outside, the passing lights of the East Pittsburgh Valley flashed more sluggishly
through the windows of the train and a tug of inertia told
Kachigan they were slowing even before he heard the hiss of
the air brakes under the train. His frown deepened. His tentative escape plan had depended on the assumption that the
train would be traveling at high speed for a while. There
wasn't much emergency brakes could do to startle anyone at
a dead stop.

"Come get yourself a drink, Alex," Dettis said, pouring
whiskey into another shot glass with surprising steadiness despite the sway of their rapid deceleration. "You deserve it."

"I'll say." The salesman shot his expensive linen shirt cuffs
down, then came across to join the railroad boss. "When you
told me to find those plans, I had no idea—"

Whiskey splashed across his cut cheek, making him cry out
in sharp pain. "That was for being stupid tonight," Ox Dettis
said bluntly. "And for all the other times you've been stupid,
too."

Greer cursed and scrubbed the stinging alcohol from his
face, getting bloodstains on his fancy shirt cuffs. The look he
gave Dettis contained the same blank disbelief he'd given Kachigan when he'd been accused of murder. "What other
times?" he demanded. "I wrote those South American contracts just the way you told me to—"

"And never stopped hanging around that female reporter,

even though I warned you about her," his employer shot back. Their train slowly drifted to a stop, brakes releasing their grip with a final cough of compressed air. A moment later Kachigan heard the rumble of a second locomotive in the winter night. Steam had wreathed their windows, but the bump and shudder of railroad cars being joined at the end of the train was unmistakable. "But that wasn't the stupidest thing you did, Alex. Oh, no. Somehow, you managed to work for me for three whole years at Westinghouse and in all that time never even realized there was *another* traitor working in the damned company with you!"

"What?" Fortunately, Alexander Erskine Greer's incredulous cry drowned out Helen's startled gasp and Kachigan's Armenian curse. "That can't be true! All those damned engineers *love* George Westinghouse. He's not a manager, he's one of them."

"No doubt." Dettis showed his teeth in an expression more like a snarl than a smile. "But there's someone in that company smart enough to *steal* patents and plans instead of just mismanaging the sales contracts on them. Smart enough to *blackmail* engineers instead of just annoy them with impossible deadlines they still manage to meet. Smart enough to *kill* the people who got in his way, instead of—"

Dettis broke off, but it wasn't because of the stunned look in Greer's blue eyes. A heavy tread echoed from the rear platform of the private railroad car, followed by the click and slide of the adjoining door. A moment later a familiar whiskered face appeared at the far end of the sitting room, as calm and thoughtful as if this were a gathering of electrical engineers instead of policemen and industrial spies.

"Evening, Orrin," said George Westinghouse. An unusually direct glance at Kachigan and Helen betrayed a tension that didn't show on his face, but it faded when he saw that they were undamaged. "Right on time, as always."

"The Pennsylvania Railroad's never late, George. You know that." The tone of Dettis's voice surprised Kachigan—brusque and rough as always, but for the first time in memory more cordial than hostile in tone. It reminded him of the way policemen who were ruthless rivals for the same promotion, could still support each other when it came to an outside threat. "I assume you being here means you agreed to my deal."

Westinghouse gave him an oddly dignified look of reproof. "You didn't need to bribe me into cooperating by offering to turn over an industrial spy—or by holding two honest police-men and a young lady hostage. All you had to do was tell me one of my engineers was setting pressure-sensitive bombs on railroad property."

Dettis grunted. "So you admit it?"

Westinghouse brought his hand out of his overcoat pocket, fingers curled around a familiar assemblage of springs and switch plates. "I won't deny we made these, even if they were experimental prototypes. And there's only one person I know who had the expertise and the motivation to use them." He raised his voice loud enough to penetrate back to his own private car. "You can come in now, John."

Kachigan frowned, but with the locomotive engines geared down, he could hear more than one set of footsteps crossing the linked platforms. A moment later the back door opened and John McCaplin came in with his usual discreet tread. And behind him, so small she couldn't at first be seen in the shadows, came the silver-haired figure of Leonora Grissaldi.

"Leo!" Helen's voice scaled upward in protest. "Mr. Westinghouse, she's not the anarchist bomber! She's only doing this to find out who your spy is—"

"Helena, *statazit,*" Grissaldi said, sounding more amused than annoyed by that impassioned defense. "You're right about why I do this." She slanted a wry look up at her employer, now regarding her with sidelong exasperation. "But Giorgio knows too much about my university days in Vienna to believe the rest. I promised him to behave here in America, but this damned arrogant Pennsylvania Railroad—" She shook her head, gossamer hair flying around her bony face. "I couldn't resist using Lullio's *scatto de molla* to teach them a lesson."

Ox Dettis cursed and slammed down his glass, looking almost as stunned as Kachigan felt. "*You're* the one who set all those bombs along the railroad?"

"Sure, why not?" Grissaldi smiled at the railroad boss's

furiously reddened face. "All the trackmen know me, I walk the dogs every night along the tracks. Who would suspect the little old Italian lady from Adderly?"

Kachigan glanced down at Helen, seeing the shared dawn of realization on her face. It had been Grissaldi's face Emma Goldman must have recognized from among those sketches, and Grissaldi's presumed retirement from anarchy to work for Westinghouse that Goldman had been reluctant to discuss.

"So, Orrin." Westinghouse cleared his throat with a sound like a gorilla's warning grunt. "I presume you'll have Dr. Grissaldi tried for her crimes in court, according to the rule of law? That was part of our deal, remember?"

"Hell, yes." Dettis swung a hand out to catch at Greer's shoulder and push the blinking salesman a foot closer to his boss. "But I don't care what you do to this idiot. He was supposed to be making sure you didn't have enough spare money lying around to start offering pension plans and sick leaves, not to mention getting this whole damned valley clamoring for the eight-hour day. What he mostly ended up doing was annoying your engineers and harassing your stenographers."

Westinghouse's bushy eyebrows lifted, but it was with an unexpected smile. "I've told you a dozen times, Orrin, you've got to hire good men and pay them a living wage if you want to get something done right."

Dettis grunted, not sounding amused. "Maybe that works with your damned overeducated engineers. I've always found that a slap on the side of the head goes a lot farther with railroad laborers." He scowled at Grissaldi. "I think you ought to try it sometime. Come here, old lady."

"I think not," Grissaldi retorted, and took a step closer, not to George Westinghouse, but to Art Taggart. "You have two good county detectives here, eh? They can arrest me and take me to jail for you."

The railroad boss's bald head crimsoned again. "On one condition," he said grudgingly, and pointed a finger straight at Helen. "You don't write any damned articles about the Pennsylvania Railroad getting bombed by a little old lady."

She paused, her fingers tightening for a moment around Kachigan's. "All right," she said, surprising him. "But on one condition of my own, Mr. Dettis. You have to tell Mr. Westinghouse who the *second* spy in his company is."

That demand dropped silence across the railroad car. Dettis's pale eyes narrowed to slits, and the cloak of anger he always wore thickened to ominous proportions.

"I never said there was a second spy—"

"Oh, yes, you did. And even if Mr. Westinghouse doesn't believe me, I can prove it." Helen jumped recklessly to her feet and started scrabbling in her coat pocket. Kachigan heard the rustle of paper and frowned, wondering how she could use his evidence book and a scrap of newspaper to outface the railroad boss. "You see, I found all of Ada Deems's original telegraph forms back to the *New York Herald* when I searched her apartment. So even if you think you can blackmail that second spy into working for you now, I'll make sure—"

"That's a lie!"

The unthinking protest burst so abruptly through the railroad car that it took Kachigan a moment to track down its unlikely source. John McCaplin stared back at him in appalled silence, as if he couldn't believe himself that he'd cracked his discreet silence and risen to that bait.

"What's a lie, John?" Westinghouse asked, frowning. "What Dettis said about the spy—"

"No," Kachigan said, rising to stand beside Helen. Her silence told him that she hadn't expected her bluff to play out quite this way. "What Helen said about the telegraph forms. There weren't any left but blanks in Ada Deems's apartment, and McCaplin knew that. Because he took away the ones she'd written her telegrams on, after he set the bomb that killed her."

The silence that followed his words sizzled with multiple layers of anger. Westinghouse was scowling back at Kachigan in disbelief while Grissaldi glared up in Italian fury at the secretary who'd escorted her here. The most violent look of all, though, was the one O. X. Dettis threw at Helen Sorby.

"I should have tracked you down in Trafford and killed you," the railroad boss said bluntly. "If it wasn't for you, I'd have finally had someone *smart* on the Westinghouse payroll—"

"John!" Westinghouse swung around, so distressed that he made direct eye contact with his private secretary. "This can't be true—"

"Can't it?" John McCaplin's outer layer of self-effacing deference visibly rippled and fell away, leaving his shrewd intelligence for once glinting in the open. "Why not, *George*? Is this particular piece of machinery not behaving according to specifications? Not keeping its mouth shut about stupid decisions, since it knows its opinions won't even be considered? Not minding when pensions are planned out for laborers and machinists, but not for office staff?"

"I never—" Westinghouse stumbled over the rest of that sentence, but Kachigan wasn't sure if it was the glare of McCaplin's resentment that silenced him or his own awareness of guilt. "But why would you sabotage our company? Who was paying you—"

"No one," the secretary said, with an oddly bitter laugh. "No one I contacted trusted a secretary to know enough to derail the famous inventor Westinghouse. So I decided to pay myself, first in patent sales and then in stock options that I could buy for a song after I sent your company into bankruptcy. All it needed was the plans for those Brazilian plant— but even the most antisocial of your damned engineers wouldn't cooperate, not even when I threatened to blackmail him for selling his own invention to the Europeans."

"And so you borrowed your boss's private railroad car and killed him in it," Kachigan said flatly.

"That's right." Another layer of polished civilization seemed to shed like a snakeskin with that admission. "And his sweet kissing cousin was obliging enough to threaten me with exposure three days later, so I didn't even have to feel bad about having set one of Osborne's bombs for her that morning. In fact, the only thing I regret is not bringing a gun for you—"

His sudden lunge at George Westinghouse caught Kachigan off guard, but from his corner in the car, Taggart must have seen McCaplin tensing for it. The big detective threw himself between them with more brute force than skill, shielding Westinghouse but also losing his grip on McCaplin's shoulder as the secretary twisted away. McCaplin broke free and dove for the door.

By then, Kachigan's muscles had unlocked enough to launch him in pursuit. It wasn't until Helen shouted and threw herself at his ankles, toppling him with a crash to the carpeted floor, that he realized the railroad car was rocking with the thunder of pistol shots. Without even moving, Dettis was shooting through the thin mahogany front panels of the bar, the holes exploding closer and closer as he tracked McCaplin across the end of the car and through the windows outside. Glass shattered and the banshee screech of a ricochet sizzled through the sudden cold.

Kachigan cursed and rolled Helen over so that he lay between her and the line of fire, expecting the thud and burn of a bullet in his back at any moment. Instead, what he heard was the frustrated click of a hammer falling on empty chambers.

"Go after him!" Dettis shouted to his outside guards, his voice sounding strangely tinny after the roaring cracks of gunfire. Kachigan rolled to his feet, seeing Westinghouse standing unhurt and astounded in the midst of shattered glass and splintered wood. Taggart must not have been wounded either—he was already pounding down the railcar's steps to join the railroad police in their chase. Kachigan paused long enough to see Helen scramble to her feet uninjured, then vaulted over Greer's crumpled body and skidded out into the winter night.

They had stopped in a dark and empty part of the Pitcairn yards. He could see the glow of the roundhouse in the distance and hear the clicking of some railroad signals closer by, but the view was mostly limited to the silent bulks of detached railroad cars all around them—coal carriers, flatbeds, and boxcars strung together on each railroad spur like dark freshwater pearls. The winter sky was clear but moonless, reflecting back none of the snowy glitter on the ground. It made the shadows between the freight cars as thick and hard to see through as steel-mill smoke.

Kachigan took his bearings from the muffled sound of shouting beyond the parked railcars. He scrambled over the nearest coupling, leaving the isolated glow of the private cars

behind. The next spur was filled with empty flatbeds, allowing
him to catch a glimpse of motion beyond another set of tracks,
a hundred yards down the valley. He turned and ran that way,
his shoes slipping more than he'd expected on the cinders that
filled the hollow between rail beds. After a moment he realized
he wasn't running on cinders at all, but on soot-encrusted
snow.

"Stop!" That was Taggart's booming voice from somewhere up ahead, ragged from gasping but for once not at all
lazy. "Police!"

That sparked a distant shout of laughter. "No kidding!"
shot back McCaplin's voice, no longer anxious or restrained
but breathlessly exultant. "Same game as it ever was, detective. Catch me if you can!"

Kachigan frowned at the clarity of the response, then realized why it bothered him. McCaplin's voice had echoed down
from *above*, unmuffled by layers of intervening train cars. He
must have climbed the ladder up to the top of a boxcar somewhere. Kachigan heard the running thump of feet, then silence
followed by a loud thud and then more thumps. Westinghouse's private secretary was jumping from car to car and
track to track, spanning the narrow gaps between trains much
faster than his ground-level pursuers could scramble across the
car connectors that barred their paths.

Kachigan glanced around and cursed, seeing only empty
coal carriers around him, useless for running across. He spun
around and vaulted a coupling, ran another hundred yards, then
rolled beneath a line of high-bellied metal-carrying cars,
slowly making his way back toward the empty track they had
come in on. It was a hell of a gamble, he knew, but he also
knew that McCaplin was nothing if not smart. The direction
he'd led the pursuit when he was on the ground was probably
the exact opposite of the direction he'd actually intended to
go. That would give him the best chance to escape—and make
Kachigan, originally the farthest behind, now the only one who
stood a chance to catch him.

The overhead thumps grew louder as he ran, approaching
at a narrow angle. Kachigan gritted his teeth and hurled himself between the next set of connected cars with more speed

than grace, swerving onto the shoulder of the single empty track that led into this pond of beached railcars. He could hear McCaplin's rhythmic footsteps paralleling him down the tops of the left-hand cars, but the secretary couldn't run up there forever. Eventually, the parking spur would run out of cars, and he'd have to come to ground or be trapped there. Kachigan squinted down the dark alley ahead of him, praying that his feet wouldn't şlip on the uncertain snow. The dim glimmer from the distant locomotives up the track showed him three more boxcars on the left-hand spur—and then nothing.

He dragged in a deeper gasp, feeling his cheek spasm with pain and his aching lungs protest the intrusion of bitterly cold air. Despite the way his feet slid and slipped for purchase, he forced his stride to lengthen. This would be his one chance to grab McCaplin—he wasn't going to get another.

The footsteps overhead abruptly stopped. Kachigan had taken three more steps before his cold-numbed brain made sense of that premature silence and brought his own run to a graceless, skidding stop. Either McCaplin had jumped off the train on its other side, or—

The blow plummeted into him without warning, an impact of falling body weight so ruthlessly targeted against his back that it sprawled him facedown against the snow without any memory of falling. The weight rolled away, and an instant later a booted foot began to slam into his ribs, so many times in quick succession that any doubt Kachigan had about McCaplin's ability to murder vanished in a flare of pain. The private secretary had been even smarter than he'd thought— not only had he doubled back on the chase, he'd swiftly decided to eliminate the one man standing in his way on the ground. A few more blows, and nothing would bar him from the freedom of a westbound freight except Kachigan's crumpled body.

Two things saved Kachigan's life: the snow and O. X. Dettis. The soot-covered remnants of Saturday's blizzard were still deep enough here in the shadow of the long-parked cars that his fall had driven him more than half a foot into it. He deliberately burrowed deeper, letting his coat bunch up and take the brunt of McCaplin's assault, even as he heard the whistle of a locomotive down the track. He didn't know whether Dettis had seen their distant struggle, or just gotten a warning shout from one of his men, but either way the railroad boss wasted no time. The joined locomotives shot the small train up to speed with an inexorable roar, barely burdened by the two private cars wedged between them. When the glow of its head-light began to burn at the edge of Kachigan's vision and the roar of its engines filled the night, he let himself grunt and slump into an abrupt limpness that he hoped would pass for unconsciousness.

The kicking at Kachigan's ribs paused, just long enough to let him wrench himself around in the kicked tangle of snow and coat and wrap desperate hands around McCaplin's ankle. They fell together across the humming railroad tracks, strug-gling with more ferocity than finesse. To Kachigan's surprise, the self-effacing secretary fought like a backroom brawler, swinging a knee at his groin and gouging a thumb toward his eyes with equal ferocity and ruthlessness. He blocked the first blow and jerked his head back from the second, then grunted and used a barroom trick of his own: pulling back and then crashing down on the other man with sheer momentum to slam him into the railroad ties. If he was lucky, that blow would drive out enough of McCaplin's breath to subdue him until the other pursuers to catch up. Kachigan knew his own pum-meled lungs couldn't keep him going for much longer—

"*Milo!*" Helen's ringing shout carried through the night, rising to a terrified scream as clearly as the train whistle that accompanied it. "Milo, *move!*"

Kachigan obeyed her without meaning to, staggering back from McCaplin and spinning toward the sound of her fear in a mindless rush that placed her safety above his own. He barely had a chance to take in the slowing blur of the bullet-torn private railroad car on the next set of tracks when a harder blast of wind slammed at his back and shoved him facedown into the snow for a second time. The wind was followed by an earsplitting roar of three heavy freight locomotives at the peak of their power, whistling past at barely a foot's distance. Kachigan hugged the ground, not daring to stand in case he was close enough to be decapitated by a passing car. He had the awful feeling that he was.

The freight train's whistle shattered the night in another warning blast, followed a moment later by the hoarser scream of all its air brakes engaging at once. There was no way to hear anything else beyond those two banshee sounds, but Kachigan had grown up next to a railroad track. He knew what that combination of noises meant.

The last car of freight train clattered past, pulling blessed silence in its wake like a trailing cloak. Kachigan levered himself to hands and knees, then paused to gather his breath and his nerves. He could feel the aftermath of his near miss running through him in fine, almost imperceptible shivers. By the time he'd managed to haul himself up to his knees and look across at the set of tracks he and McCaplin had been struggling on, all that was left to see was a stomach-turning length of wet darkness that trailed down the snow in the direction the train had gone. McCaplin's body must have been caught in the wheels and dragged away.

"Milo! Are you all right?" That was Taggart's worried, gasping voice, but the hands that dropped on his shoulders a moment later were too small and too fierce to belong to his partner. Kachigan craned his head around to see Helen Sorby glaring at him through a tangle of knotted hair. Unlike Taggart, he thought wryly, she'd saved her breath for running. And for yelling at him.

"*Idiot!*" The scornful word lost a great deal of its sting when it was followed by her frantic patting at his arms and legs, to make sure all the parts were still attached in their proper places. "You were right on the main line! Couldn't you hear those trains coming at you?"

"Thought it was Dettis, coming closer." He stopped her unnecessary medical examination by the simple expedient of grabbing onto her and hauling himself to his feet. Helen snorted in disgust, but made up for that, too, with a swift, heartfelt hug. Kachigan ignored the protest from his bruised ribs and hugged her back, only stopping when he heard the crunch of more footsteps on the sooty snow. He looked around, blinking at the sudden glow of oil lamps.

Taggart was already there, of course, looking sleepy and amused. "I can see you're all right," he said. "I'd better go check on McCaplin."

Kachigan winced, hearing the distant hiss of steam and compressed air from the freight train, now halted somewhere down the tracks. Shocked voices drifted back to them on the cold night wind. "I don't think there's much left to check."

The big man grunted. "Yeah, probably not. But Ox is going to be ticked enough at us as it is. If it turns out the dead secretary is actually one of his railroad goons, we might all end up decorating the main line."

He moved away as Dettis and Westinghouse arrived, one limping and both scowling. But where Dettis's red face wore only the usual angry aggravation, the expression on the famous inventor's face was one of concern and disbelief.

"Miss Sorby!" he said sternly. "Are you all right? Jumping from a moving train like that is risky for anyone, and most unwise for a woman!"

Kachigan added his disapproving scowl to Westinghouse's, although he didn't know why he bothered. Helen Sorby might berate others for the stupid things they did, but she was far too stubborn to admit to her own follies.

"I was trying to save lives," she said now, frowning back at Westinghouse. "It seemed worth a little risk to keep two men from dying."

"*Two* men?" Dettis demanded. "You wanted to save that bastard McCaplin? What for?"

"For the same kind of fair and legal trial that Leo deserves to get!" Helen shot back. "In this country, even being guilty doesn't mean you get thrown in jail without proof!"

"Where's Leo now?" Kachigan asked, glancing back toward the train. "Is anyone guarding her?"

Westinghouse shook his heavy head. "No one needs to. She's guarding Greer, and I don't think she'd let him get away even to save her own skin. She wants to make sure everyone finds out how he sabotaged the Brazilian contracts so the banks can't foreclose on us." He glanced at Dettis in the darkness. "That means Greer will have to stand trial, too."

The railroad boss snorted. "Do whatever you want with

him. Just make sure he doesn't mention my name at the trial."

"Don't worry, Orrin. I keep my promises." Westinghouse was still staring at the other track, his face grave in the darkness. "Poor John. He was a perfect secretary, the best I ever had. I wonder what made him turn to crime."

"Maybe it was being treated like a perfect secretary," Helen said acidly. "If you gave your office staff half the consideration you give your factory workers—"

Kachigan cut off her diatribe by tightening the arm he still had wrapped around her waist. "You can tell Mr. Westinghouse about that later, when we come back and talk to him about adding Giovanni Giocco to his police force. Right now I think we should ask him to take us back to Wilmerding so we can let Thomas know you're all right."

"Thomas!" As he'd expected, that reminder tumbled her from socialist indignation to sisterly guilt. "I forgot all about him waiting for me outside the castle."

Kachigan smiled and swung her back toward Westinghouse's private car. "With any luck," he said, "he's gone across the street to the bar and forgotten all about you, too."

17

"YOU'VE BEEN FIRED."

Helen paused halfway down the main stairs of Essene Settlement House, blinking at Thomas in surprise and gathering suspicion. The early-morning slant of sunshine across the front foyer threw his bearded face into shadow, making her doubt the astonishment she heard in his voice. Her exasperated twin hadn't found a bar to wait in the previous night, and he'd let her know in no uncertain terms that he hadn't enjoyed standing around in the snow while she'd had all the fun—as he put it—of being shot at and chased by trains. Helen had fully expected him to exact his revenge this morning, resigned to finding salt in the china pot instead of sugar, or onions sprinkled in her pancakes. So even though the folded letter he held out to her looked like the familiar ivory stationery of the East Pittsburgh Valley Christian Benevolent Association, it wasn't until she came downstairs and saw the spidery handwriting for herself that she truly believed it was real.

"I found it pushed through the mail slot when I came down this morning," Thomas said. "It wasn't enclosed or addressed, that's why I read it."

My dear Miss Sorby, read the forthright writing. *I write in great haste and distress to tell you that despite all my objections, the board of trustees has decided to relieve you of your post at Essene House for moral turpitude and dereliction of your duties.*

Helen glanced up at her brother, so utterly startled that she didn't even feel incensed. "Moral turpitude?" she repeated, thunderstruck. "But we threw out all the swindlers and the prostitutes, and cleaned Essene House up!"

"Keep reading," Thomas advised. Amusement had begun to tug at his eyes and mouth now that his astonishment had faded. She had the feeling that only the early-morning quiet in the settlement house kept him from bursting into laughter.

Reverend Wheeler says he bitterly regrets this action, but insists that he saw you leave the Trafford City Inn on Sunday morning in the company of a young man. When he made so bold as to inquire at the desk, thinking the gentlemen perhaps to be your brother, he found that you had taken a single room under the name of Mr. and Mrs. Sorby. I suggested to him that perhaps this was part of your undercover investigation of the Westinghouse plant, as indeed I am convinced it was, but no amount of remonstration on my part would sway him or the other ministers on the board. Alas, my dear, we live in an age when the appearance of impropriety is more important than its actual presence or absence. The only concession I could wring from them was to be allowed to warn you in advance so that you could tender your resignation and avoid the indignity of being fired.

The missive was signed, barely legibly, *Jarena Lee.*

Helen took a deep breath, trying to sort through the chaotic mix of shock, dismay, indignation, and guilt that had rushed into the vacuum left by disbelief. After a long moment's struggle, what emerged was a resigned and ironic sigh. "So much for my career as a settlement-house director. At least now I can get some writing done—"

Thomas demolished the silence with a roar of pent-up laughter, the kind a loving brother holds in until he's sure his sister's heart isn't broken. "I won my bet with Aunt Pittypat! She thought you could last at least six months, but I told her a fortnight was more like it, three weeks at the outside—''

"*Thomas!*" Helen reached out to swat her letter at him, but the clang of the doorbell saved her twin from further bloodshed. She spared a quick glance down at herself to make sure her sleepy fingers had found all the tiny pearl buttons of her shirtwaist and put her wool skirt on straight, then went to open the door.

"What can you find to yell at Thomas about at eight in the morning?" Milo Kachigan asked by way of greeting. His thin face looked tired and he wore the same suit he'd had on the day before, but his clean collar and the tidy bandage taped across his chin told her he'd been home for at least an hour or so since she'd last seem him. "And anyway, shouldn't you still be sleeping? You must have been up half the night."

Although Helen had been about to make exactly the same comment to him, the insight startled her into silence. She glanced down worriedly at her clothes again, but saw nothing obviously amiss. "How on earth did you figure that out?"

Kachigan stepped through the door, bringing a newspaper out from behind his back and handing it to her. "Good detective work," he said, smiling. "Look at the headlines."

She shook out the folded paper, seeing that it was the early edition of the *Pittsburgh Post*. Wedged between a dire report about inflation and a story about the upcoming mayoral elections, she saw a three-column banner trumpeting MURDERS SOLVED IN EAST PITTSBURGH VALLEY. And then below that, in clear italic print, *by Helen Sorby, special correspondent to the* New York Herald.

"They wired my story to the Pittsburgh papers!" she said in dawning wonder and delight. "That means it must be the headline story in the *Herald* today—they only ever telegraph the front page—" Joy at her first honest-to-God newspaper scoop overflowed from words to laughter, from laughter to a swift, grateful hug for the man who'd given up sleep to bring it to her. He let out a painful grunt as she squeezed his bruised ribs, but when Helen would have pulled back in remorse, it was Kachigan who wouldn't let go.

"Milo, stop!" she said in breathless protest. "Thomas—''

"Has the brains he was born with," her brother informed her, snagging the paper from her grip. "I'm going out to start breakfast and read all the stuff you wouldn't tell me about last night. I'm sure you can yell loud enough to fetch me to your rescue, if you decide that's really necessary."

Helen felt her face heat up, but she didn't try to free herself after her twin's footsteps had faded. "What made you think to buy a morning paper?" she asked Kachigan instead.

"Because I know you. Just tell me you didn't send that story through the Pitcairn telegraph office," he growled unromantically in her ear.

Helen shook her head. "It was two in the morning when I finished and woke Thomas up to deliver it. He refused to go any further than the telegraph office down the block." She sighed. "And anyway, I managed not to mention Dettis or the Pennsylvania Railroad by name, although it wasn't easy. I ended up calling him an anonymous official of a local transportation concern who provided information vital to catching the killer."

"Good." This time, his words were muffled against her throat instead of her ear. "Then we shouldn't be interrupted—"

The door thundered under a peremptory knock before Kachigan could even finish the sentence. They sprang apart and turned to face it as it burst open, staring at the burly man on the other side. Helen had never seen him in person before, but she knew the cauliflower ears and bullet head from countless newspaper photos. What the papers hadn't been able to convey about Roger McGara was his smell, rank enough to make her catch her breath despite the cold winter air blowing through the open door. She didn't know how Art Taggart, standing sleepy-eyed and stolid behind his boss, could stand it.

"Kash, you Armenian bastard." McGara's small eyes were narrowed in irritation and impatience, but an odd sense of impotence swirled around the other emotions, cloaking them in deep frustration. "I should have known you had friends in high places! Otherwise, Bernard Flinn would have just killed you for getting in his way, instead of sending you to me."

Kachigan sent a puzzled look across at his partner, as if

Taggart could somehow explain this leashed-in rage. "You always knew I had friends in the press—"

"Not your damned reporter girlfriend!" McGara's fist slammed against the door frame, drawing a chorus of gasps and anxious murmurs from the stairs and landing. Helen glanced over her shoulder to see a wide-eyed audience of tenants arrayed behind them, and a little of her tension seeped away. That many witnesses would be hard even for Roger McGara to shut up. She just hoped it was his noisy arrival that had drawn them, and not her previous encounter with Milo Kachigan. "Dammit, Kash, why didn't you tell me you had George Westinghouse and Ox Dettis both sewed up in your pocket! I've got one of them ringing me up at six in the morning to tell me what a damned hero you are while the other one's throwing money at me to get you promoted to a regional detectives' office somewhere on the other side of the county!"

Kachigan exchanged cynical looks with his partner. "I think I can guess which one is which."

"Yeah, Ox wants you off his back," Taggart agreed. "I wouldn't ride the Pennsylvania Railroad for a while if I were you."

McGara scowled at him. "It's my fault—I just didn't think you were smart enough to outfox Dettis, or I never would've sent you here. Now I'm going to lose one of my best men—"

"Kachigan?" Helen couldn't keep that astonished question from escaping. "How can he possibly be one of your best men? He's the only detective you have who's not corrupt!"

"Not him—Taggart!" McGara gave the big man at his side a disgusted look. "He says if I send Kachigan out to a regional office, I'm going to have to transfer him there, too."

"What?" This time, the amazement flared in Kachigan's voice. "Art, are you crazy?"

"Probably," said the other detective. A thin slice of grin appeared under his mustache as he held up another copy of the *Post*. "But I do like seeing my name in print. Don't worry, Milo. I'm still going to make you do all the work."

McGara snorted out a fetid breath of disgust. "Don't think

this is a reward for your damned shenanigans, either of you!
I'm sending you both up to the regional office in Tarentum.
With the coal strike coming, there ought to be enough trouble
up there to keep all *three* of you busy. Think about me some
night when you're up to your teeth in labor problems and
wishing you were back downtown. And remember, this was
all because you wouldn't let one damned drunken anarchist
stay in jail where he belonged.''

"Mr. Maccoun!" Helen's conscience-stricken yelp was
loud enough to make Kachigan jump, McGara curse, and Taggart blink at her in lazy concern. "Oh, my God. I forgot all
about him!" She turned a guilty face to Kachigan. "We have
to let him out—now!"

"No, we don't," said Taggart.

She scowled across at the big detective. Loyalty to his partner might be a virtue he had in abundance, but that didn't
mean he had freed himself from all the corruption of the detectives' bureau. "Oh, yes, we do. Maccoun's innocent of
everything except being a public nuisance, and that crime was
punished by the days he's spent in jail—"

"Except he's not in jail." Taggart endured the barrage of
astonished looks he got placidly enough, merely shrugging under the onslaught. "Dan Turchan let him out on Christmas
Eve. He said his wife was tired of making all that extra food,
and he couldn't find any deputies to stand duty Christmas Day.
Maccoun hopped a freight train that night, and he's probably
somewhere in Wyoming by now."

The silence that followed that remark was profound.

"He's free?" Kachigan asked at last. "And he's been free
since Sunday night?"

"Mm-hmm."

Helen let out a deep, exasperated breath. "So all of this
chasing and shooting and running and fighting—we've been
doing it all for nothing?"

Big Roge McGara gave the kind of baffled headshake box-
ers use to clear their wits after a bout, then abruptly snorted
with laughter. "Never fails," he warned Kachigan, in a voice

from which the hostility had vanished. "The reward of virtue is nothing but frustration."

The detective threw a rueful look at Helen. "So I've noticed," he said, then startled her by reaching out to take her hand in a warm, possessive clasp. "But there's always hope."

Historical Note

The towns and landscape described in this book still exist in the East Pittsburgh Valley, although Essene Settlement House, Sally Lowry's brothel, and the Chinese restaurant at which Kachigan and Taggart eat lunch have been added to them by the author's imagination. The Pitcairn railroad yards of 1905 were real and among the largest in the world. Although O. X. Dettis and Giovanni Ciocco never worked there, Pitcairn was a dry town for many years before the Prohibition, due to the railroad's influence. The high incidence of accidents on railroad tracks is documented in most newspapers of the day, and appears to have been the major cause of accidental death at the turn of the century, much as highway accidents are today.

In 1905, the East Pittsburgh region was the world leader in high technology, thanks to the many inventions and innovations of George Westinghouse, Jr. Westinghouse was alive at this time and still working at the "Castle" and in his air-brake shop, although the engineering, sales, and secretarial staff given to him in this book are entirely fictional. The generosity and modesty of this famous inventor are as well documented as his ingenuity. In addition to inventing the air brake and "electrifying" the nation, he is credited for starting one of the first pension systems in Pittsburgh and introducing other social reforms among his labor force. His castle still survives in Wilmerding, and houses a small museum dedicated to preserving the record of his remarkable achievements. To this day, however, few places in Pittsburgh bear his name, except for a memorial bridge built across the East Pittsburgh Valley after his death.

KAREN ROSE CERCONE

__STEEL ASHES   0-425-15856-X/$5.99

In 1905 Pittsburgh
Politics Could be Murder...

In 1905 Pittsburgh, the burning of a run-down tenement—and the resultant deaths of two poor immigrants—barely made the evening papers. But two courageous figures refused to let the murders go unsolved. One was Milo Kachigan, a detective, and the other was Helen Sorby, a vibrant young political leader and social worker to the city's immigrant poor. Together they fought the discrimination that threatened to forever shield a sinister cover-up...and a heartless murderer's deed.

__BLOOD TRACKS   0-425-16241-9/$5.99

In 1905 Pittsburgh,
Industry Could be Murder...

Detective Milo Kachigan hears of a murder case in which the victim was an engineer for the Westinghouse company. Then he learns that his friend, social worker Helen Sorby, may be involved. In an atmosphere of mistrust and unrest, the quest for justice may be explosive...